BEYOND SURRENDER

Kim— O'Kane for life!

KIT ROCHA

This book is a work of fiction. The names, characters, places, and incidents are products of the writers' imaginations and are not to be construed as real. Any resem-blance to persons, living or dead, actual events, locales or organizations is entirely coincidental.

BEYOND SURRENDER

Edited by Sasha Knight

ISBN-13: 978-1541190603
ISBN-10: 1541190602

for everyone who fights the darkness

with love and hope.

for life.

1

Another man went down from a blow he should have seen coming a mile away, and Ryder gritted his teeth as he shook the sweat from his skin.

He took a deep breath as he circled his fallen opponent, both steadying his voice and raising it so that the gathered crowd could hear his words. "The city soldiers won't be punching you in the kidneys," he told them. "They'll be stabbing you. If you're forced into close contact, you damn sure better be faster than them. It's not a suggestion. It's survival."

The trainees murmured. The man on the ground looked up, and Ryder immediately wanted to unthink the word. He was barely more than a kid, one of the small-timers who'd probably been running drugs for Mac Fleming since he learned how to tie his own shoes.

Too bad his predecessor hadn't been more focused on training his people. Now Ryder was stuck with them, poor excuses for soldiers in the midst of a full-on fucking war.

He helped the kid up, then slapped him on the back. "Take a break. Get some water."

He nodded and jogged off toward the edge of the outdoor area they'd roped off on the loading dock of one of the smaller factories. It was small, too small for some of the exercises Ryder wanted to set up, but he didn't dare base his operations in a higher-profile target area. One good shell from the city could wipe out Sector Five's entire contribution to the rebellion.

Then again, if the bastards had any shells to drop, they'd have already rained them down on the sectors like candy falling out of a fucking piñata.

Ryder gestured for two more men to step forward and spar with each other, then joined Hector, his second-in-command, on the top platform of the portable stairs overlooking the dock. "What do you think?"

"I think it's a damned miracle the Flemings held on to this sector so long with these kinds of people." Hector gripped the metal railing and stared down, his brows drawn together and his lips curled into a frown. "You've got half a dozen—*maybe*—who wouldn't have washed out under Jim."

No, Jim Jernigan had ruled Sector Eight with iron will and militaristic efficiency. Most people had assumed it was out of practicality—in manufacturing, order and control meant productivity—but Ryder knew the truth.

Jim had spent decades readying himself for war.

Ryder surveyed the scene before them, lit only by moonlight and the distant, eerie glow from the lights of the city's electrified wall. "Jim's gone," he reminded Hector. "And this is what we have to work with. Think you can get it done?"

"How scary do I get to be?"

"As scary as you need to be to whip their asses into shape before—"

The night went black, darkness settling over the dock like a blanket, along with an almost ethereal stillness that took Ryder a moment to process.

The moment he did, he shot toward the street, with Hector hard on his heels. He skidded to a stop when he saw the scant lights scattered up and down the block still twinkling in factory windows and apartments.

"It's just the city," he muttered.

Hector stared. "That's not fucking possible."

Not possible—unless you had a pet hacker in your back pocket. "O'Kane," Ryder growled between clenched teeth.

"You think he turned the lights off?" Hector jabbed a finger in the direction of the city. "In *Eden*?"

"Yeah." And without a word of discussion—or, shit, straight-up warning. "Can you handle this? I need to pay the man a visit."

Hector scrubbed a hand over his face before squinting at the wall. "Yeah, I can manage shit here. It's not like Eden's gonna have time to fuck with our western border, not with their power down for the first time since the Flares. Fuck, people in there are gonna lose their damn *minds*."

"Stay safe," Ryder advised. "If something does happen, you know what to do."

He strode back onto the dock, where the low murmur had risen to a frightened rumble. "Relax," he announced. "Blackout in the city. They're getting a taste of their own medicine, is all."

He didn't wait to see if the words reassured them, because he couldn't help it if they didn't. He snagged his shirt from the bench along the wall, hauled it over his head, and started walking toward Sector Four.

People had begun spilling out of their homes at the edge of the manufacturing district. They stood, staring toward the vast darkness of the city, confused and terrified. Ryder walked past them in silence, slipping unnoticed between clusters.

The tight knot of tension at the base of his skull started to ease as he walked. He hadn't even realized until now just how much the low, incessant buzz of electricity coursing off the wall had *hurt*. It was the kind of pain that crept up on you, that built from nothing so gradually that you only appreciated how awful it had been once it was gone.

He crossed the border street from Sector Five and into Four. The bustling street had been quiet since Eden's first big attack on the sectors, the invasion that had heralded the true beginning of the war. People were seeking safer spaces these days.

Ryder couldn't blame them.

The Broken Circle, the centerpiece of Dallas O'Kane's empire, usually teemed with noise and activity. O'Kane kept the dancers hot and the drinks cold, and there was plenty enough of both—if you had the cash. The place was packed tonight, but the stage was dark and empty, and *everyone* was drinking.

A familiar figure lurked just inside the door, arms crossed over his chest, face fixed in a semipermanent scowl. In all the time he'd known him, Ryder had almost never seen Finn smile.

He didn't now, either. "Ryder. I didn't hear you

were coming."

He snorted. "Yeah? I haven't heard a lot of things."

Understanding swept over Finn's expression, and he turned to the bar. "Zan! Can you watch the door for a bit?"

The glowering man nodded. "No problem."

"Come on." Finn led Ryder along the side of the room, weaving between tables and glaring to scatter drunks from their path. On the back wall, he pushed through a door marked *STAFF* that spilled into a dimly lit hallway.

The door swung shut behind them, muffling the music and the noise from the crowd. "You saw the city, I guess. Crazy shit, huh?"

"I take it you're not surprised."

"Are you?" When they reached the end of the hall, Finn gestured him up the stairs. "You worked with Noah long enough to know that crazy motherfucker could do it. Dallas just had to take him off the leash."

Honestly, Ryder had always suspected that Noah was bullshitting about the extent of his talents, and the only reason Mac Fleming had bought into the whole thing was because of his goddamn ego. Any edge over O'Kane, and Fleming would have snatched it up with both hands.

Even if that edge had really been working for O'Kane all along.

"Never trust a double agent," he muttered. "I should know."

"Well, trust wasn't a thing we did in Five anyway." Finn paused on the landing, one hand on the doorknob. "I'm loyal to O'Kane, but I don't forget my debts. I never told him about you."

Ryder was pretty sure Dallas had figured out who

he was—and who had put him in place—the moment he took over Sector Five. "Never occurred to me. You're a man of honor, Finn."

"I'm trying to be." He lifted his arm, showing off the vibrant tattoo of a flame-haired pin-up peeking from behind a peacock-feather fan. "Got plenty of reasons to fight now."

Before Ryder could reply, the door swung open. Jasper McCray stood there, surveying them both. He was dressed like Finn, with enough leather and silver spikes and chains to keep sector artisans ass-deep in credits for months.

A hint of wry amusement tilted his mouth at one corner. "Come on in."

Finn waved Ryder ahead of him. "I'm bringing him to talk to the boss. Is he...?"

"Busy." Jasper leaned against the wall and nodded to a closed door across the room. Something thudded rhythmically against it from the other side, shaking it in its frame, and Jasper's smile widened. "Otherwise occupied?"

"I see." Ryder dropped to a seat at the table, propped his feet up, and studied the numerous screens lining the back wall of the conference room. Half of them were dark at the moment, with no new intelligence coming in from the field to display. "I imagine fucking over the city is quite a rush."

The man at the opposite side of the table regarded Ryder warily over the edge of his computer screen. "Ryder."

Ryder said nothing.

Jasper chuckled as he pulled a cigarette from his pocket. "I like this guy."

"You would," Noah muttered, going back to his

typing as the door behind him slammed open.

Dallas O'Kane strolled into the room, smug and disheveled and completely satisfied with life. His clothes were rumpled, his belt was unbuckled, and he had rising welts on his cheek that looked like a woman had raked his face with her fingernails.

Show-off.

Jas finished lighting the cigarette and held it out. Dallas plucked it from his fingers and jammed it between his lips before lazily buckling his belt. Only then did he shove his fingers through his hair and glance at Ryder. "You here about the city?"

He held out both hands. "What else? I could have used a heads-up."

Dallas hauled a chair back from the table and sank into it. "You worried this is gonna hurt you?"

He hadn't really considered that. They were at war, for fuck's sake—damn near everything had the potential to hurt him, and this was low on the list. "No, but it's hard for me to help you bring them down if I don't know what's going on."

"It'll be hard for you to help us bring them down from over in Five," Dallas countered. "We can't risk putting our plans on the networks. I could have sent a messenger this time, but what about next time, or the time after that?" He shrugged. "You stayed on the front line. I figured you wanted to be a soldier, not a general."

What he wanted to be didn't matter. What mattered was the mission, the goal that had been drilled into him for as long as he could remember, and he'd be whatever he had to be to get it done.

"I am a soldier," he answered carefully. "And I will be on the front lines when I'm needed there. In the meantime, what I want is to make myself useful, not sit on the sidelines."

"Sounds fair." Lex watched him from the open doorway, her red-tipped fingers wrapped around the jamb. "What do you think, Declan?"

Dallas leaned back in his chair, his gaze never leaving Ryder's. "I think he might be the only man alive who knew what was going on inside Jim Jernigan's head."

"That's right." Dallas might be the face of the revolution, but Jim had been planning it since they were all crawling around in diapers.

Dallas nodded slowly and then waved toward the door. "Finn, Noah. Out."

Finn rolled to his feet without hesitation and nodded at Ryder before heading out the door. Noah only paused to sweep up a tablet and say, "I'll be in the basement."

When the door swung shut, Dallas passed his cigarette to Lex and leaned forward to brace his elbows on the table. "Having your ass parked in my command center is a win for me. But are you sure you want to leave your sector when Eden's camped out on your western border?"

The man spoke as if Five was Ryder's home. "I left my sector a long time ago. The people in Five deserve all the protection I can provide, and this is the best way for me to do that."

Dallas nodded again. "All right. Lex can find you a place to stay. I assume you've got someone who can keep the medicine flowing?"

"I do." Factories were factories, and Hector had forgotten more about their practical operation than Ryder had ever bothered to learn.

"Then make your arrangements, and we'll make ours." Dallas slid a tablet down the table, and Ryder caught it as it slipped off the edge. "That has a preliminary list of all the ways Noah thinks he can compromise Eden's systems. The electricity was just the beginning. Come back here before lunch tomorrow for our daily strategy meeting, and be ready to talk about what comes next."

The blank screen reflected Ryder's face as he stared down at it. "I'll station a team near the city gate in Five. Just in case."

"Good." Dallas dug his own cigarette case out of his pocket and shoved one between his lips. "I imagine the city's gonna be busy keeping order tonight, but come dawn we'll all want to be ready."

Ryder had a binder hidden back in his penthouse, a ragged, frayed thing that Jim had been filling with information and conjecture for decades. Noah Lennox might be able to hack Eden's systems and turn off all the lights, but that book—Jim's war book?

That was the thing that could win this. And tomorrow's strategy meeting was the perfect time to reveal the depths of his mentor's determination—and obsession.

"I'll see you tomorrow morning." He stood and held out his hand.

Dallas rose to his feet and clasped it. "Welcome aboard, Ryder."

2

War was fucking up Nessa's routine.

She flinched as soon as the thought formed and shoved it away. She used the force of her irritation at herself to power through lifting the next two boxes of unaged grain alcohol onto the pallet in front of her.

War killed people. It was still killing people. In the last week alone, it had taken Hawk's mentor and one of his sisters. It had taken Noelle's father. It had taken dozens or maybe even hundreds of people Nessa had never known and would now never meet.

It had taken a whole damn sector—Six was still smoldering. The smoke from the fires had been hanging heavy in the sky for days, dampening the sun and turning the moon a sickly red-orange color that everyone had carefully avoided comparing to blood.

War was ruining everyone's lives. Everyone's but hers, because Nessa lived behind too many layers of protective cotton to come close to danger. The biggest disruption to her life had been the shift in production priorities. These days her alcohol went straight into mass-produced glass bottles instead of carefully charred barrels. In five years, maybe, she'd be feeling the pinch. She'd walk down her rows of aging barrels and see a gap in the dates—weeks' or months' worth of product that had been diverted to medicinal purposes.

If her aging barrels still existed in five years. If *any* of this existed.

Gritting her teeth, she nudged the toe of her boot under the next crate, using the tiny bit of leverage to help her lift. Her arms and back would be aching by the end of the day, but the men who usually loaded the pallets were out patrolling the sector, risking bullets from the panicked population *and* the enemy.

Her sore arms didn't rate much sympathy.

"Let me get that."

She'd only heard his voice a few times, but it didn't matter. It was carved into her memory, and it came with tingles and goose bumps and a shit-ton of warning bells. *Danger, danger, danger—*

Then she turned to face him, and it *really* didn't matter.

Ryder was just...gorgeous. Gut-punch gorgeous, with smooth brown skin and perfect cheekbones and a carved jaw and lips that looked like the only soft thing about him. The last time she'd seen him, he'd been dressed with effortless elegance in a tailored suit that showed off broad shoulders and a narrow waist.

It really wasn't fair that he could make a T-shirt and leather jacket look just as fucking elegant.

"The crate," he clarified, then swung his duffel bag off his shoulder and set it down. "Let me."

He lifted it from her arms like it weighed nothing, and she would *not* gape stupidly at the cotton clinging to his flexing chest as he hoisted the crate onto the pallet.

She. Would. *Not*.

Grasping for any distraction, she refocused on the duffel bag. Unlike his supple leather jacket, the bag was plain olive-green canvas, sturdy but banged up and frayed at the edges. It meant something important, but her scattered wits couldn't quite do the math, and he was waiting for her to say *something*. "I figured you'd be over in Five, dealing with Eden."

"No, I'm going to be here." He turned and indicated the next crate with an upraised brow. At her nod, he picked it up as well. "Dealing with Eden."

"Oh." Presumably the bag held his belongings—though Nessa couldn't wrap her head around it. How could everything he needed fit in a bag that size? Maybe if she spent a few minutes prioritizing what vital belongings she'd pack, she could avoid thinking about the implications of having all that gut-punch gorgeous temptation living on the compound with her.

He came back for the next-to-last crate, and Nessa gave herself a hard mental shake. She had to say something normal. Something cool. "Thanks for helping. I usually have an army of lackeys to do the heavy lifting. I guess I should go hit the weight room and buff up or something."

Yeah. Or she could babble at him.

He hesitated, his brows drawing together.

She wondered how flushed her cheeks were and vaguely wished for death. At least it would be quicker.

"Just ignore me. I'm a talker. And as you can see..." She waved both arms wide, indicating the empty warehouse. "I'm running low on people to subject to my talking."

"Okay." He hefted the crate and eyed her. "Do you know where Lex is? She said she'd set up a place for me to crash."

"Probably over in the bar." With the final crate loaded, there was no reason not to take him there. "C'mon, I'll walk you."

"Thanks." Ryder retrieved his bag and gave her a once-over, watching her with what she slowly realized was sympathy. "This must be torture for you."

For a second, she felt naked. Those seething, sexy brown eyes could see *everything*—her painful attraction, her awkward attempt to be smooth, her abject terror that she'd give in and do something stupid like actually want him, because it had seemed dumb before but now it seemed *ridiculous*, with him standing there with pity in his eyes—

"The hooch, I mean," he went on. "Making this raw stuff for the field. There doesn't seem to be much art in it."

"Oh." Relief drove the word out, and it put her back on solid ground. Booze was the only thing that ever did. "Yeah, well. It's not the most fun part, that's for sure. But I still have plenty of work to do. When you're making the good stuff, liquor's a long game."

"You might be surprised what a long game war can be."

"God, I hope that means you've been planning this forever and not that we're facing, like, ten years of this."

He followed her out the door and into the parking

lot without answering.

Ten years of war. She'd thought about the possibility of victory. She'd even thought about the possibility of failure—in a vague, abstract *I guess it won't matter if we're all dead by next week* sort of way. But the idea of this tense, dangerous standoff dragging into weeks and months... Into *years*?

Her gut twisted into a knot, and she walked faster. The loose gravel crunched under her boots as they crossed the cracked asphalt, and she hated how loud it was. Sure, it was early in the day, but it shouldn't be so quiet. The guys should be shouting at each other from the warehouse. Trix and Rachel should be playing music as they readied the Broken Circle for the first wave of old-timers who liked to park their aching bones in a booth and warm them up with the whiskey that had made the O'Kanes famous.

How many years could she do this without compromising their ability to bounce back? One, maybe, if she stopped worrying so much about optimal aging. But the grim reality of war had people drinking hard and often, and she was already eyeing some of the six-years that were good enough to pass muster.

More than a couple of years, and she might as well start handing out the moonshine stacked on that pallet.

Shuddering at the thought, she hauled open the back door and waved for Ryder to follow. The corridor led into the empty kitchen, all polished steel and stacked crates—the liquor restock she'd pulled last night according to the new digital system—and a shipment of lemons from Sector One.

On the other side of the swinging door, Lex was setting up trays of glasses behind the bar. She looked up, and a small smile curved her lips. "Hey, Nessa.

Ryder."

He nodded.

She straightened and leaned one hip against the counter. "I have to admit, I wasn't sure you'd come through."

Instead of offending him, the words evoked a deep, rich laugh. "I don't know how to run. I'm still open for debate on the wisdom of that trait."

"Then you're in good company here." Nessa hopped onto the counter and leaned her elbows back against the bar. See, it wasn't so hard to stay cool if she didn't actually look directly at his hotness. Though hopefully he wouldn't laugh again—the laughter did funny things to her. "Ryder was looking for you. I guess you promised him a place to stay."

"That I did." Lex wiped her hands on a towel. "Do me a favor and show him up to Ford's old place, yeah?"

Nessa's leg froze in mid-kick. "Me?"

"Yes, you."

Shit. No point in flailing for a way out. Lex had sharp eyes and had known Nessa for way too many years. The only thing worse than embarrassing herself in front of Ryder was doing it in front of the queen of Sector Four. "Sure," she said, sliding back to the floor. "By the way, the pallet's all loaded. I'll be down in the aging room this afternoon."

"Got it. Ryder?" Lex was all business now. "Meeting's at ten. You know the place. Don't be late."

"I never am."

Nessa circled the bar. "This way."

Ryder fell in silently behind her as she threaded her way through the tables to the door that led backstage. "There are outside stairs too," she told him as she started up the narrow steps. "In case you don't wanna wander through the bar every time you leave."

Leather and cotton rustled as he climbed the stairs after her. "I can find my way."

Of course he could. He was a damn sector leader, for fuck's sake, which was why her whole body pulsed with an awareness so intense that she could feel the heat of him behind her on the steps. Her body *loved* inappropriate men.

She reached the top of the steps and the door to Ford's old apartment. It felt weird opening it without knocking, even though Ford and Mia had been gone for over a month. Someone needed to pick up the pieces in Eight now that the city had assassinated the old leader, and Ford had worked for Jim Jernigan for years before ending up in Sector Four.

Though he wasn't the only one who had. "I guess you knew Ford," she said as she flicked on the lights. They came on strong and bright—having Mia and Ford in control of the wind farms in Seven had at least gotten them off unreliable generators.

"Not well." Ryder glanced around the office. Ford's desk and filing cabinets had been moved, leaving a wide-open space in the middle of the rest of the furniture. "Jim tried to keep me away from him as much as possible."

"That sucks." Ford could be a stick-in-the-mud and a stubborn ass, but he was *their* stubborn ass, and she couldn't quite stop herself from defending him. "Jim missed out, driving him away. He's evil-genius-level smart."

But Ryder agreed with her. "Yeah, that's why he did it."

"Because he's smart?"

"It sounds crazy, I know." He studied her

incredulous expression, then set his bag on a table by the far wall. "But the thing you have to understand about Jim Jernigan is that the man guarded his secrets. Only people he trusted absolutely could get near them. And he didn't know if he could trust Derek Ford. What he *did* know was that Ford was smart enough to figure out all those secrets on his own, if he had the chance." Ryder shrugged. "So Jim didn't give him the chance."

She shoved her hands in her pockets and leaned against the wall just inside the door. "So it's true, then? I mean, that's the rumor. That Jim had been planning his own revolution basically since the Flares happened."

Ryder unzipped his bag and pulled out a binder, so worn that a jagged crack between the spine and front cover had been repaired with tape, and the protective plastic covering had started to peel back at the edges. He stared down at it for a moment, then held it out.

Nessa accepted it gingerly, afraid it would fall apart if she handled it too roughly. When she set it on the table, it fell open in the middle, revealing pages filled with tiny handwritten notes and sketched diagrams. More notes were scribbled on top of the first set, angry red slashes through words and corrections recorded in the margins. The next page revealed close-set type with the same frantic, scrawled comments filling every available bit of white space.

Page after page, and it took her a minute to see past the sheer *crazy* of it—like pre-Flare-conspiracy-nut-holed-up-in-a-cabin-with-a-murder-wall crazy—to process the words. Then one in particular caught her eye.

O'Kane.

The page was filled with terse words that summarized Dallas's connections to the power structures of the other sectors, potential methods he could use to seize that power, even what-ifs that talked about ways he could generate influence in Eden.

Beneath that, a brief list of bullet points stared up at her: concise little sentences in neat, clean type, each one a plan to assassinate Dallas should the need arise.

A murder book. It was an actual fucking crazy-as-balls murder book. "Uhhh…"

Ryder cleared his throat. "Sorry, some of it is pretty old. And...specific. It doesn't outline Jim's plans, see—it outlines *every* plan. Everything he could think of that might happen or need to happen, no matter how unlikely it was."

She turned another page and found a second bulleted list, this one outlining possible strategies for securing Dallas's loyalty. Was that soothing or even scarier? Nessa couldn't imagine living in a world this fluid, where everyone was both a potential ally and a potential enemy. There was nothing concrete here, no solid foundation. Just page after page of terrifying possibility.

Judging from the cramped, frantic notes and paranoid additions, it hadn't been so great for Jim's state of mind, either. "Wow," she said, closing the binder gently. "And I thought my grandpop was paranoid."

"Jim had good reason." Ryder set the binder aside and crossed both arms over his chest. "Do you think he would have survived the last forty years if anyone in the city knew he thought about these things, much less tracked them like this?"

"No," she conceded. She might keep her nose buried in her booze, but she wasn't stupid. She'd known Dallas her whole damn life, and *he* wasn't stupid, either. He'd spent a lot of years making sure Eden thought he kept his brains in his dick. "Pop used to say it's not paranoia if they really do want to kill you in your sleep."

"Wise words."

She waited for him to say something else, but he was just watching her. *Looking* at her, and she felt intensely self-conscious as the silence stretched. He might make a T-shirt and leather come across as elegant, but her boots were scuffed, her jeans were ripped, and she'd cut the neckline out of her T-shirt because the fabric bothered her, but she kept forgetting to give it to Lili so she could hem the ragged edges. A month of war meant her pink and purple hair showed an inch of black at the roots, and she'd piled it on top of her head in a sloppy ponytail because she hadn't been expecting sexy company.

She looked like the kind of street kid who rolled rich guys like him for their wallets, not the kind of person you shared important, sensitive information with. Shifting uncomfortably, she nodded toward the binder. "Why'd you tell me? That's some serious big-deal shit."

He frowned, a thoughtful expression that stopped just shy of turning his handsome features into something forbidding. "I don't know. You're easy to talk to, I guess." A hint of mischief glinted in his eyes. "Or maybe the babbling is contagious."

Holy shit, he was teasing her.

To hide her sudden, flustered flush, Nessa turned and waved toward the back part of the apartment. "There's a bedroom and bathroom through there. If you go back down these stairs, you can cross to the other side of the stage. Down those stairs is the other kitchen. Lili usually keeps some leftovers in the fridge. Up will take you to the conference room. If you need to find something else, I'm usually in my warehouse. I'm the only one sticking in one place these days."

"Thanks," he murmured. "For the tour."

Oh Jesus, not teasing. He was being charming. She chanced a look at him, just long enough to see that those dangerous brown eyes had warmed. There were little crinkles around the edges, and his soft, sensuous lips were—

No. She was not going to think about his lips. "You're welcome!" she said cheerfully as she backed toward the door. "I'll catch you later."

She didn't give him a chance to escalate to actual flirting before she was out the door and clattering down the steps. She hit the ground floor and leaned against the wall for a second, her heart racing and her stomach full of butterflies.

This was a crush. A stupid crush. He was different from all the men around her—sleek, sophisticated, elegant. Like Jared, really, and she'd had a whopper of a crush on him the first time she'd seen him stroll into the Broken Circle wearing a tailored suit with all the arrogance usually reserved for the O'Kanes.

That had faded. This would, too.

And if it didn't, she'd just remind herself that he'd been raised by a psycho sector leader with a murder book. Dallas might be responsible for winning this war, but Nessa was the only one who could give them the means to keep going once it was over.

No dangerous men for her. No matter how much they made the butterflies dance.

3

Dallas O'Kane's reaction to Jim's binder was the polar opposite of sweet little Nessa's—pure, straight-up delight.

"That crazy motherfucker," he murmured, making it sound like the highest compliment he'd ever offered. He turned another page and burst out laughing. "God, he wrote down every time he pushed my fucking buttons. Remember this one, Lex?"

She leaned over his shoulder and scanned the page. "The meeting in Two. How could I forget? You were ready to beat him to death with his own dick because he asked if he could buy one of Cerys's girls and have you train up another me."

Dallas snorted. "I should have seen it. He was

always too good at pissing me off. I could keep my cool with the rest of them, but he knew just where to jab."

Ryder leaned forward. "Yeah, about that—"

"Don't you dare apologize." Lex straightened and shook her head. "It's a damn shame. All that time, we thought he was an asshole, and it turns out he was a goddamn *scientist*."

"It's a tragic loss," Dallas said, his voice edged with something that could have been sympathy. "I wish I'd gotten a chance to know this devious bastard."

The words hit Ryder like a blow, right to the center of his chest. The sincere regret in Dallas's voice was the kind of eulogy Jim had deserved. His obsession had been matched only by his brilliance, and his paranoia only by his determination.

Ryder had to clear his throat to speak. "Every bit of information we need to win this war is in there," he rasped. "We just have to find it."

Dallas smoothed his finger along the edge of one ragged page. "I never thought I'd be the one saying this...but maybe we should let Noelle scan it or whatever she does. Get it into her tablet so she and Jeni can cross-reference it with what we've got."

"Whatever you need to do." The time for guarding the information—at least from the other sector leaders—had passed.

Not that there were many of the sector leaders Jim had known left. Cerys was long gone, with Two bombed to hell. The leaders of Six and Seven had died in the wave of assassinations that had claimed Jim's life. Now, people wearing O'Kane ink controlled fully half of the sectors—Two, Three, Four, and Eight. A majority, if you didn't count the ones that had fallen to Eden's control.

That only left Ryder and Gideon Rios, the god-king of Sector One. And Gideon's favorite cousin, One's proverbial prodigal son, belonged to Dallas, too. The man would listen to his cousin's counsel and fall in line behind O'Kane.

Dallas closed the binder and slid it to Lex. "Anything that can keep Eden off-balance is a win right now. I want them scrambling."

Ryder rose to get a better look at the map spread across the table. "The city has Six. How are things in Seven?"

"Ford's still holding the wind farms." Dallas leaned forward and studied the map with narrowed eyes. "By the skin of his teeth, though. Gideon's had to send soldiers over to help protect them. If Eden can't get that electricity back, they'll burn it to the ground to keep us from using it."

"They'd be stupid not to."

"I wish they were a little stupider." Dallas sighed and shook his head. "Doesn't matter, in the end. The power's good for morale and makes things more comfortable, but we know how to live without it. What I care about is where they're gonna hit next."

There was no doubt about that, never had been. "Easy. They want your head, and they'll have to come through Five to get it." He traced out the path with one finger.

Dallas tapped his finger on the other side of the map, on the border between Two and Three. "And if they have two brain cells to rub together, they'll try to cut us off from Gideon and his army of the devout."

Lex looked up from flipping through the pages of the binder and regarded Dallas thoughtfully. "That's their mistake, isn't it? They're still thinking of the sectors as separate entities, individual armies to divide and conquer."

Staring down at the map, Ryder slowly realized what she meant. "We'll have them flanked. Surrounded on all sides. Even if they take Two, they won't be able to hold it. We can pick them off, thin their numbers."

She nodded. "When they've lost enough of their troops, they'll pull back into the city. They won't have a choice."

"The military police are well trained, but there's only so many of them." Dallas made a rude noise. "And once we breach that wall, the Special Tasks soldiers won't be fighting us. They'll be standing guard over whatever rathole the council scurries into."

Unless the generals at the Base decided to join the fight, after all. With their support, the city would crush the rebellion. "How good is the intel that the Base intends to stay neutral and sit their asses at home?"

"As good as it can be," Dallas said. "I figure the fact that we're still standing here is pretty compelling proof. No point in letting us get this far if they were gonna do something."

"Hard to argue with that," Ryder admitted.

Lex huffed out a soft noise, somewhere between a rueful laugh and a sigh. When Dallas looked her way, she tipped the open binder toward him.

He leaned over to skim the page. When his gaze hit the bottom, he raised both brows in return and shrugged.

She flipped the binder around and laid it on top of the map, displaying the page on Nikolas Markovic, the youngest member of Eden's Council—and the one Jim had chosen as the likeliest to show sympathy for their cause. "You have Markovic on the inside?"

"I *had* Markovic on the inside," Dallas drawled, sitting back in his chair. "Now I have him in a cozy, secure location under medical supervision."

This time the sound Lex made was undeniably a sigh. "Christ, Declan, you make it sound like we kidnapped the bastard. We rescued him," she explained. "From a cell in Eden. He'd been locked up for months—tortured, starved, you name it."

That was the kind of shit that could kill a man in all the ways that mattered, even if he was left still breathing. "Is he going to make it?"

"I think so." Dallas tilted his head toward Lex. "She's less sure. Maybe I just need to believe it. Because he could do the one thing that'll end this war fast and clean."

Spark an insurrection within the city. Jim had had the same notion from time to time, and there were at least a hundred different scenarios for how it could play out scribbled down in his goddamn book. It was a nice fantasy, the idea that the oppressed in Eden would rise up and fight against the Council that had built its power on their broken backs.

But that was all it was—a fantasy. Ryder knew that better than anyone. "It'll never happen, so don't break your heart wishing for it."

Lex's brows drew together in a stormy frown, and Dallas protested. "If we get the right sort of shit onto their vid network—"

Ryder cut him off, blood pounding in his ears. "The last man who tried to organize the people in Eden got murdered for his trouble. He was ready to go toe-to-toe with the Council, to *fight* them. My father offered the people hope, but they couldn't stand against the city when the bullets started flying. And I had to listen to my mother cry herself to sleep for the next twenty years."

Dallas hesitated just long enough for the words to hang between them in the tense silence. "We won't count on it," he said finally. "We won't count on anything but ourselves and our people."

"You *can't* count on it, O'Kane." Two deep breaths weren't enough to calm him, so he took a third. He knew it looked like temper, a fit of childish pique, but the memory of his mother's agonizing, unfathomable grief had seized him and refused to let go. "You can't."

"Then we'll focus on the rest," Lex said gently. "We'll evacuate as many people as we can from Two. Anyone who can't stay and fight. If we get ahead of the city's invasion, we can minimize casualties."

"Mad can arrange it," Dallas agreed. "Gideon's good at taking care of people. We'll let him handle the refugees." A soft knock sounded on the door, and Dallas reached forward to flip the binder shut. "You and I will focus on bringing Eden to its knees."

"It's what I was raised to do." Ryder meant the words to sound lighthearted, or at the very least confident, but they held all the edge of a confession.

Dallas heard it. He eyed Ryder for another long moment before raising his voice. "Come in!"

The door swung open, and Dallas's people began to file in—Jasper and Noelle, Bren and Six over from their current base of operations, and Jyoti and Mad from Sector Two. Hawk and Cruz. Some carried stacks of paper, others tablets and notebooks. Noah carried a slim computer tucked under one arm.

They were all prepared, not just to listen but to *discuss*. To share information and help Dallas and Lex make their decisions, a collaborative effort that now stretched across the whole of the sectors. It was everything Jim had never had, had never trusted anyone to really give him. It was teamwork.

Maybe Dallas could get this done, after all.

markovic

On the good nights, he woke in a panic, scared right out of sleep by the sound of his own breathing, by unremembered nightmares. He'd gasp for air, try to claw his way back to sanity before the nurses came running. He'd fight for control, because control was everything.

Those were the good nights.

The bad ones were unspeakable. He'd jerk awake in the darkness, and everything would be gone—the curtains surrounding his hospital bed, the soft but shrill sounds of the equipment monitoring his vital signs, the tubes running fluids and nutrients straight into his veins. Gone, and he was back in that cell in Eden.

Back in hell.

In that cell, he wasn't a man anymore, wasn't *him*. Nikolas Markovic ceased to exist, replaced by an animal too starved and tormented to lay claim to humanity. On those nights, the bad nights, he lost it all again. Even his name, and that was the worst part. The lowest moment in his incarceration, the point at which he'd almost given up.

That was his dirty secret, the one he would take to his eventual, hard-won grave—if his captors had been willing to let him die, he would have pulled the trigger himself.

This was a good night. He could still remember his name—*Nikolas Nikolas my name is Nikolas*—though repeating it over and over was the only way he could get his hands to stop trembling enough to lower the side rail on his bed.

My name is Nikolas.

It didn't feel safe, lying under the thin sheets, dressed in an even thinner gown. Nothing did until he got his feet on the floor. He swung his legs over the side of the bed and pressed his feet to the polished tile. It was colder than a mountain lake, colder than the popsicles his mother used to freeze for him in the dead of summer, but it was solid.

He tried to stand. Did. Only sheer force of will held him there at all, but after mere moments, he collapsed back to the mattress with a pained grunt.

"You're up late."

Panic clawed its way into his throat again, but Nikolas swallowed it. Hid it until he recognized the dark-haired man standing in the doorway as Dylan Jordan, the doctor who had been treating him. "I want out of this bed."

Dylan crossed his arms, holding an oversized

tablet to his chest. "I'm afraid—"

"Out of this hospital, for that matter," Nikolas continued. "And I want to wear pants. Real clothes where my ass doesn't hang out of the back. Shoes, too."

The man sighed, peeled his glasses off his face, and rubbed his eyes. "Mr. Markovic, you need to be here. Your condition isn't critical, but it isn't exactly what I would call stable, either." He consulted the tablet. "You came in with severe malnutrition and dehydration, multiple contusions in varying stages of healing, broken bones..."

Hearing the reminders of his torture laid out like that should have sent him spinning again, anxious and terrified. But it was too clinical for fear, nothing but a bunch of fancy words that did jack shit to describe what had actually gone on in that cramped, claustrophobic little cell.

He surveyed the doctor mildly. "You're forgetting the cuts and burns."

Dylan sighed again, then pulled a sleek metal stool closer to the bed. "You want out of here. Why? What's so important?"

Nikolas swallowed the hysterical laugh that bubbled up in his chest. It was a fair question, a valid one. He was tired, and he hurt, and under any other circumstances, he'd gladly fall back into bed and sleep for a month.

But he didn't have that kind of time. "I can't just lie here, not with a war going on. Your people—" A pain shot through his side—sudden, excruciating—but he left the hand that instinctively twitched to clutch his ribs lying on the bed beside his leg, the perfect picture of casual rest, and breathed through the momentary agony. "Your people may die, but we both know the truth. Mine will be suffering."

Dylan stared at him, his eyes and expression inscrutable. Finally, he nodded. "We'll start with a meal. If you can keep it down, we'll get you off the IVs." He paused. "And we'll find you some clothes."

"Thank you."

He had too much to do to linger in a sickbed. Any day now, Dallas O'Kane would come calling, expecting him to do his part for the war effort. Oh, Nikolas had no doubt that whatever O'Kane wanted he could provide from this very room, if necessary—information, security codes, contacts. Perhaps even to record a stirring speech for Nikolas's loyal constituents back in the city, urging them to fight the oppressive leaders who had tried to kill him.

Let O'Kane demand all that. Eventually he would find out the truth—when the real fighting started, Nikolas planned to be in it, on the front lines, rifle in hand. Because he had some goddamn vengeance to exact.

4

It took hours for Nessa to regain her composure. She steadied herself with routine. War or no war, the liquor had to flow. Water had to be filtered to remove any shit the city had added. Malt had to be ground into grist. The draff went into huge barrels lining the wall near the far bay doors, and a check of the dwindling number of empty containers sent her back to her office.

A pang of loneliness struck without warning as she activated her tablet and typed out a message. Mia had been the one to recognize the potential of the used grain. On top of having a sharp mind, she *hated* waste—wasted time or wasted materials.

Mia had been the one, with Dallas's permission, to reach out to the ranchers in Sector One. The Reyes family had the largest herd of cattle and horses in the sectors *or* the communes, and had been more than willing to establish a trade relationship. Now, instead of the O'Kanes wasting time and manpower throwing out the spent grains, the Reyes family paid for the privilege of hauling it away to feed their cows.

Pop would have *loved* Mia. He would have loved her quick wit and would have cackled over her ability to turn everything into profit. He would have told her that if he was twenty years younger, he'd steal her away from Ford.

Nessa missed the hell out of both of them.

With the message sent and her upstairs tasks complete, she tucked a smaller tablet into her back pocket and headed for the aging room, the one place that always set her world upright.

Instead she found Ryder standing between her and the elevator, and the last few hours of composure building went to shit.

He'd discarded his jacket, and that black T-shirt hugged his shoulders and upper arms like it was seeing them for the first time in a decade. Nessa couldn't blame the T-shirt. Clinging to him appealed to her, too.

He turned at her approach. "Hello again."

At least the tongue-tied stupor faded faster this time. Maybe having him around was good—she could build up a tolerance to all his hotness. "Hey. You exploring, or lost?"

He cast a leisurely look around, like the hallway outside of her office was something fascinating to behold. "A little of both. Headed downstairs?"

"Yeah." Maybe that was why he'd wandered back here. Most newbies were fascinated by the aging room. "You want a tour? I know Jas gave you one, but no one knows the place like I do."

He gestured toward the elevator. "After you."

The elevator was huge—big enough for pallets and barrels to go in and out—but she still felt the flutters as the doors rolled shut. Just her and Ryder, together, alone.

It was the closest thing she'd had to a date in months.

She jammed the down button with her finger and listened to the creaks and groans as the elevator began to descend. "So did you have a good meeting?"

He leaned against the wall and crossed his arms over his chest. "Define *good*."

"Don't ask me, man. I'm not the war girl. I'm the booze—"

The pop just sounded like another creaky elevator noise at first—but the grinding didn't. Nessa slapped her hand to the wall as the lights flickered and the elevator shuddered.

Then darkness enveloped her.

For a second, all she could see was the afterimage of Ryder's face. She pressed her hand harder against the wall, trying to ground herself as the world dipped, disorientation hitting her hard. It was dark, *completely* dark. No stars, no moon, no hint of light under the crack of a door.

No up or down. No *anything*.

Her breath rattled in her ears, too loud, and her heart thumped until she felt the pulse of it in her fingertips. She wanted to speak, to say something, anything that might prompt a response from Ryder. Something to prove she wasn't alone.

Her teeth dug into her lips. If she stopped biting them long enough to speak, she might whimper.

His deep voice materialized in the darkness. "Nessa?"

She had to reply. She had to be calm. Slowly, carefully, she opened her mouth and let her voice escape on a whisper. Maybe a whisper wouldn't convey her terror. "I'm here."

The rustle of movement. "Are you okay?"

Apparently whispers conveyed terror just fine. Irritation and pride almost overrode the sick feeling in her stomach, but another unsteady breath sent her spinning again. Was the air thinner? It couldn't be—it had to be imagination and dread and the memory of a hundred nightmares where she gasped for oxygen that was in short supply.

His hands settled on her upper arms, somehow finding her without hesitation even in the darkness. "Hey, listen to me. It's a power failure, that's all."

She kept one hand on the wall and swept the other out until it crashed into him. His T-shirt was soft under her fingertips, but his chest was solid. She spread her fingers wide, bracing herself against him until *up* and *down* made sense again. "Sorry. I can't—" Her voice cracked, and she swallowed a hysterical laugh. "I don't do small, dark spaces."

"Not many people do." The observation somehow managed to sound sincere instead of flippant, not to mention *profound*, which was ridiculous.

Maybe she just wanted it to be profound. A universal truth, so she could keep pretending the trip from Texas had never happened. That she'd grown up safe and cozy on Dallas's family ranch, and then had miraculously appeared here, safe and cozy in the heart of the O'Kane compound.

Everyone around her had lived harsh, sometimes

brutal lives. She'd had three weeks of uncertainty and danger. Three weeks out of more than twenty years. If anyone found out she cracked that easily, they'd make sure she spent the next twenty tucked in a nice bunker somewhere.

Even knowing that, she couldn't stop herself from inching closer to Ryder. Her leg brushed his, and her hip bumped against his thigh. Every point of contact oriented her, and she didn't feel quite as adrift. "Don't tell anyone, okay?"

"That you don't like the dark?"

"That I'm freaking out." She tried to laugh, but it came out forced and breathless, and she didn't care if it was dark, she still felt *naked*. "They get overprotective."

His low chuckle washed over her. "They care about you. You can't fault them for that."

Guilt needled her, because he was right. Who the fuck would fault Dallas and Lex and all the others for caring so much that they did whatever it took to keep her safe?

An asshole, that's who. A selfish asshole. "Yeah, but no one has time to be worrying about me right now. So...keep this between us. Please?"

"Sure." He moved a little closer. "I have a theory. You want to hear it?"

She wanted to hear anything that filled up the emptiness surrounding them. "Yes."

"There are two kinds of people who hate the dark," he murmured. "The people who just do, and the ones who have a damn good reason." He paused. "Which one are you?"

She still had one hand pressed to the side of the elevator car. The metal had warmed beneath her fingers, but it still felt cool compared to him. A shiver ripped through her, and she gave up that last outside point of reference and leaned into him. Her hand landed on his bare arm, and she didn't even try to be cool.

She was clinging to him. Maybe more tightly than his T-shirt was. "It's a stupid story. Everyone I know has worse ones."

"Is that how we're supposed to judge these things?"

"I don't know. It's the sectors, right? If you're alive and warm and not hungry, what do you have to whine about?" She traced a nervous circle on his shoulder, hypersensitive to the brush of cotton under her fingertips. "It's worse outside the sectors, though. At least there's infrastructure here. Utilities. Someone's in charge, even if it happens to be an asshole."

"Ah." The noise was lower, and a little rough. "You're not from here."

"Texas," she replied softly. "Before the Flares, my parents worked for Dallas's family on their ranch. They died when I was little, but my grandfather was there, too. He taught Dallas everything he knows about liquor, and when Dallas set up shop here..."

"You came north too." One of his hands slipped from her shoulder to her back. "Makes sense."

It had. The ranch had been fading rapidly. After Dallas's mother died and Dallas took off, one of his cousins seized control. Pop clashed with the man more often than not over the increasingly harsh treatment of the workers. He had started keeping Nessa close as the mood around them turned sour, and she suspected they might have ended up leaving even if the message hadn't come from Dallas.

"Dallas sent someone with a truck." The words came slowly, haltingly, because she'd never told *anyone* this story before. "Chuck. He seemed okay at first. He helped Pop pack all our shit and some of our equipment. But once we got on the road, it was slow going. You never knew when you'd come across a road that had been washed out, or abandoned cars just sitting there, blocking everything."

"How long did the trip take?"

"Three weeks." She swallowed hard and leaned her forehead against his shoulder. His hand on her back was warm. Comforting. She stopped trying to fight the tremor in her voice. "We ran into trouble nine days in. Some gang of thieves started following us that morning. Pop made Chuck circle around to the shack we'd stayed in the night before. It had this root cellar..."

The smell of it still hit her sometimes. Musty and old, but mostly dirt. The walls had been carved out of the earth, and there'd been dirt on all sides. The last time Jeni had coaxed her up to the roof gardens, the smell of freshly turned soil had compressed Nessa's stomach into a tight knot.

"He said he'd be right back," she said, fisting her hand in Ryder's shirt. "But he moved this ratty rug over the trap door and put the table there in case they'd tracked us to the shack. So they wouldn't find me."

"Jesus," he breathed. "Nessa—"

It had been so dark, with just the thinnest beams of light sneaking between the floorboards around the edge of the rug. And then even those had started to fade. "He never told me what happened, but it must have been bad. Maybe Chuck tried to double-cross him, or maybe he split. I don't know how Pop killed all those guys on his own. But it took him two days."

Ryder remained silent, but his hands tightened.

"I was thirteen. Not as buff as I am now. I tried to get out, but the table was so heavy..." And her grandfather had been furious with himself for not thinking ahead. For not anticipating the betrayal, for not being able to kill six men half his age faster. For getting wounded so badly that Nessa had to choke down her own terror and sew him up before he bled to death in that shitty little shack and left her alone for real.

"He came back for me." That was the part she clung to as hard as she was clinging to Ryder now. "I had someone who always came through for me. How many other people can say that?"

The hand on her back began to move in slow, soothing circles. "Not enough."

It felt good. The tingles were back—the silly crush butterfly kind—but something else joined them, a warmth that unfurled in some place so deep and lonely inside her, she'd never dared to look at it straight on. "So how do we judge it?" she asked hoarsely. "I had a couple of shitty days. Fuck if I'm gonna cry over them to people who survived shitty decades."

"Maybe not," he conceded. "But you also have to understand that there are people who've had shitty moments that might not have lasted more than a heartbeat—and it still fucked 'em up bad."

True enough. Some moments were so terrible, that was all it took. It wasn't like being in that cellar for two days had cracked her. No, it was those terrible seconds after she'd collapsed back to the dirt floor, her arms burning and her hands scraped raw from trying to shove open the trap door—

I can't fix this.

Helplessness. Was there anything worse in the world?

Her heart was still racing, but she got her first deep breath, and the air tasted fine. Not stale, not like dirt. She dragged in another and got Ryder this time—aftershave and soap and the *absence* of the familiar tang of liquor. "I'm okay." She didn't even know which one of them she was reassuring. "Maybe a little fucked up, but I'll be okay."

Silence again, but it seemed heavier somehow—like he was trying to find the words to speak this time instead of waiting for her to go on.

With her forehead resting on his shoulder, so close to his chest, his heartbeat filled the space words had abandoned. Strong. Steady, but a little fast. All the soothing, innocent ways they were touching sparked a sudden, overwhelming tension.

If she didn't defuse it, she might do something crazy. "Weren't you a spy or something? Can you, like, pry the doors open and backflip out of here?"

"There's a hatch on the ceiling of the car. I could climb out, but without knowing what kind of safety features this bucket has, I'd rather not. It might start moving again with me on top of the car." How could she *hear* him smile in the utter darkness? "Or is that your devious plan to get rid of me?"

That was just unfairly competent. Stupidly, ridiculously sexy. Maybe if she scoffed hard enough, he wouldn't notice her insides melting. "Whatever. I'm an O'Kane. If I wanted to get rid of you, I'd be direct."

"So everyone says." His hand dropped lower. "That could be part of the game, too. Convince everyone that O'Kanes are so blunt, they'll never believe you're all sneaky as hell."

His fingertips were brushing the waistband of her jeans where her T-shirt had ridden up. Another inch and he'd be touching the bare skin at the small of her back, which had never seemed like a giant erogenous zone before five seconds ago.

She was going to die. Just fucking implode. *Here lies Nessa, perished from sexual frustration-induced cardiac arrest.*

His fingers dipped down past the waistband of her jeans, and he froze. A moment later, he tugged something from her back pocket, and the elevator car lit up in the glare from—

Her tablet screen.

Oh *fuck.*

She didn't quite leap back, but she put some space between them and hoped the ghostly light didn't show the color in her cheeks. "Shit, I forgot I had it."

The elevator lurched with a loud, mechanical whir, and the lights flickered on a moment later, revealing Ryder's broad grin. "Distracting a pretty woman so much she forgets the salvation in her pocket? I'll take it."

God, he was breathtaking when he smiled.

And the bastard probably knew it. At least growing up around the O'Kanes had given her the skills required to deal with arrogant men. She plucked the tablet out of his hand and rolled her eyes. "Don't get a big head," she told him, trying to channel all the tart and sass of Lex at her finest. "Deflating the male ego is every O'Kane woman's favorite hobby."

His grin didn't fade, but the look in his eyes turned into something almost speculative. "I'll remember that."

The swaying car slowed to a stop, and it took forever for the wide doors to roll open. Nessa stomped on the urge to flee the elevator like a hapless little bunny running from the big bad wolf.

She was a fucking O'Kane, for Christ's sake. She

was queen of the distillery, princess of fine liquor. Her leather boots might be scuffed with hearts doodled on the steel toes and pink laces, but she'd crushed plenty of cocky men into dust beneath them.

And this was her empire.

She waved her arm, gesturing for him to precede her. He strolled out of the elevator and clasped both hands behind his back. "So."

"So." She followed him into the aging room, and the last little bit of fear dissipated. "Do you want the short tour, the long tour, or the increasingly drunk tour?"

"The *real* tour," he answered immediately. "Not the one reserved for visiting dignitaries and other useless chumps."

Lots of people wanted the real tour. Not many got it. Dallas was overprotective for a reason, after all. More than one would-be competitor had tried to lure, bribe, threaten, or seduce the secrets of O'Kane success out of Nessa.

One asshole had actually come close.

But Ryder wasn't some random bootlegger with delusions of grandeur. He had his own damn sector. He was dangerous, for sure, for a million reasons. Especially the murder book—she couldn't forget Jim Jernigan's goddamn murder book. But somehow she doubted Ryder's master plan involved stealing the secrets to her whiskey and setting up his own operation.

"All right." She swiped her thumb over the tablet and pulled up her list of tasks. "Congratulations. I'm promoting you to buff minion. See if you can keep up."

"Just tell me where you want me."

He was teasing her again. The innuendo landed in her pool of inner calm like a rock, and she wished Lex's witty retorts were as easy to channel as her attitude. She would have shot back something sexy and suggestive, flirtation wrapped in invitation.

Nessa had snark and bluster. “Depends on how useful you turn out to be.”

Ryder laughed. “Probably not very. What do we do first?”

There were so many tasks that fell on her shoulders, more than she could possibly complete in a given day. So she picked her favorite. “We’re going to find some whiskey that’s ready to bottle.”

5

Seeing Finn smile—when bloodshed wasn't imminent, anyway—still managed to jar Ryder. Seeing him smile this much…

Well, it was just fucking weird.

"I managed to snag an extra steak for you when the shipment came in from One." Finn grinned at him. "Wait until you taste this shit. Fresh off the ranch, with that rub Lili makes. Compared to this, that slop we ate in Five was barely food."

"It was barely food by a lot of standards." It shouldn't have surprised him that O'Kane had connections this widespread and useful—it was one of the things Jim had often repeated about the man. "How does Dallas get his hands on this much beef, anyway?"

"Trade. There's a lot of grain that gets used up

and chucked while we're making the liquor, but I guess cows like it just fine. So now whenever we're full up on it, Nessa sends a message, and boom. All the fucking steak we can eat."

"Guess we'll have to toast Nessa for more than the whiskey."

Finn shot him a surprised look. "You've met Nessa?"

Ryder snorted. "That's one word for it. She's been giving me hell since I got here."

Finn's smile returned, fond this time. "Yeah, that's her thing. Probably because no one dares to give her hell back. She has a couple dozen violent-as-fuck big brothers and sisters who'll slam down on anyone who tries."

That explained the haunted look in her eyes. Ryder had been the golden child before, sheltered and protected from things that other kids around him weren't. "Sounds lonely."

"Lonely? How do you—?"

The high-pitched wail of a siren cut through his words. Finn stiffened, then changed directions. "That's the alarm. Something's going down."

Ryder followed him out the back of the main building where most of the O'Kanes lived, through a narrow alley set with a table at one end and targets at the other, and into a cavernous, L-shaped warehouse.

Most of the building was filled with pallets and crates, stacked in long rows along the walls—storage, then, except for an area right at the entrance that held racks of guns and shelves of ammunition.

People were already gathering—O'Kanes he'd met during the conference that morning. Cruz buckled a heavy belt around his hips as they approached, his expression serious. "We need as many soldiers as we can get over in Three. Six and Bren are exchanging fire with a Special Tasks squad near the hospital."

A single squad of Eden's best-trained soldiers could take out every person Dallas had holding Three. "Can they beat a retreat?" Ryder asked.

Jasper barked out a laugh as he zipped himself into a tactical vest. "I thought you'd met Bren and Six."

Fair enough. Ryder grabbed a rifle from the rack and helped Finn lift a crate of ammunition into the back of a truck idling just outside the door. Adrian Maddox accepted it and slid it next to another crate full of surveillance tech. "I sent Flash out with half the new recruits to patrol the streets here. Just in case this is a distraction."

"And Zan and Ace are holding down the compound with the rest." Hawk hauled open the driver's side door. "We waiting on anyone else?"

"No, let's go." Jasper slapped one hand against the side of the truck and climbed into the back. "Make it fast, Hawk."

Finn waited for Ryder to hop into the bed of the truck before following him. The grin his friend wore this time was familiar. "Been a while since we rolled out together to do some damage, eh?"

"Yeah." Not that Fleming had ever sent them out to back up his other men. Usually by the time he put Ryder and Finn on the job, it was about damage control—killing whoever hadn't fallen in the fight in the first wave, and, above all else, protecting his investments by bringing back the drugs or the money. Sometimes both. "Not much like the old days, though."

"True," Finn agreed. "Same fighting and bleeding. Way better reasons."

Jasper checked the magazine in his pistol, then reached for his rifle as the truck bounced over ruts and swerved around potholes. “Special Tasks team in Three. What do you think—random trouble, or are they looking for something?”

Neither option appealed very much to Ryder. “Hard to tell. The city could be sending them ahead of the regular troops, hoping to wear down any defenses they encounter. Or…”

“Or they know there’s something important out there.” Cruz didn’t look up from the tablet in his hand. “This isn’t far from where that assassin jumped Dallas. Eden probably wants to know what he was doing.”

“They can keep wanting,” Jasper shot back. “They won’t find the hospital.”

If only they could be sure. Dallas had taken every precaution in converting the underground tunnels in Three into a hospital, even going so far as to conceal the entrance inside the most nondescript, unassuming building Ryder had ever seen. But the place still had undeniable foot traffic moving in and out on a daily basis. It would survive bombing and reconnaissance flyovers, but there were some things you just couldn’t hide from curious human eyes.

“What are our orders?” he asked quietly. “Defend our people, or take the squad?”

Cruz didn’t give Jasper a chance to answer. “We’re taking the squad.”

So they’d be going up against this squad with two former Special Tasks soldiers, a handful of O’Kanes, and whoever Six had managed to train up in her new sector. Ryder shrugged. “I like our odds.”

“So do I.” The pop of gunfire outside rose over the deep rumble of the truck’s engine, and Jasper pounded the frame again. "We'll move out from here on foot."

The vehicle jerked to a stop, and they filed out of the back of the truck. Jasper gestured to Hawk and Finn, then winced when another volley of gunshots echoed through the streets, louder in the absence of noise. "We'll go ahead, and you two can bring the supplies. We'll be fine on ammo for a while, so bring the medical kits and tech first."

Hawk hoisted a heavy bag from the truck. "Got it, boss."

Ryder turned to follow Jasper, but Finn caught his shoulder. "Be careful. Remember, we got steak waiting."

His concern was as touching as it was disconcerting. "Relax, man. You know me—I'm too stubborn to die."

"Stay that way," he commanded before releasing him.

They took a zigzag route, moving up some blocks and down others. Jasper came to a halt in the shadow of a crumbling old building that had been shored up and reinforced with a stone half-wall on the first level. The dented metal door at the corner of the building slammed open, and covering fire rang out as Bren waved them inside.

Four armed women knelt along the reinforced wall, watching the building across the street through makeshift gun slits that had been knocked through the brick. Another tended to a girl who couldn't have been more than sixteen—and had a sluggishly bleeding bullet hole in her upper arm.

"Give me an update," Jasper barked.

"We have them pinned down for now." Six gestured across the street. "My three best shots are covering the other sides of the building, but sooner or later they're gonna risk an escape. I don't know if we can cover them all."

"Sure, we can." A voice crackled over the boxy speaker propped on a crate beside Six. "Ever hear of an old game called Whack-A-Mole?"

Six's sudden grin was bloodthirsty. "Okay, Laurel can cover them, but the rest of us can't do fucking sniper math in our heads. Sometimes we miss. And I'm not letting any of these bastards get away."

Bren crossed his arms over his chest. "We could go in, clear the place. But these guys are Special Tasks. It could get ugly."

It couldn't be any worse than Six's wrath if these assholes managed to slip the net. "Count me in." Ryder stepped forward. "I live for ugly."

Jasper and Bren conferred, while Ryder and Mad covered Hawk and Finn as they brought in supplies. They carried two stacked crates between them, and Jas paused in his conversation just long enough to snort. "Showoffs."

Bren was focused on something else entirely. "Did you bring it?"

Instead of answering, Mad flipped open one crate, revealing a sleek, matte-silver drone with several lenses attached to the bottom and a monitoring system.

Jasper whistled, impressed, but Ryder could only stare. It was the kind of technology that he'd only seen in Sector Eight—and that was because Jim had made the fucking things. "Is that what I think it is?"

Bren pulled the drone from its molded case. "It's the same model the city uses for unarmed reconnaissance. It's lightweight, fast, and hard to spot against the sky, night or day. Best of all..." He flipped a switch on the bottom of the drone, then booted up the remote monitor. A few seconds—and a few keystrokes—later, an image filled the screen. Everything captured by the cameras was rendered in bold, bright outlines of orange and red and green and blue.

It was Ryder's turn to whistle. "Heat signatures. You're going to take a peek through the walls."

"It's the safest way." Bren tapped another key, and the drone flight system whirred to life. It floated up off his hand, and he passed the joystick-type controller over to Six. "Once this thing is in position and we get a good look at what they're doing in there, we can plan our attack."

No wonder they had one walking casualty, and no fallen. Bren and Six together made one brilliant, ruthless team.

Six watched the monitoring screen as she maneuvered the drone into place, while Bren studied the feedback and fine-tuned the images. After a full sweep of the building, they knew exactly what was going on.

Two men, their outlines plainly visible even through the dampening brick, stood watch at the south entrance. Another man guarded a floor-level window. The rest of the heat signatures were clustered in one central area, far away from the exits. And they weren't just standing around, either. They were bustling about, industriously undertaking some sort of task, though Ryder couldn't make sense of it. They weren't providing first aid to their injured, and it didn't look like they were deep in discussion about how to get the hell out of their current situation.

So what the fuck were they doing?

It hit him in a rush that drove an instinctive noise of protest from his throat. "The tunnels. Is there access in that building?"

Six shook her head. "The tunnels in this part of the sector are a mess. Half of them have collapsed, or they lead to dead ends."

That meant half of them might still be passable. In the Special Tasks squad's shoes, when measured against certain death, those were odds Ryder would take.

Jasper had obviously come to the same conclusion. He turned to Cruz. "I probably don't need to ask, but those guys carry C-4, right?"

Cruz nodded. "Enough to blow their way through a wall. Or the floor."

If the squad made it into the tunnels… "So we move fast," Ryder said.

"I want in." A woman with brown hair streaked with red stood in the doorway. She wore handguns on her hips and tucked into thigh holsters, and balanced a wicked looking rifle on one shoulder.

"Laurel." Bren scrubbed a hand over his face. "Who's watching the south side of the building?"

"Kay has it under control." She strolled into the room, kicking a broken brick out of her way. "And I mean it—if you're going in, I want a piece of the action."

Bren turned to Six, who jerked her head in a nod as she checked her own gun. "You can come, but you stick with us and cover our backs. No superhero shit, chasing down Special Tasks soldiers on your own. You hear me?"

Laurel handed off her rifle, a tiny smile forming at the corners of her mouth. "Yes, ma'am."

Jasper squared his shoulders and surveyed the room, looking every inch the military tactician that Dallas O'Kane had molded him into. "Bren, when we get in there, I want your sole focus to be whoever might have a detonator in his goddamn hand. No one's getting blown up today, all right? Everyone else—eyes on your targets. It might be close quarters, so watch your asses."

Six started passing out tiny earpieces, identical to the ones she and Bren already wore. "We only have a few—"

"Give one to Ryder," Jasper instructed as he accepted his own. "He'll take point."

So much for generals staying off the front lines. But Ryder was glad—both for the vote of confidence *and* for the chance to play an active role. He situated the earpiece, then flashed Six a thumbs-up as her test whisper carried clearly through the device.

Jasper exhaled sharply. "Let's move."

They filed out the side entrance as quietly as possible, Ryder and Six at the head of the group. Their boots crunched on the cracked, debris-strewn asphalt, and a volley of shots rang out from a broken window, the one where the Special Tasks soldier had taken up position. Six muttered a command, and her people inside the building responded with suppressing fire. Ryder ran across the street, trusting them to cover him.

They made it safely to the corner of the building, and the gunfire died away as they surrounded the south entrance. Jasper held up one finger, then a second. Before he could finish his count of three, a thundering explosion shook the ground beneath them.

They were out of time. Heedless of the fact that the squad might very well have rigged the door to blow as well, Ryder kicked it hard, sending the dented metal slamming in against the interior wall. It left Six with a clear line of sight to the soldier covering the window, and she took it, bringing the man down with one clean shot to the head.

After that—chaos. Three of the men dove for the gaping hole in the middle of the room, the only possible escape now. Jasper took one out, but the other two made it, disappearing in a heartbeat.

Ryder went after them, ignoring Cruz's warning shouts and the hail of bullets flying all around him. Nothing was as important as making sure those bastards didn't get away.

The tunnel was dark as the grave. Ryder stopped for a moment, dragged in a single, calming breath, and ran in the direction of the heavy, receding footsteps. He was closing in—he could *feel* it—when a gunshot exploded in the small space. The report was so loud it hurt his ears, hurt everything, but he didn't care. He didn't care because he saw the muzzle flash, and knew exactly where to aim his own shot.

He squeezed off three rounds, one right after the other. By the time Ryder's ears stopped ringing, all he could hear was the wet sound of bloody, dying wheezes.

He was closing in to finish the man off when a blow caught him on the chin—the second soldier, who must have been lying in wait. Ryder was still staggering when his attacker took off, but he had no choice.

He gave chase. Three turns through inky darkness, and he nearly stumbled over his prey before slamming into a pile of rubble blocking the tunnel.

Dead end.

His racing pulse pounded in his ears, and he had no idea how well-armed his opponent was. So he went for brute force, grappling the soldier against the fallen rock and punching him in the head.

For a Special Tasks soldier, he fought dirty, kicking

and scratching. He slammed Ryder's head against the wall, then knocked him down. But he couldn't keep him there, and Ryder reversed their positions with a roar of rage, his boots scuffling on the dirty ground.

They tumbled, rolling over rough chunks of concrete, and sharp pain blazed along Ryder's ribs. At first, he thought he'd cut himself on debris, but when he lashed out instinctively, a knife clanged unmistakably into the darkness only inches away.

The soldier spat a curse and wedged his forearm across the front of Ryder's throat, throwing all his weight behind it. It hurt like hell, not just from his burning lungs and the lack of oxygen, but from the sheer force on his windpipe. If he didn't shake the bastard, he was going to die in a dark tunnel beneath Sector Three.

Not exactly a blaze of glory. No fucking way was he going down like that.

The soldier was so focused on choking him that he didn't seem to notice Ryder moving. He reached out, and his fingertips brushed one of those huge, jagged lumps of shattered concrete.

If he'd had any breath left, he might have laughed.

But the world was starting to fade away, and Ryder felt himself slipping into an even deeper darkness. Mustering the last of his strength, he swung the piece of concrete and smashed it into the side of his attacker's head. The man pitched off him with a grunt that sounded more animal than human, and Ryder allowed himself the luxury of one ragged, searing breath before diving after him.

He kept swinging the rock. The edges bit into his fingers, but he ignored the pain. It was a small price to pay for staying alive, so he kept crashing his arm down, again and again, long after the man beneath him stopped fighting.

A dim light filled the tunnel. High on adrenaline, Ryder whipped around, the hunk of concrete raised. Laurel froze, her face cast in the unforgiving light of a chemical glow stick, her pistol at the ready.

Ryder saw the concrete for the first time. It was dark with blood—and other things he didn't really want to think about too closely. He dropped it immediately. "Sorry."

"No problem." She lowered her gun, but her guarded expression stayed. "We couldn't raise you on comms."

The earpiece was gone, knocked loose sometime during the fight. He opened his mouth to tell her so, but her gaze skipped down to the fallen soldier and back up—quick, furtive—and she took a step back.

Ryder didn't look. He didn't need to. He could feel the sticky mess that had once been the man's head drying on his hands.

Jasper met them at the last turn, his usually lazy voice tight with tension. "Maybe Six should have been warning you not to dive into tunnels all alone instead of Laurel here."

Ryder shrugged. The movement seared through the slice on his ribs, so he grinned, too. "Got the job done, didn't I?"

"Yeah. But the cost could have been high." Jasper paused, then sighed. "Have a little mercy, huh? Dallas'll never forgive me if you get dead on my watch."

"Pinky swear," Ryder lied dryly. War was war, after all. The same story, repeated for tens of thousands of years. Some who fought lived and others died, and you never knew which you were destined to be.

6

Nessa was getting good at interpreting the mood of a party.

Since the start of the war, the O'Kanes had gathered in the old warehouse more nights than not. Sometimes the parties were every bit as wild and debauched as the good old days, with liquor and dancing giving way to sex in every dark corner—and plenty of the more brightly lit ones. Sometimes they were quieter. People would sit around and tell stories over slow sips of the best liquor, their gazes drifting over familiar faces as if they were trying to replace the horrors of the day with something good—or fix those beloved people in their memories, just in case it was the last time.

Sometimes it was just the drinking, because even O'Kanes couldn't party through the pain all the time.

Those were the bad nights. The nights when the dark corners stood empty, because those who had partnered up already wanted to drag their loved ones home and cling tight, like they could fuck away the darkness.

On those nights, Nessa left early. It hurt less than watching everyone peel off in twos and threes and even fours—and it hurt way less than when some of them stuck around out of pity for her.

This party wasn't a bad one. She knew it from the moment she cracked open the warehouse door. Music spilled out—loud, with a thumping bass line, and from the doorway she could see the dance floor was crowded.

The knot of tension making her shoulders ache eased. Whatever had provoked the alarm today might have been bad, but it couldn't have been *too* bad. But as she hesitated and scanned the crowd again, the knot returned.

Ryder wasn't there.

It probably didn't mean anything. Fuck, she of all people knew how impenetrable the brotherhood of the O'Kanes could seem from the outside. Maybe it hadn't occurred to anyone to invite him.

And maybe she was making up an excuse to go and check.

Before anyone could see her, Nessa ducked back out the door. The night air was chilly, like the warmth had been leached from it as soon as the sun set. It had been years since she'd noticed how much the temperature dropped after dark, but the tense moments in the elevator had stirred up too many memories of Texas—including its balmy nights.

She was off balance. Caught between memories of the past and the uncertainty of the future. And she *really* wanted to lay eyes on Ryder. Just so she could know he was okay.

Not that she'd tell *him* that. She circled back to her office in the new warehouse and used her thumbprint to open her safe. Bottles of liquor were stacked neatly inside—the very best of her small batches, bottles so rare they went for thousands of credits on the black market.

She picked her favorite and retraced her footsteps. The lights in the parking lot illuminated the iron staircase along the back of the Broken Circle, and she felt exposed as she clattered up them. She was being ridiculous. Pathetic, really, like her crush had taken over her brain.

But she needed to know.

She knocked on his door, trying not to bounce with impatience. "Ryder? It's Nessa."

No one answered, but boots thumped across the floor. A moment later, he opened the door, then immediately turned away. "What is it?"

He was shirtless, which probably would have been a full-on fucking butterfly fluttering invasion in her gut if she hadn't seen the slash across his ribs before he turned to hide it. "Holy shit, are you okay?"

"Fine." He had a suture kit open on the desk, along with a few med-gel applicators and a bottle of the cheapest whiskey the O'Kanes produced, the shit so raw Nessa had tried to talk Dallas out of selling it. The people who still bought it had probably burned their taste buds off years ago.

"Okay, first of all, I don't believe you." She slipped past him into the room before he could stop her and took a better look at his ribs. The wound was ugly—long and still bleeding. Even worse were the small stitches at the very bottom of the wound. "Second of all, tell me you are not up here with a bottle of rotgut, *sewing your own fucking side back together*."

The damn man *smirked*. "Okay, I'm not sewing myself up."

"You asshole." Nessa's temper boiled over. She stalked to the table and set down her bottle, then snatched up the shitty whiskey and waved it at him. "You better be using this as disinfectant because if you're drinking this shit, we're gonna have words."

"I am drinking it," he shot back. "No need to waste the good stuff when all I need is to get a little blurry, take the edge off."

"We have drugs for that, which you should know, since you make them. And people who are good at stitches. Like doctors." Of course, the doctors were probably back in Sector Three by now, in their cozy, well-guarded beds. She jabbed her finger toward the desk. "Sit your ass down."

He glared at her, but slid onto the desk without argument. "Are you handy with a needle?"

"For sewing clothes? Hell, no." She picked up the numbing spray and the suture kit and carried them over to the desk. "But Dallas's mama had me putting stitches into people by the time I was nine."

"Lot of knife fights down on the ranch?"

"More than our share." She ducked into the bathroom to wash her hands and raised her voice to be heard over the splashing water. "Mostly new guys, though. No one caused trouble a second time. Quinn chased 'em off with her shotgun if they tried."

"Quinn." Ryder repeated the name slowly, rolling it over his tongue like he was testing it out for...*something*. "I always wondered what her name was. It's not in any of the files on Dallas."

It wouldn't have been, and Nessa felt a twinge as she cut off the water with her elbow. This was why she had to be careful. Words just tumbled past her lips without stopping at her brain—and she knew way too much. About Dallas. About *everything*.

Resolving to watch her tongue, she strode back into the office and hesitated.

Ryder looked different. Maybe the rotgut he'd choked down was fuzzing his hard edges a little, because the gut-punch of his gorgeousness wasn't quite as punchy. Instead of cold and aloof and intimidatingly perfect, he looked...easier. Not softer, but warmer. His smile prickled up her spine instead of slamming into her gut, and that was way more dangerous.

She crossed to his side and focused on the only thing about him that wasn't pretty—the cut across his side. It was amazing the first few stitches were as even as they were, considering the awkward angle. He must have been doing it by feel, which made her stomach flip in a far less fascinating way. "I'm gonna numb this up, okay?"

"Don't need it," he rumbled.

"Yeah, yeah. You're a tough guy." She picked up the spray anyway. "Apparently that makes some ladies swoon, but I grew up surrounded by meatheads who liked to show off. You wanna do something really impressive? Be smart and let me handle this."

He watched her apply a thin layer of the lidocaine spray, his brows drawn together in a harsh frown. "Renee. That was my mother's name."

Maybe he was drunker than she'd thought. Or maybe he was talking to distract himself from the fact that a bootlegger with purple hair was about to start poking a needle through his skin. "Tell me about her."

"She was strong," he whispered. "I guess everyone who survived the Flares was, but she was...different. A lot of folks toughened up, but it made 'em hard on the inside. Brittle. That never happened to her."

Nessa started the first stitch, careful and even like Quinn had taught her. "What did she do? Before the Flares, I mean."

His face tightened. "Teacher."

Now she was poking at more than one wound. "I didn't know my mother," she said quickly, giving him the chance to retreat from the topic as she tied off the first knot. "But I've seen pictures. There's this one my Pop kept for me of her right before the Flares—she was at some school dance with my dad. They were teenagers, fourteen or fifteen, maybe. But they looked so *young*."

Ryder snorted. "Simpler times."

"Or more complicated." She moved on to the next stitch, falling into the remembered rhythm. "I mean after the Flares, shit was real simple. Don't die."

"Yeah." He squeezed his eyes shut.

Silence fell, and Nessa hated it. Some people seemed to thrive on it, but for her it had always felt so claustrophobic, like the empty air could crush her. Ten seconds of it and she cracked like an egg, spilling awkward truth all over them both. "Do you want to talk about her? Your mom? You got stiff, so I thought maybe it hurt. Bad memories, or whatever."

"Your hands are cold."

No, they weren't, but the lie was its own kind of truth. "It's okay, you know. *Don't ask* is pretty much the rule. And we're the lucky ones. People don't know our stories. Can you imagine being someone like Lili? All that baggage and nowhere to hide it."

Slowly, he opened his eyes. "Maybe that's better. Think about it. You'd never have to explain *shit*."

"Hey, I'm the one who likes to talk." She finished knotting off the current stitch before glancing up at him, eyebrows raised, her voice as light and teasing as she could make it. "Go ahead. Ask me anything."

A hint of a smile curved his lips. "Nah, you don't want to play that game with a deep-cover spy. Trust me on that."

"I don't, huh?" At least that dark sadness had left his eyes. The wound was halfway stitched, so she refocused on her task and pretended she was just trying to distract him, and not desperate to know what he saw when he looked at her. "Try me."

Ryder touched her chin, warm fingers stroking gently as he urged her to tilt her face to his. "Who was he?"

Her breath caught. Tingles. So many fucking tingles. "Who?"

"The guy who fucked you over so bad you won't look at me straight in the face."

Oh, *ouch*.

He'd warned her. She'd asked for it. She'd wondered how clearly he saw her, and now she had the answer. Better than the people who'd lived with her for years, better than anyone but Mia. But even Mia, with all her training, had taken weeks to find that vulnerable spot.

Ryder had only needed a couple hours.

She ducked away from his touch so she could look at the wound on his side again. "Who said there was only one? My bad dating stories could fill libraries. Smart men won't risk the collective wrath of the O'Kanes, and stupid men are lousy lays."

"Mmm." She could feel the continued weight of his stare, and the butterflies were migrating now. The back of her neck prickled, and the tingles shivered down her spine. "Right. *Don't ask.*"

She could tell him. She could spill the whole sordid story, just to prove him wrong. But shame churned in her gut as she thought about how stupid she'd been. How naïve and gullible. How goddamn pathetic.

"Fine," she grumbled. If she'd been a little more vindictive, she would have left him to finish sewing up his own damn ribs. But she *had* asked for it. "You win. Some shit sucks to talk about, even for me."

"It does," he agreed mildly. "It's nothing to be ashamed of."

Not unless she was being stupid again. The shame of that would drown her. "Can I ask you something kinda fucked up?"

"The more fucked up the better."

She swallowed hard, and only Quinn's training kept her hands steady. "Was I in Jim's book?"

"I wondered if you'd ask." Ryder caught her eye again and held it this time. "No, you're not in it. Wasn't his style, anyway. When it came to Dallas, he may have recognized the potential need to get rid of the fucker, but he never wanted to ruin him. Not like that."

It made a weird sort of sense. All of the men who had come after her had shared the same goal—they wanted Dallas's money. Jim's goals had been loftier. Power. Revolution.

Nessa could make someone rich, but she couldn't win wars.

And if Ryder knew enough to wonder if she'd ask, then he already knew the answer to his own question. It didn't matter *who* the guy had been, just *what.*

Someone who saw what Dallas had and wanted it for himself. Someone who'd seen a lonely girl as an easy target.

And God, she'd been so easy.

She felt raw. Awkwardly exposed. But for some reason she couldn't tear her gaze from his this time, like those gentle brown eyes were holding her captive. She wet her lips and pushed back, tried to balance her own vulnerability with his. "Tell me about your mother."

He drew in a slow, deep breath. "She loved animals—not just the cute, furry kind, either. Even the lizards I brought home. She was like that about people, too, no matter how fucked up they were. She liked coffee, flowers, and something called Broadway. And she pretended to like squash so I would eat it, even though it made her sick to her stomach." His shoulder flexed in a small shrug. "Only lie my mother ever told me."

The words painted a warm picture. Pain lingered in his eyes, but it was the gentle pain of loss. Nessa had seen it in Jyoti and Mad, in the precious few O'Kanes who had been lucky enough to grow up knowing love. "She sounds nice."

He cleared his throat. "She was."

She only had a couple stitches left. Her throat felt oddly tight as she finished up and reached for the med-gel. "He was an ass," she said without looking up. "He didn't give a shit about me, he just wanted me to make him as rich as I made Dallas. That's all most of the smart guys want. So yeah, I don't look smart guys straight in the face much."

He touched her chin again. Just a touch, with the gentlest of pressure, and it would have been easy for her to twist her face away again. Instead she straightened slowly, and with him sitting on the desk, she was almost eye to eye with him.

Except he wasn't looking at her eyes. His gaze dropped to her mouth, and the air between them crackled. She took an unsteady breath, fighting the sudden urge to nervously wet her lips.

He could kiss her. Right here, like this. He could kiss her, and that might be all it took to wreck her world. Because he was looking at her like he knew what to do with his mouth. What to do with *her* mouth. It wouldn't be sloppy and clumsy like the drunk fighters who tried to gag her with their tongues as some kind of weird dominance ritual.

If Ryder kissed her, he wouldn't have anything to prove. He didn't need her connection to the O'Kanes or her ability to make money. He had his own power and people and wealth. He'd just be kissing her to *kiss* her, and her body ached in a million places she hadn't realized could ache.

If Ryder kissed her, it would be the best sex she'd ever had. Even if it stopped at a kiss.

Then he looked away, breaking the spell. "What do you think?" he rasped, studying his side. "Am I going to make it?"

"Probably." Her voice was all breathless and her heart was still pounding, so she turned and hurried to the table where the medical supplies were spread out. She grabbed a bandage and then snatched up the rotgut and waved the bottle at him. "But I'm confiscating this so you don't poison yourself."

Instead of waiting for her to bandage his wound, Ryder slid off the desk and stretched experimentally. He winced a bit when it pulled his stitches, but that did nothing to diminish his sheer masculinity. "It's not that bad. The booze, I mean."

"Yeah it is." She hefted the bottle again, wrinkling her nose at the weak color. "You know, before the Flares, it would have been *illegal* to call this shit whiskey. I mean even before the laws cracked down and they started making all kinds of liquor illegal. It's barely aged, the color's fake, and the only reason people can't tell it tastes like shit is because we barely diluted it, so it probably destroyed your taste buds with the first sip."

One strong arm slid around her waist, and he hauled her against his bare chest. Before she could make sense of the contact, his mouth covered hers.

Her fingers went lax. The bottle slipped through them, hitting the floor with a thud but no shatter, and relief that it hadn't broken was the last clear thought she had. Because his lips were warm and firm, and he was teasing them over hers, the soft friction the most innocently erotic thing she'd ever felt.

She clutched at his arms for balance, but that only made the world spin faster. He was all heated skin over hard muscles that flexed when her fingers dug in, and she parted her lips on a silent moan.

Mistake. He caught her lower lip between his teeth, and his gentle tug pulled everything inside her tight and white-hot. Her nipples throbbed with the scrape of his teeth. Her skin tingled. When he soothed the spot with his tongue, she squeezed her thighs together against the temptation to crawl up his body until she could rock her way to release.

She was losing it. Losing her ever-loving mind over a fucking *kiss*—and then his tongue swept deeper, clashing with hers, and she didn't care. She groaned and went up on her toes, pressing as close to him as she could get, hating that he wasn't between her thighs.

It ended after an eternity, way too fucking soon. Ryder lifted his head, his eyes dark and heavy, and licked his lips. "Yeah. My taste buds are definitely still working."

She flushed at the suggestive heat in the words, then stiffened and pushed him back. "Your ribs. This has to hurt."

"Worth it." He ignored the bandage still clutched in her trembling hand. Instead, he snagged a clean, neatly folded T-shirt from the chair behind the desk, dragged it over his head, and retrieved the fallen bottle of whiskey from the floor. "Wasn't it?"

It had the slight lilt of a question, but the smugness in his eyes made it clear he wasn't really asking. The paper backing on the bandage crinkled as her hand fisted, and she wanted so, *so* badly to smack the smugness right off those perfect lips.

But not as much as she wanted to kiss him again, dammit.

Her knees wobbled. She tried to hide it as she stomped to the table and tossed the bandage onto it. Her precious bottle of liquor was still there, so she scooped it up and turned. "If you want to drink something, you should drink this. But only if you promise to appreciate it. You don't even wanna know how much I could make selling it on the black market."

He held out one hand.

She offered him the bottle, but when his fingers closed around it, they covered hers. His fingertips lingered as hot little points of contact before they rasped slowly over her skin. Her imagination kicked into overdrive, imagining those calloused fingertips dragging down her throat, between her breasts, over every spot that ached for contact.

Holy *shit*, she was playing with fire.

"Thank you," he murmured.

"No problem." He was still watching her, and she *knew* that look. She'd seen it dozens of times, in the eyes of every cocky, arrogant O'Kane man who'd ever locked eyes on a woman he knew he could have.

She'd always wondered what made women bolt like terrified prey in the face of that look. If a hot guy who knew what he was doing with his dick wanted to get busy, why wouldn't you jump on and ride?

Now she got it. Arousal might have made her wet enough to squirm, but the flutter in her chest was closer to panic than excitement. Wanting something this much was scary as fuck. Men were easy when you didn't care, when they couldn't rock your world. She'd played with the cage fighters. She'd rolled out of their beds decently fucked but never really touched. Their faces and names faded from memory, and if she never saw them again, it wasn't a loss.

This would be a loss. He'd haunt her dreams. He'd fill her waking hours. She'd crave him and miss him when he was gone and spend her whole life—however much of it she had left—knowing nothing could ever be this good again.

Oh yeah. She got it now, why women ran.

She also knew that running got you chased.

Gathering the shreds of her pride around her, she swept up the bandage again and ordered her knees to behave. She took two steps and slapped it against his chest. "Don't be an idiot. Put that on," she ordered, only giving him a second to catch it before she strode past him. "And you shouldn't stay up here brooding. We're having a party down at the warehouse. There's food and music and socializing. Come be social."

"I have things to do," he countered. "Work."

"If you're not gonna live, too, what's the point?" She pulled open the door and hesitated. "It doesn't have to be one or the other, you know. Maybe you have a big fancy book full of stats, but you don't *know* us. You don't know what we can do. Maybe part of your work should be finding out."

"Oh, I plan on it." Another of those secret little smiles tugged at his lips. "Don't worry about me, Nessa."

She couldn't help it. He'd already lodged himself under her skin. But she didn't have to let *him* know that. "Don't flatter yourself," she replied tartly, turning her back on him. "I worry about everyone."

If it had been true, she wouldn't have pulled the door shut quite as hastily as she did. She wouldn't have clattered down the stairs like the scared little rabbit she was trying not to be.

Her circle of worry was small and tight. She loved the O'Kanes fiercely, and most days she knew she wasn't as noble as Dallas and Lex. The rest of the world could burn, as long as her people made it out the other side.

Worrying about strangers wasn't her usual MO. Neither was worrying about some guy she'd just met, no matter how much he smoldered and how hot he kissed.

Ryder was making her stupid, and that was the one thing she couldn't afford to be right now. Because the O'Kanes would make it through this war. Her faith in Dallas had to be absolute.

And when they did, she had to be ready to rebuild their empire. No sex was worth risking that.

Probably.

7

Nessa wore cherry-flavored lip gloss.

Two busy days and two restless nights, and Ryder could still taste it. It was enough to distract him not only from the usual, day-to-day shit, but one of the most important meetings Dallas had ever called.

At one end of the table, Nikolas Markovic sat, ashen-faced, his blank eyes constantly scanning the wall of monitors. Every so often, something would spark in his dark gaze—a hint of recognition, interest, something bordering on desperation. Like he was searching for something amidst the maps and status reports.

He looked like hell. Gaunt and ragged, even though Lex and Lili had cleaned him up. You couldn't fix months of imprisonment and torture with a haircut and a shave. He still carried a haunted look, and the first time someone let the door slam behind him, Ryder thought Markovic might dive under the table.

He was a mess.

On the other side of the room, an older gentleman stood, eyeballing them all from under a messy fall of steel-gray hair. Neal Cooper, former MP and revolutionary in his own right, was a legend, a man renowned equally for his resilience and his kindness. Coop had spent years on Eden's military police force, then moved on to champion the weak and helpless in the city. The very idea of having Coop as an ally in fighting the city leaders would have made Jim weep with envy. And here he was, ready to go to war at O'Kane's side.

Ryder leaned closer to Dallas. "Is there anything you can't do?"

One side of Dallas's mouth tilted up. "Plenty. That's the point of a gang. No man can do everything, but all of us together? We can do anything."

Coop snorted. "I'll tell you one thing you can't goddamn do." He gestured to the bank of monitors covering the wall. "You can't tell what's really going on in the city by looking at this shit all day long."

"We're working on getting better intelligence," Noelle said, running her fingers absently over the tablet in front of her. The former councilman's daughter looked almost as tired as Markovic. "It's a matter of manpower at this point. There are only so many of us who can work the tech. We could put out a call..." She trailed off with a shrug. "Maybe we'd get help. Maybe we'd get city spies."

"Probably a lot of both." Dallas shook his head. "We can't risk it. We need—"

The door opened again, and Noah came through. His pale face had an unhealthy pallor, and the shadows beneath his eyes were even deeper than Noelle's. His gaze swept the room before he slid into the empty spot next to Ryder. "Sorry I'm late. That asshole almost got through again."

Coop's wrinkled face screwed up into a grimace. "Say what, now?"

"The person running security in Eden." Noah shoved his fingers through his hair, making the already unruly strands stick up wildly. "Up until now, I've always been careful. Used the exploits my grandfather programmed in. Never caught their attention. But when I came at them head-on... This girl's *mean*. And good. She calls herself—"

"Her name is Penelope," Markovic cut in. "I met her a few years ago. She'd breached one of the networks at City Center, and they were going to toss her out into the sectors. I hired her as a junior programmer instead."

Dallas went utterly still, as if it was taking all of his willpower not to pounce on the words. "How well do you know her?"

Markovic winced. "Not well enough to turn her to your cause, if that's what you're asking."

Dallas held up a hand. "Just feeling out the situation."

The man went back to studying the monitors, as if Dallas hadn't spoken.

Coop blinked, then blew his breath out between his teeth in a low whistle. "As I was saying, the computer shit's all well and good if you want to cut their power or track their troop movements. But it can't give you the whole picture of what's going on in the city. You need eyes and ears. Human ones."

A blond man across the table leaned forward. His

wrists were bare of the O'Kane tattoos, but a skull peeked out from beneath one sleeve and ravens chased each other in circles around his biceps—the mark of one of Gideon's elite Riders. "That's where I come in."

Dallas gestured to him. "Everyone, meet Zeke. Mad asked him to come over and set up shop with us for a bit. He's been riding with Gideon for a few years now, but he was born in Eden."

"Don't hold it against me." He twisted one of his hands, revealing the underside of his wrist. Where the bar code should have been, he had a beautiful tattoo of a phoenix, wings spread, bright, colorful flames licking at his skin. "I got caught breaching the networks at the City Center, too. Probably before Markovic's hacker rehabilitation initiative kicked in."

Markovic ignored him, and Ryder covered his smile with a cough.

"Anyway…" Zeke tapped his fingers on a tablet. "I still have friends in the city. Friends who've been waiting for this day for a long damn time. They're good enough with the tech to keep communication open without getting caught, but they know the people, too. They can figure out who would fight for us, who's too scared. Who just needs the right push."

Coop eyed him appraisingly. "Where are you from? There's plenty of people in the city who think they know what's what, but they don't know *shit* about what goes on outside their high-rises."

"The east tenements," Zeke shot back lazily. "North of the docks. Nowhere near as fancy as your posh little flat over by marketplace, but the roofs only leaked when it rained."

Coop's severe expression relaxed, and he barked out a wheezy laugh. "Fair enough. If your people can handle tech, may as well hook 'em up with mine. We'll have a nice little back-alley intelligence network set up in no time."

"Someone should reach out to Rachel's family." Dallas tapped his fingers on the table. "It's been too risky to contact them directly, but I'd bet all the money Liam Riley's ever made me that he's not sitting around, twiddling his thumbs in there."

Liam Riley had plenty of weapons—and plenty of men who knew how to use them. What he didn't have was support, not in the middle of the city. The smart thing would be to lay low until the shit hit the fan.

But waiting was hard, and Liam Riley had never been known for his patience.

Ryder leaned forward. "Riley has the resources to mount a proper resistance within the city walls, but it's tricky. If he waits too long to move, he may as well not bother. But if he moves too soon, he'll get himself killed—and take all your city contacts down with him."

"Liam's got a temper, but he's not a fool. If he knows the moment's coming..." Dallas shrugged. "We need to tell him. Zeke, how long will it take you to set up secure communications?"

"We can get a message out now. But better to wait and get everything you want together." Zeke laced his fingers behind his head. "We're not taking chances with this. Every account's a burner, and we'll want to rotate encryptions, and when and where we send from. Minimize contact. The second we fall into a pattern, Penelope'll be on us."

"If it takes that long," Markovic muttered.

Zeke quirked one eyebrow, his expression still full of lazy confidence. "Got something to add about your little protégé?"

The man stood up, retrieved the carved wooden cane leaning against the wall beside the door, and left.

"Whoops," Zeke murmured.

Dallas waved it away. "I'll have Lili talk to him when he's had a chance to settle down. She knows him better. In the meantime, we get our plan together. Coop—you figure out which of your people Zeke's boys should reach out to. Noah—"

"Keep Penelope the fuck out of our systems," he grumbled, already rising.

"At least keep her busy," Dallas retorted. "Distract the hell out of everyone inside those walls. We have almost all the noncombatants out of Two and Three, so buy us a little more time."

"Got it." Noah held the door for Coop and then followed Zeke through it.

As it swung shut behind him, Noelle looked from Dallas to Ryder before gathering up her tablet. "I'm going to talk to Rachel. If we're sending a message anyway…" She trailed off, then shrugged. "I don't want anyone regretting wasted chances."

"Good." Dallas smiled at her, genuine fondness crinkling the corners of his eyes. "Track down Lex when you're done and see if she needs help. I can be my own assistant for the afternoon."

"Sure you can." She paused halfway out the door to turn and give them both a stern look. "Don't forget to eat. There's plenty of leftovers in the downstairs kitchen."

Dallas rolled his eyes. "Get your pert little ass out of here, brat."

"I love you too, Dallas."

She pulled the door shut behind her with a gentle *click*, and Dallas leaned back in his chair with a laugh.

"Lex is a terrible, wonderful influence on that girl. The first day she showed up, she damn near fainted every time I breathed in her direction."

"She doesn't seem to have a problem with you now." And Dallas seemed equally unbothered.

"Nope. And that's good." Dallas dug through his pocket and pulled out his cigarette case and a lighter. "I was an asshole when she showed up. I had let myself get nice and comfy, playing with all my money and wanting power just because I didn't know how to stop reaching for it."

Overly ambitious, maybe, but it still sounded better than spending your life preparing for an uprising you weren't sure would ever come. "I need a favor."

"What sort of favor?"

Noelle's words bounced around in Ryder's brain. "I need to know what happened to Cerys."

Dallas huffed and tapped his lighter against the table. "Good luck with that. She split, as far as we know. Before the bombs hit Two."

It was all too easy to imagine—Cerys, the eternally selfish opportunist, seizing her chance to flee before getting blown off the map with the rest of her sector. Even Jim had believed it, had *died* still believing it, and maybe that was why Ryder needed to know.

He nodded to Dallas's cigarette case with an upraised brow, and Dallas passed him a cigarette and the lighter. Ryder took his time igniting the tip of the cigarette before explaining. "She didn't tell Jim she was leaving, and she didn't ask him to go with her. She always had before, every time she got sick of all the bullshit and wanted to take her money and run."

Dallas froze, one hand extended to take the lighter back. "You are fucking *shitting* me."

His shock was almost laughable. “An illicit, decades-long affair doesn’t fit with how you had either of them pegged, huh?”

“The fucking? Sure.” Dallas huffed. “Cerys caring about anyone enough to ask them to run away with her? That one’s gonna take some time to sink in.”

“She was just a woman.” Ryder paused. “Really, the fact that I can’t stop thinking of her in the past tense should tell you everything you need to know about my suspicions. Can Noah check it out? Or, hell, maybe Markovic knows something.”

“I’ll talk to them both. Jyoti, too.” His amusement faded. “There’s still a lot of rubble over there we haven’t had time to move. I don’t like to think about what we’ll find when we do.”

The only reassurances Ryder could offer him were secondhand, all whispered or mumbled stories about the horrors of war. How, after a while, they all blended together, or you stopped being able to associate the sight of a dead, mutilated body with what had once been a living person—even if they had died by your own hand. Your mind would go to great lengths to protect itself, and you would carry on.

Unless you couldn’t.

Ryder stuck the cigarette between his lips and pushed back from the table. It was premium tobacco, the kind you couldn’t get in a factory-rolled cigarette. Under normal circumstances, he would have enjoyed it, but he found himself missing the taste of cherries. “You’ll let me know?”

“Absolutely.” Dallas watched him rise. “You really should eat, you know. We only have a few hours before we’re supposed to meet with the other sector leaders.”

“Yeah, I remember.” But he wasn’t thinking about

his stomach as he left.

He was thinking about wasted chances.

Until recently, the O'Kanes had lived for one thing—the moment. They spent their time drinking, fucking, and partying, and that was *smart*, because who the hell knew when it could all end abruptly?

But it was foreign to Ryder. He'd lived his whole life in anticipation, preparing for a future war he could barely fathom, much less fear. And here he was, finally *in it*...and he didn't know what the hell to do.

If he died tomorrow, tonight—shit, within the next fifteen minutes—what did he have to show for it? A legacy of revolution, perhaps, and the very best military training you could get outside of the Base. But he'd never lived, not like these people. And it wasn't that they didn't understand the threat hanging over them all, or that they didn't appreciate the danger. They just managed to carry on in spite of it.

Ryder had never made time for that. He'd never shoved aside all his responsibilities for a few stolen moments, long enough to spark something in his gut besides the burning weight of *duty*.

Wasted chances.

He wound up in the aging room. He could hear Nessa slamming around, the occasional colorful curse drifting up from amongst the racks of barrels. He sat on the edge of the tasting table, his heart thudding, and waited.

Five minutes later, she appeared between two shelves. Her pink and purple hair was pulled up in a messy knot that bared her neck, and the thin straps of her black tank top bared her shoulders and arms. Unlike the rest of the O'Kanes, who seemed covered in tattoos, Nessa only had the O'Kane cuffs around her wrists and a delicate infinity sign above her heart.

She muttered as she approached him, scowling at the tablet in her hand so intensely she was almost to the table before she looked up. She jerked to a stop with a yelp of surprise, then slapped her hand over her mouth. "Oh God, you scared the shit out of me. How are you so *quiet*?"

"Training." He'd been taught to engage as many muscle groups as possible when moving to ensure maximum control. It wasn't exactly an easy habit to break. "Sorry I startled you."

"It's okay." She stepped closer and tossed the tablet onto the table next to him. "You taking a break between important war stuff?"

"Something like that." He stared at the soft line of her neck where it sloped into her shoulder. "This could be our last night—here, alive, on Earth, all of it."

Her breath caught. Her gaze shot to his—naked and without guile. She'd never learned to hide. She'd probably never had to. He could read each emotion as it flickered across her face as clearly as if she'd handed him a list. Fear, swallowed by intense yearning that she swiftly buried under stubborn determination. "It won't be."

"You don't believe that."

She wet her lips, and the memory of the taste of her lip gloss flooded Ryder. "I'm trying to. I have to believe it. If I give up…" She waved a hand toward the rows of casks. "I have to keep betting on the future, or we won't have one."

"No, I'm not saying give up. It's—" He wasn't making any goddamn *sense*. "I know it sounds like a line, but it's not. It's the truth. We can hope, and we can plan, but this might be it."

She sank her teeth into her lower lip and took a step closer, until she was standing between his knees. He could smell her skin now—a new scent today, vanilla with hints of cinnamon. She reached up and ghosted one finger over his mouth. "I kinda wish it was a line. Then I'd know you just wanna fuck my brains out and move along. Nice and simple. Safe."

His gut tightened. "I don't have a choice but to move along. Nice and simple...but not safe."

"No," she agreed softly. She traced the line of his jaw all the way up to his ear. "You're too smart to be safe. And you'd fuck up all my rationalizations, you know that?"

"How?" He tilted his head to the side.

"Because I keep telling myself it's okay." She kept touching him, gliding her fingertips up and over his eyebrow, her dark brown eyes alight with wonder. "I mean obviously the sex they're all having is good, but I can still pretend, you know? That I'm not missing anything that spectacular. That dumb, uncreative fighter boys can be enough."

Oh, he could show her everything she'd been missing. Things she'd never dreamed of. "Then it sounds like your rationalizations need to get fucked up."

Her lips curved into her sweet, fearless smile. "No, the smart thing would be to throw your ass out of here so I can focus. I'm good at knowing the smart thing to do." Her fingers found his lips again. "Not so good at doing them, though. I'm too curious."

"Curious enough to say yes?" It *had* to be her choice, just like it had to be his. Getting swept away in the moment might lead to regret, and that was the last thing he wanted to see shadowing her gaze.

Her hand fell away. She swayed closer, until her

lips almost brushed his. "Why me?"

He touched her hair, weaving the brightly colored strands that had slipped loose between his fingers. "Because you say what's on your mind. You call it babbling, but you don't—" He took a deep breath. Vanilla. Cinnamon. "I've spent most of my life surrounded by people I couldn't trust. Hiding who I really was from them. I feel like I don't have to hide from you."

"You don't." Her breath tickled across his chin. "I've already seen your murder book, and I still spent the last couple nights imagining all the ways I could get you into my pants."

Her pulse was pounding in the hollow of her throat. Ryder watched the spot, entranced, as he rose and grasped her hips. He lifted her onto the tasting table and eased between her thighs, switching their positions. "Tell me one."

"It started pretty much like this." She wrapped one leg around his, the heel of her boot bumping against the back of his thigh, and dragged her fingers over his belt. "Except I was wearing a skirt, which made it a lot easier to just get your pants open and get to it."

There was a time for that, shoving clothes aside, fucking hot and heavy against a wall or on the floor. This wasn't it. He tilted her head back and ran his thumb up the center of her throat. "Not the first time, Nessa."

Her breathing went ragged and she swallowed, her throat working under his thumb. "Why?"

"It's too easy." Her shirt had a scooped neckline. He traced that too, and had to close his eyes tight when she made a low, shocked noise. "Too fast, and it's all a big blur. So you tell yourself later that maybe it didn't move the earth beneath your feet, after all. No big deal."

"Oh *God.*" The leg wrapped around his tightened, but he didn't think she was aware of trying to pull him closer. "The earth's already moving. Have a little mercy."

"Not a chance." He kissed her again, but she didn't taste like cherries. Today, it was peach and ginger, and he savored it with a slow lick over her lower lip before delving deeper, gliding his tongue over hers.

For one shocked moment she was still against him, her body tense and her breath held. Then she moaned and wrapped her other leg around him. Her hands slid up his arms to the back of his head, and she dragged him closer, crushing his chest to hers.

Hungry, *starved*, like no one had ever taken the time to just kiss her. Ryder drew her arms from around his neck and pressed her palms carefully to the table's surface, one after the other, without breaking the kiss. She tugged against his grip, but he soothed her with a quiet noise lost to her mouth.

When she kept her hands on the table without pulling away, he moved on, touching the inner surfaces of her arms where they bent at the elbow. The delicate lines of skin above each collarbone. And finally the curve of her neck, just to see if it was as soft as he thought it would be.

Her thighs clamped hard on his hips. She broke away and panted against his cheek. "This isn't even fair. How the hell did my elbow become an erogenous zone?"

"I think—"

"Well, hello."

Nessa jerked back so quickly her boot slammed into Ryder's leg. Her hands flew up, and she froze with them pressed against his shoulders, a second from shoving him away. He saw the moment she realized that just made her look guiltier. He saw the moment stubborn rebellion filled her eyes.

He saw everything, because Nessa didn't hide anything. Not even in front of her leaders. "Lex."

Lex was standing at the end of the row, one elbow propped against a barrel and her chin on her hand—like she was watching a sunset or a video, not two people getting it on. "Good afternoon, Ryder. Don't you have a meeting soon?"

"Yeah." The same meeting she'd be attending, and she knew it.

"Ah." Something flashed in her eyes, but she lowered her lashes a heartbeat later. "Can I steal Nessa, or should I come back another time?"

At least she asked. Ryder slowly disentangled himself from Nessa's embrace, then kissed the tip of her nose. "Find me later."

"I'll bring dinner to your place," she replied. "After your meeting?"

"Deal." He headed for the stairs, but stopped short when Lex *winked* at him. "What?"

"What?" she echoed mildly. "It's nice to see you, that's all."

Nessa covered her face with her hands and groaned. "*Lex.* Knock it off."

"It's all right." Ryder gave them both his cockiest grin. "I can handle it."

After all, he'd heard Finn's horror stories about his arrival in Sector Four. If his friend could survive the challenges and beatdowns that had come his way while he was proving his worth to the O'Kanes, then Ryder could deal with some pointed looks and teasing.

Hell, it was almost quaint.

8

Nessa could still remember the first time she'd met Lex. She'd been a baby back then, barely a teenager, but after the trip from Texas she'd felt a million years old. Her days had been filled with work, with the banter between Dallas and his men and her grandfather's occasional growled command for them to watch their mouths in front of her.

It didn't seem odd at the time. She'd grown up on a farm surrounded by rough, foul-mouthed men. Before the trip north, she'd cut her hair short and hid her changing body beneath so many layers that most people assumed she was a boy. It had been easier to let them. Easier to be one of the guys. To be tough. Safe.

Then Lex strolled into her life, beautiful and glamorous, exuding sex and danger in equal measure, and

Nessa *hated her.*

For about twenty minutes.

She hadn't realized how badly she wanted another woman around, how much had been missing that she'd never even realized she could have. Dallas's mother had been a badass, but she was always distant and remote, a matriarch more likely to give you tough love than hugs and cuddles.

Lex had offered both, and more. She'd laughed and joked with Nessa. She'd relaxed with her. When the guys gave her shit, she gave it back with interest, and when they teased Nessa, Lex smacked them back twice as hard.

With her around, Nessa had discovered what it felt like to have a sister. And she'd figured out something just as important.

She didn't have to choose between tough or feminine. She could be both.

Lex was the one who had given her her first proper haircut, turning the short, shaggy locks into a pixie style that made Nessa feel cute for the first time in her life. Lex had taken her shopping for clothes that actually fit her, and filed the ragged edges of her nails to introduce her to the glory of nail polish. When Nessa had gotten curious about hair dye, Lex was the one who tracked down bleach on the black market and patiently applied it to Nessa's hair.

It had been more than a makeover, more than dye and polish. Surrounded by people who expressed themselves with the vivid ink they tattooed on their skin, Nessa had found her own mode of expression—by necessity, at first, since her grandfather had threatened all of Ace's favorite body parts if he tattooed Nessa before she was grown enough to know what she wanted, but then by choice.

She'd been trying to figure out who she wanted to be since she was thirteen. Other than the O'Kane cuffs wrapped around her wrists, the only ink she'd felt ready for was the tiny memorial tattoo Ace had inked over her heart the day after they'd put her grandfather into the ground.

Ink was forever. Nessa still felt too...impulsive.

Which was how she ended up on the couch in her office, staring down her first and most protective big sister, unsure if she felt guilty or defiant. Probably both. And irritated, too—that kiss had been getting *good*. "Are you gonna tell Dallas?"

Lex pulled a flask from her back pocket and began slowly unscrewing the cap. "And what, exactly, would I be telling him? Enlighten me."

God, nothing he wanted to hear. Nessa's memories of Dallas from before he left the farm were shrouded in hero-worship, and arriving back into his life as a hormonal teenager had saddled her with an embarrassingly intense crush for a while. But he'd made it clear from day one that he remembered her birth—and that baby sister wasn't a term of endearment from him. It was damn close to literal.

Which was why there was a fair-to-middling chance he'd punch Ryder in the teeth if he found out they'd been making out already. "It's nothing. Just blowing off some steam."

"That's not what it looked like."

"Really?" She wrinkled her nose at Lex and slumped down on the couch. "That's how everyone else blows off steam."

"With a nice, casual fuck in the back room, sure." She took a swig from the flask and held it out. "But those big eyes you were making at him, Nessa? Come on."

Nessa took the flask and rubbed her thumb over it. The shiny surface had the O'Kane logo etched into it, but Dallas hadn't stopped there. A crown hovered just above the skull, and the words *My Queen* flowed beneath it.

Yeah. Dallas wasn't usually subtle. Faces were gonna get punched. "That's what I was trying to get. A nice, casual fuck. He's the one obsessed with all the sexy-touching foreplay."

Lex's eyebrows slowly rose.

She was making this so much worse. Nessa scrubbed a hand over her face and took a sip from the flask. Trust Lex to have the good stuff—one of the first bourbons they'd bottled the second year, when they'd had too much leftover corn and Pop had started looking toward the future. The yeast had been *his* grandfather's secret recipe, passed down through who-the-fuck-knew how many generations, a strain Nessa lovingly kept alive, because it kept him alive.

And every time she tasted that spicy caramel and vanilla, she missed him all over again.

Which was the real answer to Lex's unspoken question, and the one thing Nessa would never allow to tumble out of her mouth. That deep ache of loneliness felt like a betrayal of everything Lex had ever given her. She had family and friends. She had a soft, comfortable life and a purpose.

She didn't like that about herself. Didn't like the dark neediness that made friends and family insufficient. Oh, she covered it with jokes about her barren love life, but until Ryder had touched her in that elevator, she hadn't realized how flimsy the cover was.

She wanted what he was offering so hard it made her dizzy. And that scared her. She took another sip before passing the flask back to Lex, unable to meet her eyes while she asked the most important question. "Do you think he's...playing me or something?"

"Ryder? No, I don't think so. It takes a special kind of sociopath to run game when it's not necessary." She sat beside Nessa, curling one leg beneath her. "And it's *not*, right? Necessary?"

"Depends on his goal," Nessa retorted, trying not to sound grumpy. "Getting in my pants? No, I pretty much already invited him. And if he's trying to do something else, I can't figure out what it would be. I'm not important to the war."

Lex choked on her bourbon. "Is that what you think he is—another money-grubbing asshole looking for a way to peel off a little of Dallas's empire for himself without putting in the work?"

"No. I *don't*." She slumped even lower on the couch, unsure if Lex's amusement was annoying or relieving. "Doesn't mean I'm right. Men aren't the only ones who get dumb when they're horny."

"Well..." Lex mused. "We can look at this logically. He *could* be out to get rich, except that he already has more money than Dallas."

Nessa stopped trying to sink through the couch. "What? How?"

There went Lex's eyebrows again. "Everything in Five is his. The Flemings are all dead, except for Lili. He tried to give her what they left behind, but she wouldn't take much. And then there's Jim Jernigan's fortune—Ryder was practically his kid, of course he left it to him." She paused. "I thought you knew. I thought *everyone* knew. Ryder's bankrolling this war."

Maybe she should have realized. But the man had arrived on the compound with a fucking *duffel bag,* for fuck's sake. Managing to make yourself rich in the sectors was hard enough. She'd never met anyone who didn't show it off. "Oh."

"Oh." Lex fell silent for a few heartbeats. "What are you really worried about, Nessa?"

Trust Lex to ask the question that cut straight to her heart. Nessa shifted until she could lean into Lex and rest her head on the older woman's shoulder. "I don't know," she admitted. "Everything's so tense, and it could explode tomorrow. And I barely know him, but he makes me feel less—" *Alone.* "Sad. Or less scared. I don't know. I just don't want the guys to scare him away."

"Ah." Lex rubbed her back in small circles. "With the way he looks at you, that would be a tragedy. I'll talk to Dallas. But, you know...he might surprise you."

Nessa doubted it, but she didn't quibble. She was too busy latching on to Lex's other words. "How does he look at me?"

"Ryder?" Lex smiled against Nessa's forehead. "Like he hasn't figured you out yet, but he really, really wants to."

Nessa closed her eyes and didn't fight the flutters this time. Maybe it was selfish or reckless in the middle of a war, but she didn't care. It felt *good*, and she needed something good. "We're gonna win this, right? Tell me we can do it."

"The city leaders think we can't, and they've been wrong about everything else," Lex whispered. "So let's just say I think our chances are good."

"Because O'Kanes can do fucking anything." But because Lex sounded tired, Nessa wrapped both arms around her. “Can I do anything else to help?”

Her answering sigh was silent, but Nessa still felt it. “We need an inventory on candles. There could be more blackouts, and we may not always be able to run the generators.”

Which definitely meant staying out of the elevator for the foreseeable future. “What about the generators in the distillery? Can I keep those going, or do I need to consider shutting down after this batch?”

“I’m not sure yet, but it’s a possibility.”

So shit really was dire. She’d been half-hoping for a denial, but Lex didn’t pull punches. And right now she needed Nessa to step up, not fall apart—even if she was facing the total disruption of her life’s work. “It might be best to scale back, either way. The guys have war shit to do, and I can’t keep us moving by myself.”

“I know.” Lex sighed again. “But it won’t be for long. And just think of how much these last few batches will be worth in ten years.”

Nessa sat back up with a grin. “Hey, I’ll let Ace make me some special War Whiskey labels. Distilled in the heart of the rebellion. We’ll be rich.”

“There you go. It’s all about the branding.”

The door slammed open, and Jasper jogged in, a little out of breath. “Sorry to barge in, but we have a problem.”

Lex straightened, and Nessa’s big sister vanished, replaced by a queen. “What is it?”

“Noah and Zeke figured out how to access the city’s troop movements.” Jasper’s expression went dark. “They’ve moved a whole goddamn platoon into Two.”

“Shit.” Nessa rolled to her feet, even though there was nothing she could *do*. The alarm would start blaring any minute, and the fighters would gear up and ride out.

All she could do was sit and wait to see how many of them came back home.

Lex rose. "I guess it's a good thing we finished the evacuations, then. Nessa?"

"Where should I start?"

"The candles, if you would."

At least it would keep her distracted. She'd do the inventory and then beg Lili for some help putting together dinner for Ryder. Because he was coming home. They were *all* coming home.

Nessa simply refused to accept any alternative.

Ryder had never seen so much blood.

Except it wasn't merely blood, it was carnage. An entire platoon of military police from the city, dozens of men, lay scattered over one of the wide streets in Two. As far as he could remember, this area had escaped the bombing that had leveled much of the sector—not that you could tell by looking at it now. The soldiers weren't just dead. Some of them were in pieces, torn or blown apart by Christ knew what.

He stood there, staring, as Cruz crouched near the center of the destruction. He'd been studying it for a few minutes, his brow furrowed. As if he was staring at a puzzle that almost made sense.

The others seemed far less serene. Finn stood next to Ryder, his stance and expression uneasy. Ace looked a little green, and before long he turned to study the road leading back to the city. Zan stood on his other side, glowering at the mess.

Retching came from behind him. Flash ambled

up and crossed his big arms over his chest. "Tank's chucked up his breakfast and is working on last night's dinner."

Even Dallas looked uncertain about the situation. Ryder focused on the V of the man's T-shirt collar and breathed slowly, trying to block out the metallic scent of blood—and worse. "Do you think Gideon had his men come down and take them out?"

After a moment, Dallas shook his head. "They would have stayed to clean up, even if they didn't have time to let us know beforehand. And I don't think this is their style. It's too..."

"Messy," Mad finished for him. "They wouldn't use explosives. They'd rather risk going hand-to-hand. It's too important for them to know exactly how many lives they've taken."

"Forty, by the way." Six stepped up next to Dallas and shoved her hands in her pockets. "As close as I can figure. Kinda hard to be sure."

Bren returned from his own survey of the battlefield with a grim expression. "They didn't get hit by a squad. See, they came marching up through there—" He pointed down at the undamaged end of the street. "Someone waited until they got here, someone who already had this section of the street wired."

"Wired with what?" Jasper asked.

"Hard to say without a better look. Mines, probably." Bren shrugged. "Took out half the men at once. You can see where the rest broke ranks and ran for it, but they didn't make it far." He glanced up, his eyes narrowed. "Cruz?"

The man was kneeling beside one of the fallen soldiers outside the blast zone. He started at the sound of his name, then rose. "This was Ashwin."

"Your Eden informant?" Ryder asked Dallas.

"Something like that." Dallas glanced at Cruz, one eyebrow raised.

Cruz met Ryder's gaze and lowered his voice. "How much did Jim know about the Base?"

Irritated, Ryder stared back at him. "What they needed him to know."

"Not enough, then." He tilted his head, indicating the carnage. "Ashwin isn't your average soldier from the Base. He's part of a covert program whose goal is to create better soldiers through genetic modification. Project Makhai."

The assumption that he knew nothing about Base operations annoyed Ryder almost as much as the fact that no one had told him the whole truth about Dallas's mysterious informant. He sucked in a breath, torn between correcting their misapprehensions with a fancy speech and getting the answers he needed.

He settled for the latter. "Even a third-generation Makhai—the ones they finally perfected—couldn't pull this off without help. No way did your Makhai friend manage to shoot a dozen guys before they ran for cover."

Surprise widened Cruz's eyes. Dallas just snorted. "Fucking Jim Jernigan. Of course he knew."

Ryder shrugged. "Someone had to make their equipment."

Cruz was still watching Ryder—speculatively, now. "You're right. Even most Makhai soldiers wouldn't have been able to do this, but Ashwin is the best. You saw him the night Eden invaded the sectors. He charged their lines and left nothing behind him but bodies."

"I remember." And he should have made the connection—between Ashwin heading alone into enemy lines and Cruz's obvious deference, it was clear now what Ashwin was. "If he's such a badass, neutralizing whole platoons all by his lonesome, then why don't you just round him up and send him into Eden?"

"Because I can't find him, for starters. He shows up when he feels like it, and leaves the same way." Dallas scrubbed a hand over his mouth and turned his back on the sea of dead bodies. "And to be perfectly damn honest? I don't wanna rely on his self-control next time he gets in a murdery mood. Maybe we'll be the ones who look like enemies that day."

A chill seized Ryder. "You think that's a possibility?"

"I'm not ruling it out. He's a powerful weapon, no doubt. But I prefer the ones I can aim in the right direction. The ones that don't go off until I'm damn well ready." Dallas exhaled roughly and raised his voice. "Flash?"

"Yeah, boss?"

"Strip the bodies of tech and weapons."

The big man strolled over to where the new recruit stood and slapped him on the back. "You heard the man, Tank. You start over there, with the guys who aren't in pieces."

"What about the bodies?" Cruz asked.

Dallas turned to survey the destruction again, his jaw tightening. "Leave them. Let the next recruits who roll out of those gates wonder just what the hell we do to people who come to play."

It was an ugly game, but that was all the leaders in Eden understood. That was the scariest thing about war—not the things you might see or suffer, but what you might be driven to *do*, all in the name of victory.

Because victory meant survival. Anything short of tearing down the city would count as defeat, and no one he knew in the sectors would live through the aftermath. The rebellion leaders would be the first ones executed, but the Council wouldn't stop until all of Dallas's people, especially, were dead.

Even Nessa.

Ryder squeezed his eyes shut and let the rage wash over him. This anger was old, almost as old as him, but knowing that Nessa was in danger lent it a new, burning edge. They wouldn't care that she'd never lifted a weapon, that all she wanted to do was keep her grandfather's legacy alive any way she could. To them, she was an enemy, and they would kill her.

Which meant Dallas was right. The rebellion had to succeed, so they couldn't show mercy. They couldn't afford to.

Ryder opened his eyes. "These men are just the first wave. They'll keep coming."

"I know." Dallas eyed him. "Do you know about any other secret weapons over there in Eight that Ford and Mia haven't already unearthed?"

"A few." It seemed wrong to smile through his rage, but that's exactly what he did. "They're not in Jim's book."

"Let's go make a list. And let's make every step they take into the sectors cost them."

9

Nessa didn't venture off the compound very often. For all that she bitched and moaned about Dallas keeping her chained to the production room, there were advantages to being a liquor prodigy and a princess. When she wanted food, one of the guys ran to fetch it for her. If she needed supplies, she sent the newest recruit.

It had been weeks since the last time she'd put so much as a toe out into Sector Four, and the changes were enough to slam her right in the chest.

The streets were quieter. Not just unused, but *empty*. She passed boarded-up doors and carts that had been abandoned. Some people had left the area closest to the wall when it had been electrified, but only a few had come back to reclaim their spots now that Dallas had turned it off.

For a place that had always felt so vibrant—dangerous, maybe, but seething with *life*—the fearful silence felt too much like giving up.

The feeling got worse when she reached the market square. There was more activity here—people gathered in clusters, talking in low voices. Men with guns patrolled with a sense of purpose that made her suspect they were part of Jasper's newly organized militia.

But when she stopped in front of her favorite noodle stall, she found it stripped bare, with no trace of the sweet, gray-haired lady who'd always flirted with Pop while sneaking Nessa sticky pieces of peanut candy. The stall next to it was empty, too, but the upended table and tangle of broken dishes told a darker tale.

People were running. People were *dying*. And Nessa wished desperately and selfishly that Lili hadn't been too busy to help her cook dinner, because seeing the raw truth of what the war was doing to Dallas's people hurt.

The crotchety old lady who sold pizzas and meat pies was still there, at least. She grumbled under her breath as she packed up Nessa's order, issuing her litany of complaints about the state of the sector in a voice just low enough that Nessa could pretend not to hear. But the sheer normalcy of her ever-present griping made Nessa want to grab her face and kiss her.

She gathered up the food instead, leaving behind an obscenely large tip. She did the same at the pastry shop, ignoring the proprietor's wide eyes as she left with her purchases. The people who stayed through it all deserved loyalty in return.

It was the literal least she could do.

The sun was dipping beneath the wall when she arrived back at the compound. The metal stairs to Ryder's apartment shook under her boots as she stomped up them, her nerves swallowed by her eagerness to see a friendly face. She banged on his door with her elbow, and shoved one of the bags at him when it opened. "I hope you're hungry."

He cleared his throat lightly and swallowed hard. "Uh, sure."

She knew that look. It was a *terrible shit went down today* look. She'd gotten enough of an update from Noelle to know everyone had made it back safely, but Noelle had seemed reluctant to share details.

Now Nessa wished she'd pressed. "If not, that's okay, too. I brought more liquor."

"No, thanks. The food's good." He set the bag on the desk and took the rest from her. "I'm not much of a drinker."

"I've noticed." She kicked the door shut and followed him to the table. "Do you just not like it?"

He didn't answer right away. When he did, his voice was rough. "I don't like feeling out of control. I'm not used to it."

He said it in that tone of voice too many of the O'Kanes used sometimes, the one that really meant *I never got to be a kid.* Which didn't seem to fit with the way he'd talked about his mother. He'd felt loved, she was sure of it.

Then again, she knew love wasn't always enough to make a kid feel safe. "What was it like, growing up in Eight? Ford never wanted to talk about it, but I've heard it's really...rigid."

Ryder pulled up a chair expectantly. After a second, she realized he was waiting for her to sit. So she did, letting him push the chair in for her. His fingers brushed the base of her neck for one electric moment.

Then he stepped away. "Sector Eight is all about structure. It has to be, in some ways—you can't run production on that scale without reliability and order. But that's just the surface, you know? The cover. You've seen Jim's book, and you know what he was planning. That was *my* life."

She stared at him, not quite comprehending at first. Then she looked at his perfectly formed muscles again and remembered how he moved—quietly, deliberately, with a control and focused grace only one person she'd ever met could match.

Cruz had been raised to be a warrior. Apparently, so had Ryder. "So Jim made you a soldier?"

"Jim kept a promise." Ryder paused, the wrapped meat pies in his hands. "My father tried to lead a revolt against the city, back in the early days after the Flares. He didn't make it. Jim always told me that was my legacy. That someday I'd finish what my father started."

"Oh, God." Her stomach knotted. "I'm sorry. I didn't know."

He huffed out a breath. "About which part?"

"Your dad." The meat pies smelled good, and she knew they'd taste good, too. Flaky crust stuffed with whatever meat and cheese and veggies the shopkeeper had been able to get her hands on. But Nessa could only break off the edges. "How old were you?"

"Young." Instead of sitting across from her, Ryder positioned his chair right beside hers. "I barely remember him. Sometimes I think I don't, not really. I only remember things people have told me."

She shifted her leg until her knee bumped his. "I get that. I remember my mom a little bit, but not my dad. But Pop told me so many stories about them, I kinda made my own memories."

"Something like that, yeah." He looked at her, his gaze skipping down to her mouth before returning to meet her eyes. "My father wanted to leave the sectors, head out past the communes to the mountains. He was going to build a cabin out there, away from all this."

"Yeah?" She'd seen her share of people living rough off the land on her way north from Texas. Some of them had looked so snug and cozy that she could imagine living that way, too—for a few days or a week or something. The idea of being away from network access and movies and music and what passed for *civilization* for too long made her skin itch with anticipated boredom.

He stared down at the untouched pie in front of him. "When this is all over, I'm going to do it. Go build that cabin."

His words from that afternoon drifted back to her. *I don't have a choice but to move along.* That's what he'd meant—when this war was done, if they came out the other side alive...

He was leaving.

Easy. No strings attached. It should have made all this feel safer, but instead it twisted an odd sort of sadness through her. She covered it by shoving aside her dinner and reaching for dessert. "Do you even know how to do that? You couldn't have gotten much experience living off the land in Sector Eight."

"I like to read." He shrugged. "And I've picked up a few things here and there."

She popped open the thin cardboard container to reveal golden-brown puffs of fried dough, some dusted with powdered sugar, some coated in a sugary-sweet syrup that probably wasn't real honey but was close enough.

She lifted one and bit into it, savoring the sweetness as she let go of that little stab of sadness. This was exactly what she needed, after all. A glorious fling with a firm expiration date. "I'm sure you'll be good at it, what with all your super-spy powers. We could drop you in the woods with a hatchet and come back a month later to find you with indoor plumbing and surround sound."

He smiled, that slow tilt at the corners of his mouth that she saw when she closed her eyes now, the one that made her pulse race. "Nice to know you believe in me."

"Of course I do." She popped the rest of the fried dough into her mouth and grasped for any hint of cool. "Except for your taste in liquor. But no one's perfect."

"I'll try to stay humble." His hand closed around her wrist. "May I?"

"May you—?" It was all she got out before he tugged gently, and then she knew *exactly* what was about to happen and could only wait, breathless, as anticipation stretched seconds into years.

Her pulse was pounding under his warm fingers before he got her hand anywhere close to his lips. His gaze caught hers. Held it. Their knees brushed under the table again, and she inhaled sharply as awareness danced over her skin.

She held her breath, and didn't let it out until he dragged his tongue over the pad of her thumb. All the air rushed out of her on a soft moan. God, he was barely even touching her, but the *look* in his eyes—

Like this was just the first taste. Like he'd lick her everywhere, all the places that were tight and throbbing. Like he'd take his time, and Nessa knew she was out of her depth and way out of her league, because he was still cleaning the sugar off her thumb with slow licks and she was ready to promise him damn near anything if he didn't stop.

But he did. Only instead of releasing her hand, he twined his fingers with hers and turned his attention back to his food.

It took her two unsteady breaths to decide not to murder him. It took two more for her to realize that hadn't been his big opening gambit in his seduction plan—he was just casually, accidentally smoldering at her.

Well maybe not accidentally. He knew what he was doing. She was the one flailing, because he wasn't playing by the rules of any game she'd ever learned.

"Do you really think I can make it?" he asked quietly.

"Out in the woods? Sure." Anyone trained to be creative and disciplined would have a shot, but it wasn't like he'd have to leave without resources. According to Lex, he could buy half the sectors. It was the truth, so it came easily. Except it wasn't the whole truth. "But it sounds..." *Lonely.*

"Crazy?"

"Quiet," she countered. "But I like to have people around to listen to me talk."

He seemed to consider that for a moment, then grinned again. "Gotta get through this war first, right?"

She couldn't help it. She laughed. And then she stopped trying to figure out the rules and did exactly what the fuck she wanted to do—because war. Fucking *war*. She could be gone tomorrow, her office as empty as those abandoned stalls, and she would have wasted these precious minutes.

She scooted her chair closer and leaned into him. He was warm all along her side, and tall enough that it didn't hurt her neck to rest her temple on his shoulder. The urge to climb into his lap and tear off his clothes hadn't abated, but the desire that came with it melted through her skin, settling deep inside as a gentler kind of heat.

"I don't want to think about the war," she said softly.

"Me neither." He moved, wrapping his arm around her and pressing her to his chest instead of his shoulder. She could hear his heartbeat—a little fast but steady, thumping beneath her cheek.

Expiration date. She had to keep that front and center if she wanted to survive this. Like a safety rope or a net, something to stop her from crashing too hard to earth. Because this was the part she craved, the part she'd never gotten from fucking guys she didn't really like, even if the sex was okay. She saw it every day around the compound, with every secret smile and casually exchanged caress. The O'Kanes practically oozed it from every pore—except with her. She got all the affection and none of the heat.

Having both was intoxicating.

She closed her eyes and inhaled. His soap was unfamiliar, something clean and woodsy, like he was already living out in some snug little cabin somewhere. She rubbed her cheek against the soft cotton of his T-shirt and shivered when his fingertips brushed her hip. "Distract me?"

"You haven't finished your dinner."

His voice was a low, velvety murmur that stroked inside her skin and made her squirm. "Ryder…"

"Shh." The couch was only steps away, but instead

of leading her to it, he picked her up and carried her. He laid her out on the soft, supple leather, then stretched out over her, his hard heat a stunning counterpoint to the cool leather.

He blocked out the world like this. Breathing raggedly, she braced her hands on his shoulders, frustrated by the thin fabric keeping her from touching skin. She told herself to *move*, to gather the T-shirt in her fists and tear it over his head, but her body wouldn't obey her. Her fingers trembled.

She was nervous. Even though it wasn't her first time, even though she'd spent her late teens wandering blithely past orgies—

Ryder wasn't some overeager fighter boy whose ego she could crush with a few words. He wasn't harmless or inexperienced or powerless. He was strong, and smart, and in complete control of himself and this moment and everything that was about to happen. Even as the realization gave those butterflies in her stomach a fierce kick, it stirred something else.

Relief.

She might be nervous, but he wasn't. And he was going to make this *so good.*

His lips brushed hers, then returned for a fierce, deep kiss. Like the one from that afternoon, hot and hungry, licking past her lips and drowning her in the taste of him. Moaning, she slid her hands around him, and now her body was obeying her commands. Or maybe it was just instinct, the same instinct that had her rocking up against him as she jerked his shirt higher.

Her questing fingers found warm, smooth skin. She dug her nails into the small of his back, and he made a low, sharp noise in the back of his throat, one that vibrated through her mouth as he plunged his hands into her hair. His fingers tightened, clenching into fists, pulling at the strands until the sting of it flared through her like tiny electric shocks.

She wanted more. She wanted all of him. One leg was trapped against the couch, but she wrapped the other around his hips, dragging him closer. She moved her hands higher up his back, spreading her fingers wide over the flexing muscles. She could die happy like this, rocking up against him.

Then she shifted her hips. His dick ground over her clit just right, and she *was* going to die. Dead, flying apart, coming with two layers of denim still separating them.

He kept kissing her, his tongue gliding over hers, both distracting her from and adding to the tension he'd sparked. He rocked, not just his hips but his whole body, a gentle movement that lit up a thousand nerve endings all at once.

Arching her back rubbed her nipples against his chest, soothing some of the throbbing, but it pushed him away from that perfect pressure against her clit. She whimpered her frustration into his mouth and arched, trying to get him everywhere she needed him, all over her all at once. But he was unmovable—nothing stopped his slow, methodical rhythm.

No swift, fleeting death for her. The pressure was twisting and building, headed someplace glorious and inevitable.

Ryder caught her lower lip between his teeth and slipped one hand beneath her shirt, his fingers hot through the thin lace of her bra. The first stroke jolted through her, all sweetness and no sting. A little pain would have made the pleasure easier to take, but he just kept caressing and circling, relentlessly gentle.

Nessa tilted her head back, and *there* was the sting. Just the barest scrape of his teeth along her lip as he released it, but she shuddered. "God, why are we still dressed?"

He reached between them and tugged at the buckle of her belt. "You don't want to be, just say the word."

"What word?" She tried to peel his shirt off, but it caught on his arms, and he was like a rock—focused on his current task, not altering course for anything. She consoled herself with stroking the skin she could reach. "You can have all the words. Any word. Just get naked with me."

He stripped his shirt over his head. Her breath caught, and for a moment all she could do was *stare*. His deep-brown skin was decorated with breathtaking black ink, and she mentally apologized to Ace for disloyalty as she traced one wondering fingertip over the elaborate compass decorating his shoulder.

Then she followed his collarbone down to his chiseled, perfectly defined chest, and something different unfurled inside her. She'd watched with carnal appreciation as well-built men beat on each other in the cage each week, but Ryder was different.

She didn't just see the strength and power in the graceful flex of muscle beneath her hand. She saw the discipline, the control. A lifetime of self-denial. They'd started forging him into a weapon before he was old enough to know who he wanted to be. This perfect body must have taken endless work and training, hours upon hours of pushing life aside so he could be ready for his mission.

Nessa didn't know what to do with all the tenderness welling up inside her. It was smushy and overwhelming and not remotely conducive to getting her brains fucked out. So she shoved it back down and dragged her nails lightly over his chest and down the center of his body.

His abs rippled under her touch, and he let her tug at the warm leather of his belt before seizing her wrist. "Your turn."

Her nerves roared back as he guided her hand to her T-shirt. No one had ever turned *her* into a weapon or encouraged self-denial. Nessa had bitched and moaned her way out of every attempt at self-defense training until Dallas had gotten her a gun and told Bren to train her with it.

Most of the time, she felt just fine about her body. But she still squeezed her eyes shut as she wiggled her way out of her shirt and tossed it to the floor. Her hair fell around her shoulders and tickled her skin, and she pushed it back from her face to peek up at Ryder.

He stared down at her—chest heaving, hands flexing at his sides. "The bra, too."

A silky order, and Nessa played along. She had to arch to get one arm behind her, and the clasps seemed to have turned into labyrinthine puzzles. She blamed the heat of his gaze—she could *feel* it, like the tingling pressure when someone was almost touching you, but everywhere.

She cursed and finally got the bra undone, flinging it away with no regard for where it fell. Nothing mattered but getting his hands on her before she came out of her skin.

Ryder smiled, slow and hot, and quirked one eyebrow as he reached for his belt.

She didn't wait for the command this time. She groped for her own, tearing the leather open and popping open the button on her jeans. “Boots,” she managed. “I need to take mine off.”

“Relax.” He drew her hands up over her head and pressed them to the leather cushions as he leaned over her. Another soft kiss, and he trailed his lips down to her jaw. “Just...relax.”

His mouth slid down, and she burned wherever he touched her. The tender spot beneath her ear. The place where her neck met her shoulder. The hollow at the base of her throat. The spot to the left of her collarbone where she had a funny little cluster of freckles.

Her heart pounded. She tried to get a full breath. “I can’t relax. You’re trying to foreplay me to death.”

His brows drew together. “I don’t think that’s a thing.”

She wiggled her wrists in his grasp. When that didn’t work, she rocked her hips up with a groan. “It is totally a thing. You’ll see when I die.”

He laughed softly and returned his attention to the spot just beneath her jaw. “If you die, I’ll stand corrected.”

The murmured words against her skin sent a shiver through her. Then he parted his lips and teased the spot with his tongue, and her toes curled in her boots.

It was relentless. It was inexplicable. No—that wasn’t true. She’d been to enough parties to know some people delighted in taking teasing to extremes. She just hadn’t expected Ryder, with all his stripped-down minimalism and efficiency, to be one of them.

He sure as hell wasn’t being efficient now. She’d been wet forever, and if he worked into her now, she’d probably come on the second thrust. She’d never even gotten herself this cranked up with her own fingers, because *she* sure as hell wasn't into self-control.

Maybe she was missing out.

Ryder stroked his hands down her arms as he eased down, licking a path past her collarbone to the center of her chest. She tried to obey and relax into the pleasure. But there was so *much*, and she couldn't stop the way her body jolted when he grazed one of her nipples with his teeth.

She wanted to grip the back of his head to hold him there, but he still held her arms trapped, so she dug her head back against the couch and whimpered. He couldn't stop—the sudden ache blooming inside her was like a compulsion. "Ryder, *please*—"

"I'm here." He soothed the aching peak with his tongue as he shifted his weight, and his fingertips tickled down her stomach and eased into her open pants.

Oh God, oh God, oh *God*. She dropped her freed hands to his shoulders and clung to him, her attention swinging dizzily back and forth between the slick heat of his tongue circling her nipple and the slow progress of his fingers.

The word *anticipation* hadn't had meaning before this moment. It took hours and days and weeks for him to graze her clit, and any possible self-consciousness about just how wet she was vanished like smoke. So did the distraction of his tongue.

So did the world.

He groaned against her breast as his fingers slicked over her. Then he lifted his head, his jaw tight and his eyes blazing. "You're so fucking wet."

"Told you," she moaned, digging her nails into his shoulder. "Death by foreplay."

"You're very much alive." His fingers pressed deeper. "I can feel your heart beating."

She shuddered and tried to shift her legs wider. But with her pants still on everything was tight and intense and impossible to escape. Her pulse pounding in her ears, she stared up at him. "Do it. Ruin all my rationalizations. Ruin me."

He leaned in for a kiss, and the moment his lips touched hers, his fingertip glided over her clit. Slow at first, just like his kiss, so gentle she shuddered through little shocks that only coaxed anticipation tighter.

Her hips twitched, the movement beyond her control, and the babbling started. Pleas, tripping over each other to roll off her tongue, and she could barely understand herself with the words muffled against his lips. But they echoed in her head, a litany rising with her need.

Please.

Right there, right there.

Yes. Yes yes yes. Yesyesyes—

His fingers pressed down firmer, and right where she needed them, and she wanted to scream her relief when that heat pulsing through her grew to a tight point and then snapped.

The orgasm hit her hard. It hit her *deep*. The first fire of it burned through her, that swift release she was so used to wrenching free with her own fingers. But everything was clenching now, and the fire didn't burn out. It swept out in another wave, clenching her fingers and curling her toes, until she was pretty sure she only had one word left.

Fuckfuckfuck.

Ryder didn't stop. He murmured words she couldn't quite hear—or maybe just couldn't understand—as he pushed her higher. Harder.

She was coming again. And still coming. Both at

the same time, all tangled together. She panted against his cheek, riding his hand with no shame or control. She rode it until the sensitivity overwhelmed her, and her nerves fritzed out and she couldn't stop her hips from writhing away.

"I can't—" she gasped finally, limbs trembling, voice hoarse. "No more, no more."

His hand stilled. He was breathing almost as hard as she was, and the hot rush of every exhalation over her ear and neck added to the sensory overload. Gently, bit by bit, he pulled his hand away.

Nessa melted back into the couch as tiny aftershocks zipped through her. She had real flutters now. Actual physical flutters—and not in anyplace nearly as poetic as her heart. Her pussy was clenching around nothing, and the hollow emptiness was the only part of this moment that didn't feel perfect. Her body clearly had no fucking survival instincts, because it was ready for his cock. Craving it, even, tempting her with the satisfaction of having all that emptiness filled.

His fingers had just about stopped her heart. His dick might actually send her into cardiac arrest.

And fuck, now she was rambling in her head. The orgasms had broken her.

He watched her, his expression soft. "You okay?"

"I don't know," she admitted. He was still stretched over her, warm and strong, and the gentleness in his eyes made it so easy to snuggle into him. She felt safe like this, even knowing he was eroding the foundation of her sheltered little world view. "That was...wow. It was really wow."

He ducked his head with another of those heart-melting smiles. "I didn't quite catch that. Wow, you said?"

She didn't know if her cheeks could flush any harder. She screwed her face up into a scowl and smacked his shoulder with her fist.

It bounced off.

Of course it did. A laugh sputtered out of her, ruining her attempt at severity. "Don't get smug. I hate smug men."

"You don't hate me." He rose on his knees between her thighs, all those delicious muscles flexing as he moved, and finished opening his pants.

His left hand was still wet with her arousal. She watched, entranced, as he freed his dick and wrapped his fingers around it.

The first slow stroke tugged at all those pulsing places inside her. He was magnificent, *shameless*, dragging his fingers over the length of his shaft, totally unconcerned by her rapt fascination.

No, not unconcerned by. That tiny tilt of his lips grew into a smile, because he *loved* her rapt fascination. And he was making a liar out of her.

He was so smug, and it was so hot.

Watching his face, she reached for him. He sucked in a sharp breath when her fingers bumped his, and she held his gaze as she slipped past his fingers to circle the head of his cock.

"Fuck." His head fell back and then forward, his hips rocking slightly, pushing into her grip. "Again."

Not so perfectly controlled anymore, and definitely not denying himself. Nessa slid her thumb up to repeat the movement and made a loose fist of her fingers so he could fuck into her hand.

Her fingers glided down his shaft when he thrust again, her own wetness easing the way. It was crude and intimate at the same time, and she had to watch.

Her fingers looked small, wrapped as far around him as she could go. He'd more than fill that empty ache, and part of her wanted to crawl over him now and take him as deep as she could.

But he'd be so gentle. He'd reach for all that control, and she wanted this. The naked look of pleasure on his face as he thrust forward again, one hand trembling on hers and the other clenched at his side.

There was no slow build. His cock twitched in her grip, and he tightened his hand around hers until it almost hurt. "Harder."

Hypnotized, she followed his lead. Pumped her fingers up and down, not resisting when he took over the movements. A few more short, rough jerks, and he choked out her name. His jaw clenched and his eyes closed, and she wondered if she'd looked like that in the moments just before she came. Like it felt so good it hurt.

Knowing she'd helped bring him here made her head swim. She couldn't tear her gaze from his expression, not even when he came. She felt it, spurting over their joined hands, landing on her stomach—and she didn't care.

His face. His *face.* For one beautiful second, he was naked and unguarded—his features slack with relief, his lips parted in satisfaction.

He should always look like this. Sated. Happy.

Perfect.

He opened his eyes slowly, their depths shadowed only by lingering heat, and stared down at her.

She was broken. She had to be. Because she was sprawled on her back on a couch, half-dressed, her hand and stomach sticky because a sector leader had just jerked off all over her. And all that inappropriate tenderness was bubbling up so fast and hard her lips curved into a goofy smile before she could stop them. "Wow."

His smile matched hers. "You said that already."

"Well, it still applies." She twisted her hand to twine her fingers with his. "Plus, it sounds more romantic than *you missed my tits*."

That shocked a laugh out of him as he rose from the couch and righted his clothes. "You O'Kanes are foul. I like it." He disappeared into the next room, and she heard the water in the bathroom sink cut on. When he returned, he was carrying a damp hand towel.

Before she could stir herself to reach for it, he'd already settled on the couch next to her legs. That momentary lapse in control had vanished, but there was something...nice about relaxing under his gentle touch. The towel was soft, the water was warm, and he took his time, turning what could have been an awkward practicality into its own quiet pleasure.

He was taking care of her. And she didn't hate it.

"Still hungry?" he rumbled.

"Maybe a little." She squirmed upright and crossed her arms over her naked chest. "I hope I didn't throw my bra into the food."

He retrieved his shirt from the floor beside the couch and pressed the cotton into her hands. "Not quite. I think we're safe."

The shirt was huge and smelled like him. She barely managed to keep herself from rubbing it against her cheeks as she pulled it over her head. "Thanks."

"Anytime, Nessa."

It sounded sincere, and deeper than a simple shirt. It encompassed every filthy, glorious thing they'd done and would hopefully do again, and those sweet moments of tender caretaking.

It didn't sound like an expiration date.

10

Ryder couldn't spend one more goddamn day looking at the monitors that covered the walls of the O'Kanes' war room. It was too sterile, all data and maps, so far removed from the messy reality of what they'd seen in Sector Two that it felt disrespectful, almost cowardly, to sit in there while real shit was going down outside.

Which was why he gladly geared up when Dallas asked him along on a tour of the sector. He didn't care if it was ugly, or even dangerous. It was better than sitting in a room that increasingly felt like a prison, safely distanced from the horrors outside.

They stopped in the marketplace first. Many of the shops and carts surrounding the square had been abandoned, but there were still a fair number of people milling about, hurrying from one stand to the next.

The buzz of conversation faltered as people noticed Dallas. A handful quickly turned their backs and scurried into alleys. Even more froze in place as he passed. Some bowed their heads, and a few looked ready to drop to their knees.

Whispers rose, and Dallas ignored it all as he crossed the open space. "Good news is, most of the people who flat-out hate me are long gone."

"Just *most*?" Ryder's hand itched for a weapon. "Now you tell me."

Dallas winked at him. "If you only keep the people who love you around, life is boring. You get complacent."

Before Ryder could respond, Dallas gestured to their left and led him toward a stand overseen by a glaring, gray-haired woman. The shelves were stacked with the meat pies Nessa had brought him, and the smell of baking bread and spicy meat drifted from the open door behind her.

As soon as they approached, the woman balled up her fists and braced them on her hips. "Did that girl tell you about the milk?"

"The milk?" Dallas asked, both brows rising.

She scowled. "The *milk*. Ever since this war started, I can't find nearly enough. Do you know why I need milk?"

"I expect you plan to tell me."

She huffed. "Cheese. All these young men you're training to fight just eat and eat. They eat everything I can make. I sell out before lunch every day, and my regulars have to go someplace else."

"Well, we can't have that." Dallas pulled a few rumpled bills out of his pocket and passed them to her, then picked up a pair of paper-wrapped meat pies. "I'll tell you what, Miss Pearl. I'll get you all the milk you want. Maybe some fresh beef, too. I'll give you a real sweet deal on it."

Her wrinkled face scrunched in suspicion. "And in return?"

"You pass that deal along to the militia." Dallas handed Ryder one of the meat pies. "Just a little discount, so I know none of them are going hungry."

She muttered something that sounded vaguely obscene, then jerked her head in a rough nod. "If the deal's sweet enough."

Dallas grinned at her. "I'll send Hawk over to negotiate. You need anything else, you let him know, okay?"

Pearl grumbled her assent. Then, as Dallas turned to leave, she said, "O'Kane. Wait."

When they turned back, she was already bustling through the door into the small kitchen beyond. She came back with a cardboard box and thrust it out. "For Lex. Don't you steal any."

"Wouldn't dream of it, Pearl." He nodded to her and led Ryder back into the square. When they were far enough away, he rattled the box. "That woman would tell God and the Devil both everything she thought they were doing wrong, and charge them for the privilege, but Lex comes around and she's all smiles and free food."

It was a common reaction to Lex, from what Ryder had seen. "That lady of yours has everyone charmed. Even Jim was almost fond of her, and he wasn't fond of anyone."

Dallas smiled, and it was the closest Ryder had ever seen his eyes get to softening. "She's special. And she knows how to make *them* feel special. That's not something a lot of people get to have these days."

"No, it isn't." The bustle in the marketplace had mostly resumed, and Ryder couldn't help wondering if those initial frozen reactions weren't about Dallas personally, but about the perpetual target on his back. "Where to next?"

Dallas polished off a third of his meat pie in one bite and nodded across the square as he swallowed. "I want to check in with Stuart. He's the best leather-worker I've ever met—and the unofficial leader of the crafters. If it happens in the market, he knows about it."

Halfway to the shop he'd indicated, a plump woman with a pretty face stepped out of one of the shops and hurried toward them, a paper cup in each hand. "Here," she said, offering one drink to each of them. "Pearl should have given you something to drink."

"Pearl was busy complaining," Dallas replied with a grin. But he tucked the box for Lex under his arm and accepted the cup. "How're you doing today, Pam?"

"Good, good. Things are good. So much better now that the wall's off."

Her gaze slid to Ryder and back, as if she wanted to say something else. Dallas caught the look and tilted his head toward him. "This is Ryder. He's helping me with this beef we've got with Eden. You can say whatever you want in front of him."

She glanced at Ryder again and twisted her hands together. "It's not so much... It's just—" She exhaled in a rush and gave Dallas a pleading look. "Lou's been fretting about the fight. About not doing his part. He's been talking about going over to join up with the men Jasper's training."

"Ah." Dallas folded the paper around his food and

shoved it into his pocket. Then he grasped Pam's shoulder lightly. "Jas knows about Lou's bad leg. He won't take on someone who'll just get himself killed."

"That means Lou will do something even stupider." She swallowed hard. "I thought maybe if we could help some other way, one that didn't wound his pride. He can cook, and everyone needs to eat. If you made a special request…"

"All right." Dallas squeezed her shoulder. "I'll talk to Lex. I got sector leaders in my office damn near every day, and only about three people on that compound who can serve up a meal without poisoning folks. We'll figure something out."

"Thank you." She clasped his hand for a moment, then smiled at Ryder and inclined her head. "Sorry to interrupt."

"It's fine, Pam. You have a good day."

She scurried back to the shop, and Dallas took a sip from his cup. "Fuck, that synthetic stuff Jim cooked up in Eight is close, but there's nothing like honest-to-God real coffee."

The rich scent drifting up from the cup in Ryder's hand reminded him of his mother. Jim had created the coffee replacement for her, but whenever she'd managed to find even low-quality coffee beans, it was like Christmas. She babied those bitter little gems, grinding them by hand and coaxing every bit of flavor from the grinds. She'd even tried growing it herself, but the plants died before they ever produced flowers.

She wept over the limp stems and brown leaves, and told him the story of how she'd met his father in a shop that sold nothing but coffee. There was one on every corner, she said, laughing like it was some joke only she understood.

She never drank real coffee again.

Ryder drained half of his in one searing gulp. The liquid blistered over his tongue, but he shook off the pain and squared his shoulders.

Stuart's shop turned out to be an actual *shop*, with racks of leather jackets and shelves stacked with pants and boots. Corsets covered one display table, deep browns and blacks decorated with lace and silver. Another table held nothing but leather wrist cuffs, some sporting silver studs and some with delicate rings.

"O'Kane!" A big man at the front of the store rose when they entered, an easy smile coming to his face. The counter in front of him was strewn with scraps of leather and tools, and the piece in front of him looked like an almost finished gun belt. "Good to see you."

"Same." Dallas shook the big man's hand. "I'm giving Ryder here a tour of the marketplace. Thought I'd check in and see how it's going."

"Shit is what it is, right?" Stuart held out his hand to Ryder. "You're the gentleman who took over Five."

"I am." The man had a strong grip, but not the purposeful knuckle-crushing he'd experienced elsewhere in the sectors.

"Right on."

Dallas picked up a bandolier and turned it over in his hands. "Is this what you're doing with that scrap leather? Noelle mentioned something about it."

"Yep." Stuart pulled up a stool and bent over his worktable again. "Anything I had bits of lying around—full-grain, bonded, you name it. Patched-together pieces of shit—don't tell anyone I made them."

Dallas gave the piece in his hand an experimental tug, then grinned. "Still quality work. And the boys will find it useful."

“It’ll get the job done,” Ryder agreed.

“I guess.” Stuart shrugged, then tapped an awl on the scarred wooden surface of his table. “Been hearing some rumbles, O’Kane.”

“Tell me.”

“Folks are saying some ugly shit went down in Two. A bunch of Eden soldiers, dead as hell.” He eyed Dallas sharply. “Christ knows that’s not the bad part. People are also saying it wasn’t us. Your men, I mean.”

Dallas nodded, his expression easy. Relaxed. If Ryder hadn’t been there in Two with him, he wouldn’t have been able to guess the slaughter had bothered him. “It wasn’t pretty, that’s for sure. But *us* is bigger than the O’Kanes right now. Remind people that we have all the damn sectors united—and the only people who need to be scared of that are the ones who think those walls will protect them.”

Stuart’s craggy face split into a grin. “That was a damn good speech, O’Kane. Downright motivational. You practically write my shit for me.”

So that explained how Dallas managed to not only keep an eye on his people, but speak to them, as well. The kinds of people who built their lives in the sectors didn’t trust power, full stop. To them, a benevolent dictator was just as bad as a despot. It didn’t matter whether the man in charge was cruel or kind, he still wielded power over your freedom, your fortunes.

Your lives.

But if an average man, one of their own, trusted Dallas enough to speak for him? That meant Dallas trusted him enough to let him, to give him that power. And that made all the difference between a dictator and a leader.

Dallas and Stuart spoke for a few more minutes,

but Ryder wasn't listening. He was thinking—about power, and about *community*.

He didn't know the first thing about the people in Five. He knew some of the men who worked for him, and more who had volunteered to train, but he left them mostly to Hector. Truthfully, he didn't want to know them. He didn't know where to begin.

Dallas O'Kane cared about Four. About its economic well-being, the lives and livelihoods of the people in it, even the buildings. The man probably knew every stone and brick in the whole fucking sector, the same way Dallas's mother had undoubtedly known every hill and valley of her ranch back in Texas.

It was a knowledge born of love, of legacy. Dallas was fighting this war to protect his home. Ryder was fighting it because the war *was* his destiny.

What would he have when it was over?

Nessa. Flashes of memory invaded his senses—the curve of her hip, her smile, the taste of spices on her tongue. Reluctantly, he locked those thoughts away. They'd agreed from the outset that their arrangement was temporary, an attraction they could both only afford to indulge in the moment, under these very specific circumstances. Changing the rules of engagement now would be dirty, beneath him.

Besides, Nessa was the heart of O'Kane's empire, the beating center of it all. Her family would need her when the war was over and it was time to rebuild. She'd never abandon them, not for the world.

"Hey." Dallas snapped his fingers in front of Ryder's face. "You got some deep thoughts you want to share?"

Was Dallas a fucking mind reader, or did he just give off that vibe on purpose? Maybe that was his game—stare at you like you'd done something wrong, and you'd trip over your own feet to admit what he didn't even know yet. "Deep thoughts, sure, but they're not for sharing."

"Uh-huh." Dallas lifted a hand in farewell to Stuart and headed for the door. "It's a good ten-minute walk to the warehouse where Jas is training fighters, so how about *I* tell *you* a story. It's a good one. Real cautionary-tale stuff."

"I can't wait."

"It's about the first time I led men into a fight." He held the door open for Ryder and followed him out into the street. Instead of returning the way they'd come, he took a sharp left down an alley so narrow, the rough stone was completely in shadow.

"Texas was rough," he continued in an easy voice. "My mama held her family's ranch through grit and will, but there were plenty of people who looked at a woman in charge and saw weakness."

"I hope your mother taught them painful lessons about stupid assumptions."

"Over and over again. So when the people whose land bordered ours needed a little more space—and they decided to push out in our direction—they didn't come at us nice and clean and in the open." Dallas's jaw clenched. "Those motherfuckers poisoned our water supply. Half the ranch was sick before we figured it out. Seven people died."

"Jesus." Ryder stopped and stared at him. The tactic was brutal but effective. Jim had considered that Eden, if pressed, might do the same. But the fact that the sectors surrounded the city afforded protection—in order to poison everyone outside the walls, the city would have to poison itself. "What happened?"

"I gathered everyone who could stand steady enough to hold a weapon, and then I got them *mad.* Fuck, *I* was mad. I was, twenty, maybe. *Maybe.* I've always had a temper, but back then I didn't know how to keep it in check." Dallas slanted a look at him. "And I didn't know well enough to leave the folks who'd lost loved ones at home. They were looking for revenge, and they didn't much care if they survived it. They went down first, and almost took the rest of us with them."

It felt a little too pointed to be coincidence. "Are you telling a story or trying to ask me a question?"

"Who says it has to be one or the other?" Dallas shrugged and stared ahead again. "One of the men out for revenge was Nessa's father. She was just a baby, barely walking yet. The poison got her mother, and then I got her father killed because I couldn't recognize a man who wasn't in any shape for battle. I made her an orphan."

The story was horrific, unthinkable, yet the sincere, self-directed blame in Dallas's voice still made Ryder want to laugh—not out of mirth, but disbelief. "Is there *anything* you won't take credit for?"

"Not credit. Responsibility," Dallas countered. "And no. Right now, the fact that my decisions have consequences is something I'm holding on to real tight. Because it would be easy to let it go, and I don't think you'd want me running this war if I did."

It was nothing less than a confession, and it deserved to be answered in kind. "You know, not everything in Jim's scary little book was his idea."

Dallas snorted. "Shouldn't be surprised. You're smart, but you're a devious motherfucker, too. You took over Five from the inside without spilling a drop of blood. That might be a first for the sectors."

Ryder shrugged. "I made it a point never to do anything I couldn't live with." Just in case he made it through this war, he couldn't want to walk a path of self-destructive vengeance.

"Good." Dallas stopped abruptly and turned to face him. "Lex told me I'm not allowed to be an asshole about this, but I am not fucking around here. If you hurt Nessa, even a tiny bit, I'll make Jim's scary book look like a fucking princess tea party. Do we have an understanding?"

"O'Kane—"

"If I'd been a little smarter, a little *better*, she'd still have a father. She's family, in every fucking way that counts. I will ruin anyone who makes her cry."

Maybe Ryder had a bit of a death wish, after all, because he couldn't help imagining Nessa's reaction to Dallas's proclamation, and he had to bite the inside of his cheek to keep from grinning. "I hear you. Yes, we have an understanding."

"We'd better," he rumbled, glaring at him for another moment before he resumed walking. "It'd be really fucking inconvenient if I had to kill you."

"Uh-huh." More inconvenient for Ryder than anyone, because he had no doubt that Dallas would do it. "For what it's worth, she could have done worse than you for family. A lot worse."

Dallas laughed roughly. "Don't bother with flattery. My ego's already as big as it can get."

"Flattery's for people who don't have more important shit to say."

"I suppose it is." Dallas slapped Ryder's shoulder—maybe a bit harder than necessary, but still friendly. "Let's win this war, and we'll both have enough ego to last a few lifetimes."

Ryder finally let loose with the chuckle he'd been holding in. "Whatever, O'Kane. Something tells me that in the ego department? I'll never catch up with you."

11

The upstairs warehouse area that had become Tatiana's workspace wasn't as pretty as her shop had been, but it *smelled* the same. No matter how tightly she packed away the oils lining the huge steel shelves, the fragrances always escaped in teasing hints. Nessa could lose hours sampling each one in turn—and probably would have, if she'd had hours to spare.

No one did, not anymore. Even girl-bonding time had been taken over by the practicalities of war. Instead of soaps or lotions, one side of Tatiana's massive worktable was lined with the latest batch of the unaged grain liquor. Bottle after bottle of clear, stringent liquid, each waiting for some mysterious combination of the herbs Rachel and Jeni were sorting at the other end of the table.

Nessa didn't like watching. They were basically murdering her booze.

Jeni frowned down at a pile of brittle, dried *somethings* in front of her. "Do we have any more calendula?"

Rachel looked up from counting out sticky-looking brown plant buds. "Just the fresh ones in Jyoti's greenhouse. We're saving those for oil, though—topical use."

"Zan reached out to a contact down south, but we haven't heard back yet." Tatiana carried another basket to the table and straddled the bench. "We have plenty of skullcap, though. Nessa, do you want to help slice the ginger?"

"Sure." She abandoned the shelf of fruity-smelling oils and joined the other women at the table, stopping only to stroke little Hana's cheek. Amira's daughter was strapped into a high chair just far enough away from the table where she couldn't grab things, banging two wooden blocks together.

At Nessa's attention, she lifted one chubby hand, offering her a block with a drooling smile.

"You keep it," she murmured, ruffling the girl's dark hair. "I gotta play with the grown-up toys today. We'll build you a castle tomorrow."

The baby babbled as Amira smiled indulgently. "Don't let Hawk hear you say that. He'll hit the workshop and actually build her a tiny castle."

Nessa laughed and settled on the bench across the table from Jeni. "That reminds me. I owe you and Hawk a wedding present. Maybe something from the vault, if you think he'd like it."

Jeni waved that away and began to break up dried sprigs of herbs into a mortar. "It'll keep. Everyone's so busy right now."

Amira passed her the pestle, along with an

encouraging smile. “This shit won’t last forever.”

No, it wouldn’t. It *couldn’t.* They’d fight and they’d win or they’d fight and they’d die, but one way or another, there was a time in the near future where none of them would have to worry about Eden anymore.

And then Ryder would leave.

Fighting back a frown, Nessa accepted the ginger and a knife from Tatiana. Thinking about Ryder was dangerous. Thinking about him would lead to babbling about him, and her mood was too precarious for teasing. “How are you feeling, Rachel? Cruz hasn’t raided the ginger stash in a while.”

“Better, thanks. Much better. I think the worst of the morning sickness might be over.” She knocked on the tabletop.

That should soothe Cruz, who’d been fighting two different wars lately—the easy one against Eden, and the impossible one against Rachel’s discomfort and the fundamental nature of pregnancy. Cruz took taking care of Rachel and Ace so seriously that Nessa had always rolled her eyes and wondered why they put up with it.

Maybe it wasn’t as much of a mystery now. Having someone take care of you could be kinda nice.

“Poor Cruz.” Jeni laughed as she ground the herbs into fragrant green bits. “He’s so excited, he just doesn’t know what to do with himself.”

So was Ace. Nessa had known Ace for half her life, and if she’d had to guess about his reaction to knocking someone up, she would have put her money on sheer panic. But Ace was as smug as if he’d invented the concept of making babies himself.

Even more unthinkably, he had a workroom up here above the warehouse now, too—a place to stash all his painting supplies and half-finished canvases. His old studio had become a nursery, complete with cheerful dragons chasing each other through fluffy clouds all around the walls and up onto the ceiling.

It was so violently adorable, Nessa wanted to puke on him.

"Hey." Tatiana nudged her arm. "You okay?"

Nessa blinked, and realized she'd been glaring at the ginger, her knife frozen above it. Flushing, she quickly resumed slicing. "Yeah, I'm fine. Just tired. I never thought I'd be glad to shut down production, but I can't run that place myself."

Rachel glanced over at her, then squinted sharply.

Oh, shit. She'd lied. In front of *Rachel*, who was one of the only people who could actually tell. Her cheeks grew hotter, and she stared down at the ginger, not seeing it.

Don't think about Ryder. Don't think about Ryder. Don't think about—

"I got naked with Ryder."

Everyone around the table froze.

"Not all the way naked. Just like half-naked. Three-quarters naked at most." Oh shit, oh shit, oh *shit*. Everyone was staring at her, and they weren't *talking*, and the silence pressed in on her until more words spilled out. "I don't want it to be a big thing, because then all the guys will *make* it a thing. But if I'm not talking about it, then it's a big thing because I talk about everything..."

Rachel squealed and drummed her hands on the table in a quick, staccato beat. "Oh, my *God*. Shut up and tell us about half-naked. Tell us *everything*."

Nessa's breath escaped her in a *whoosh*. So did all the tension she hadn't even realized had settled itself at the base of her neck. She felt fifteen pounds lighter, not to mention a little giddy. So many times she'd been in Rachel's shoes, demanding all the details and hoarding them as a shield against disappointment.

Finally, *she* was the one with a story. "It was... It was just hot. He smolders all over the place. He's so serious and focused and he kept going *so slow* I wanted to kill him..." She trailed off, trying and failing to find the words. No wonder they'd never been able to describe that moment when patience—or even impatience—was rewarded a million times over.

The words didn't exist.

"Look at her face." Jeni covered her cheeks and laughed. "I think I might blush."

"Shut up," Nessa grumbled, but she could feel her lips forming that goofy, ridiculous smile she'd seen so many times on other faces. "You guys, I'm serious. As soon as Ace and Jas and Dallas find out, they're going to make it weird. They always make it weird."

"Or maybe you've just found the upside to our little revolution," Amira suggested. "They're too busy right now to make it weird."

"Who's gonna make what weird?" Ace asked from behind her.

Rachel disguised her laugh with a cough and dropped a bundle of herbs to the table. "Didn't anyone ever tell you that it's rude to sneak up on people?"

"That's why I do it," he replied cheerfully, and Nessa wondered if she could turn her cheeks any color other than bright red in the next five seconds.

No, probably not.

Ace strolled around the table to drop a kiss on Rachel's head, but kept going until he reached Hana's high chair. The baby grabbed for him with an excited burble of laughter, and Ace swept her up into his arms. "Well, Hana? What were they talking about?"

Hana babbled something in babytalk and grasped a fistful of Ace's hair. He grinned like it was the cutest thing he'd ever seen, and Nessa moved *puke on Ace* up three spots on her mental itinerary.

Amira propped one hand on her hip. "Hana won't rat us out. Girl code."

"Girl code, huh?" Ace settled Hana against his side, seemingly oblivious to the tiny fist tangled in his hair, and made a goofy face at her. "I think you'd tell your favorite uncle, wouldn't you, sweet pea?"

Oh, God. Five spots. *Ten* spots. Puking on Ace was definitely near the top of her to-do list.

Until she looked at Rachel.

Her friend stared at Ace with a dreamy, almost unfocused expression, one that radiated happiness and tenderness and a strangely satisfied hunger. It was such pure, unfiltered joy that it spilled over everyone in the room, provoking fond smiles and settling in Nessa's gut as a dangerous mix of yearning and envy.

All the smushy relationship baby shit might be revoltingly adorable from the outside, but the view from the inside just looked...adorable. And kind of glorious.

cruz

Cruz still remembered the first time he spoke to Ashwin Malhotra.

He'd been exactly ten years old. Exactly, because it was his birthday—an occasion marked on the Base with physical and mental fitness evaluations instead of presents and celebration. He passed with top marks in every category and received a new uniform—his official entrance into the ranks of the elite soldiers.

Then he received his first official beating as a new recruit.

There were six of them, all in their mid-teens, all well into puberty with height and reach that Cruz couldn't match. He held his own as best he could with the training he'd been given, but pain had been as inevitable as the lack of intervention. The Base encouraged elite soldiers to define their own hierarchy, and they weren't interested in soldiers who couldn't survive within it.

Those boys might have killed him if Ashwin hadn't arrived.

"Go."

It was the only word he said, the only one required. The boys scattered, because no one fucked around with the Makhai soldiers—even one who was still a teenager. Ashwin had probably been no more than seventeen or eighteen years old, but he seemed as powerful as any adult as he helped Cruz off the floor. His face remained impassive as he pulled Cruz's broken finger back into alignment and checked him for more serious injuries.

Too wary to argue, Cruz had obeyed when Ashwin prodded him in the direction of the clinic. But he gathered enough courage to ask one question. "Why'd you stop them?"

They walked in silence for so long, Cruz had been sure Ashwin intended to ignore him. But then the answer had come, impassive and cold. "You represent a massive investment of Base resources. You're small now, but within three to four years, your height will put you in the top percentile. It's inefficient to risk compromising your viability."

That chilly, impersonal logic had defined his relationship with Ashwin over the years. There were no more severe beatings—not until his teens. By then, Cruz had grown a foot, then two. He towered over the other recruits and worked hard to build muscle to match his height. Ashwin never intervened again, because he didn't need to—Cruz might have been at risk of pain and discomfort, but not incapacitation, and

Ashwin only cared about outcomes. The end game.

Efficiency.

The man standing across from Cruz in a dead-end alley behind the market square looked like Ashwin Malhotra. He had the familiar light-brown skin and closely shorn black hair. He wore fatigues and weapons with an absent ease that spoke of a lifetime association with them.

But the dark-brown eyes that were usually so cold, so *empty*, seethed with a wild panic his impassive expression couldn't hide. He'd appeared without warning, though Cruz had detected no indication he was being followed. And even as his old friend stood there with his hands resting easily by his sides, Cruz couldn't stop measuring the distance from Ashwin's left hand to the gun strapped to his thigh.

Not that he needed it. If Ashwin wanted to kill him, he could do it with his bare hands.

"Lorenzo Cruz."

His voice was rough, unsettled. Fraying around the edges. Cruz wanted to be wrong about why. "Ashwin. We've been wondering where you were. You made quite a statement over in Sector Two."

Ashwin ignored the words, as if the slaughter in Sector Two was irrelevant. "I need to know where she is."

She. Weeks ago, Ashwin had come to him to cash in on a long-owed favor. The request had been deceptively simple—find Dr. Kora Bellamy among the people giving aid after the bombings in Sector Two, and hide her someplace safe.

The true favor had been to *keep* her hidden, even when Ashwin himself came asking. And after the unbridled massacre in Two, Cruz couldn't help but wonder if this favor was going to get him killed.

"She's safe," he said carefully. It would take at least a second to get his hand on his gun. Hand-to-hand might be safer—Ashwin was genetically enhanced, but Cruz could use his lack of control against him. If it came to that.

With Rachel pregnant, he couldn't let it come to that.

The man absorbed the words without immediate response. His lips pressed together in an uncharacteristic display of emotion, but when he spoke, it was close enough to coolly rational that it might have fooled anyone who hadn't known him *before*. "I know what I said, but I'm revoking the request. I've arranged for a secure location. Tell me where she is, and consider your debt repaid."

Cruz didn't doubt the man's ability to prepare a safe house. Whatever he'd set up, no one in the city or the sectors or the entire *world* could find Kora and hurt her.

Which didn't make it safe. Not if Ashwin was unraveling in there with her.

"You have to trust me," he began, his eyes trained on Ashwin, waiting for the slightest hint of movement. "When you're feeling more—"

Even watching for it, Cruz didn't see the explosion coming.

One second, they were on opposite sides of the alley. The next, Ashwin was slamming Cruz into the brick wall hard enough to knock the wind out of him. Ashwin's hand closed around his throat, pushing him up onto his toes, and his rational mask shattered. "*Where is she*?"

Cruz's fingers brushed the butt of his pistol, but

Ashwin was too crazed to sense the slow movement as he eased it from the holster. The man's eyes blazed and his fingers tightened, leaving behind the precise application of force. Even if Cruz had wanted to answer Ashwin's snarled question, it was impossible.

He demanded it again anyway. "Tell me where she is."

Cruz slapped his free hand against Ashwin's and mimed speaking. Ashwin's grip loosened in response, but he didn't let go, those steely fingers crushing Cruz's last hope of getting out of this without violence.

There was no reliably nonlethal place to shoot a man, but Cruz jammed the barrel of his pistol against Ashwin's thigh and fired, praying he missed the femoral artery.

Ashwin staggered back with a grunt of surprise, and Cruz's boots thumped hard on the pavement. He allowed himself one painful breath before launching off the wall. Ashwin's wounded leg gave way with the impact, and they slammed to the ground.

Before Ashwin could recover from the shock, Cruz had him pinned on his stomach, his arms twisted up behind his back. "If I owed you a little less," he croaked, "I'd hand her over to you and let you run. My family and my sector would be safe. All I have to do is sacrifice a woman who doesn't deserve it."

Ashwin snarled, still past reason. "I wouldn't hurt her."

"Right now you would."

"No." Ashwin hissed and twisted in Cruz's grip, and *Christ* the man was strong. It took all of his considerable weight to keep him pinned down, even with Ashwin bleeding from the leg. "I would never hurt Kora."

"Then why did you ask me to hide her?"

Silence. Cruz listened to the man's unsteady breaths and groped for a way to end this that didn't involve another bullet—this one in the back of Ashwin's head.

According to Base guidelines, a Makhai soldier who developed a fixation on a person was damaged goods. He was a danger to everyone around him, especially the person in question. Official policy prescribed immediate, brutal recalibration—months of dangerous drugs meant to purge emotion and association and every trace of humanity left in the soldier. If that failed—and it was expected to fail—termination swiftly followed.

That was the official word, but the soldiers talked. Whispers traveled between workers and staff. And the one rumor that wouldn't die was that Ashwin would now be a danger to everyone around him *except* Kora.

A feeble hope. A grasped straw based on gossip and old stories. Cruz still reached for it. "You would hurt her, even if you didn't mean to, because I've known you most of my life and you're scaring the shit out of me. Fear hurts, Ashwin. It can break a person. If you try to take her somewhere right now, you'll terrify her. You'll *hurt* her. You can't keep her safe, not until you get yourself under control."

Ashwin went utterly still beneath him, as if processing the words. Maybe considering fear for the first time. Cruz wasn't sure how the man experienced emotion. If Ashwin could comprehend something as basic as giving in to terror, or if whatever they'd done to him on a cellular level had rewired his basest instincts too much.

The silence echoed. Cruz raised his pistol, silently apologizing to the man who'd saved him all those years ago, the man who might not even exist anymore.

"All right," Ashwin said quietly. "I'll stay away from her until I get myself under control."

Cruz didn't release the gun. He eased up, giving Ashwin the chance to try to overpower him. But Ashwin didn't move until Cruz was on his feet, and even then he only rolled to his back and sat up slowly.

Ashwin examined the bleeding hole in his leg for a moment before dismissing it with the same disregard he'd had for the violence in Sector Two. "Keep her safe until the war is over. Promise me."

"I already promised."

"And...after. If I can't..."

It was the first time Cruz had ever seen the man hesitate. He couldn't fathom how Ashwin viewed the world, but he recognized this on a gut level—the agony of knowing you couldn't protect someone who mattered. At least with Kora safely tucked away in Gideon Rios's household—and practically adopted into the royal family—Cruz could allay Ashwin's fears with honesty. "She'll be taken care of. During the war and after. I promise."

Ashwin nodded and rose without flinching. He strode past Cruz, but stopped at the edge of the alley. "This quiet's about to break. Dallas should see to his intel sources."

Cruz opened his mouth to ask for more details, but Ashwin vanished around the corner. He briefly considered trying to chase the other man down, but it would be pointless. Even with a gunshot wound to the leg, if Ashwin wanted to disappear, he would. And if he'd been willing—or able—to be more precise, he would have been.

Willing or able. Cruz didn't know how to define

either word when it came to a destabilized super-soldier on the brink of emotional collapse. But he had the answer to one question that had been plaguing Dallas.

Unless the objective at hand pertained directly to Kora Bellamy's safety, the O'Kanes couldn't trust Ashwin to be on their side.

12

The vibe in Dallas's command center had grown decidedly grim, and it was starting to make the back of Ryder's neck itch.

Half the monitors along the back wall were blank now, devoid of the constant stream of updates that had once flashed across their flat surfaces. A quick scan of the remaining screens revealed nothing new—which, considering the influx of information that usually cascaded across them, was almost as scary as nothing at all.

Around the table, things were just as dire. Tension etched new lines in Coop's already craggy face. Lex frowned down at a sheaf of papers in her hand, and even Zeke, the pretty-boy hacker from One, was unusually subdued.

Dallas refilled his coffee from the pot sitting between him and Ryder and scanned the table. "All right, Coop. The suspense is killing me. What's so ugly it's got you looking like that?"

Coop exhaled and slowly stood. "I caught the latest from a couple of my kids. Eden must be running low on troops, because they've started recruiting civilian soldiers."

"Fuck." Dallas thumped his mug down so hard coffee sloshed over the sides. "*Fuck*. Cannon fodder, that's all they'll be. Are they recruiting or conscripting?"

"Oh, these folks are joining up." Coop shook his head. "No force necessary."

Zeke's fingers hovered over the surface of his tablet. "My friends got this out to me. It's been on all the networks, every hour on the hour. Make sure you're not eating anything when you watch it."

He touched the tablet, and the screens went dark for a moment before blazing up again, every one showing part of the video Zeke had queued up. Underscored with slow music, including a deep, almost militaristic drumbeat, it played a vast, familiar scene of carnage—the aftermath of Ashwin Malhotra's massacre in Sector Two. At first, the images flashed in black-and-white, then they slowly bled to color, revealing the full, gruesome extent of the death and destruction.

Whoever was in charge of the city's propaganda was a goddamn, hell-bound genius.

"Mother*fucker*—" Dallas bit off the curse and braced his hands on the table, half rising from his chair. "Eden and their damn surveillance drones. I should have thought of this."

Lex gripped his forearm. "Settle down. If they hadn't had this footage, they would have manufactured something."

He sank back into the chair, his jaw clenched, as the image faded into Eden's skyline, superimposed with a nearly transparent, waving flag. A smooth, perfect female voice began to extol the virtues of the city, and Coop muttered a vicious curse.

"So this is how they'll con them." Dallas glared at the screen as if he could incinerate it with a thought. "And why the hell not? It's worked for the last forty years, hasn't it? *Do what we say or the evil sector gangs will kidnap you from your beds and send you straight to hell.*"

"It gets better. Or worse, if you're us." Coop ran a gnarled hand through his hair. "They're lining up at recruitment offices, ready to do their duty. In return for *faithful service—*" he spat the words, "—the Council is promising them homes and land."

"In the sectors," Lex finished. "Kill those of us who won't fall in line, and the sectors will be half-deserted. They'll have plenty of space for people loyal to the city to rebuild."

It shouldn't have worked. The folks so eager to sign up should have realized that trading their lives for a slim chance to settle the war-torn sectors—and become their brand-new line of defense against outside attack—was a deal so far in Eden's favor that it should have been laughable. But they weren't laughing. They were singing patriotic anthems, kissing their wives and kids goodbye, and signing away their lives.

And he and Dallas were the ones who would have to kill them.

Ryder clenched his hands on his knees—under the table, out of sight. "How many recruited so far?"

"Rough estimate? At least two thousand." Zeke's

face was grim. "Best guess is that they have at least five hundred MPs left, on top of that. We can't find anything on Special Tasks."

"There were a hundred and seventeen under Ashwin's command when he left the city," Dallas said quietly. "We've probably taken down a couple dozen since the bombing in Two."

But not enough. "How long have they been showing this?" Ryder asked.

"And how the *hell* did we not see it before now?" Dallas demanded, trading his disbelieving look between Zeke and Noah.

Noah was the one who answered. "That goddamn security girl, Penelope. If Zeke's friends hadn't sent me the code, I wouldn't have fucking believed it, but she mapped the network somehow. *All* of it—even the access points my grandfather removed from Eden's documentation. She has a list of the IDs of every computer, tablet, and fucking *coffee maker* that's ever connected to a sector WAP. She's combined that with geolocation—"

"In *English*, someone," Dallas snarled.

"All of the broadcasts out of Eden are locked down," Zeke said. "If you try to open them outside of Eden, the file corrupts itself. If you try to tamper with the file without knowing what you're doing, it dumps all your data, transmits it back to Security, and trashes your system." The corner of his mouth tilted up. "That's the English version. It's a little more complicated than that."

"It's also a pain in my ass." Noah blew out a breath and waved a hand at the tech powering the screens. "But not impossible to work around, thanks to Dallas's hoarding tendencies. I set up virgin tablets and spoofed the—"

"I swear to Christ, Noah—" Dallas warned.

Noah held up both hands. "English. I protected us, for now. But I'm going to assume she's got a whole room of hackers working around the clock to come up with new ways to screw us. We may need to lean more heavily on Zeke's contacts."

"They're up for it." Zeke braced his elbows on the table. "They've already made contact with Coop's friends *and* Liam Riley. The whole Riley family has gone underground, and they're not the only ones. These propaganda vids might sway the people who are used to feeling comfortable, but there are plenty who still know who the real bad guys are."

Lex turned to Dallas. "We don't have a choice now. We have to use Markovic. He's the only one with a hope in hell of countering this bullshit."

Dallas looked back at the screen, where the final image of the video sat, still and chilling. "We can't match this sleek, shiny stuff. It'll have to be raw. Real. And he'll have to be ready to pull it off."

She nodded absently, her fingers steepled under her chin. "Get me a copy of this video, and I'll make it work."

"Done."

Noah glanced at Zeke again, who cleared his throat and met Ryder's gaze. "Dallas asked me to keep my eyes open for intel on Cerys."

Ryder managed not to flinch. "Yeah?"

"With Penelope's focus on us, one of my friends was able to slip past her. Three days before the bombing in Two, there was an order logged. The Council sent a Special Tasks squad to bring her in for questioning. After that, she just vanished."

Across the table, Lex had gone pale. "Could they be holding her?"

Coop crossed his arms over his chest and shook his head. "Can't say. I got a good look at the Council's prisoner roll when I busted Markovic and your friends out, but half the people in custody weren't on it. Strictly off the books."

If there was even a remote possibility that Eden's leaders were holding Cerys, Ryder needed to know. For Jim's sake. "How do we find out?"

Zeke shrugged, though his eyes held sympathy. "Check every cell, one by one?"

"So...win the war," Dallas rumbled. "It's already on the itinerary."

It would have to be soon. The advantages that the sector rebellion had fought hard to earn over the city were dwindling by the second—and Eden was growing stronger, or at least more desperate.

Ryder rose. "We may have to consider that thing you wanted to avoid, after all."

"I know." Dallas sighed and picked up his cold coffee. "Lex?"

She looked up from the note she was writing, pausing in mid-word. "Mm-hmm?"

"Tell Bren we might need to make a new door in those walls."

"Oh, I think he's already prepared for that." She laid down her pen. "Are we?"

"Hell if I know." He waved a hand toward the monitors. "But we'll be a lot closer if we can counter this shit. Noah? Figure out how you're gonna get us onto every TV, tablet, and flat surface in that city."

Ryder still didn't think it mattered *what* Markovic had to say. The chances of winning over the people of

Eden, of rallying them to rebellion, were slim to none. But Dallas and Lex were right—they had to counter the brutal picture the city leaders were painting of the sectors. They had to instill enough doubt to make people question the party line, stay out of the army. Stay out of the *fight*.

If not, more people would die, and their blood would be on his hands.

13

People didn't usually knock on Nessa's door.

Unlike most of the O'Kanes, Nessa had never chosen a suite in the building that housed the more comfortable living quarters. As soon as they'd claimed the new warehouse as their own, she'd staked out a giant second-floor meeting room with an adjacent bathroom as her personal domain.

Over the years, she'd softened the stark space with scavenged area rugs and art from all over the world. Her bed was vast and buried in enough pillows to make it feel less lonely at night—when she slept in it. More nights than not, she sacked out on the couch in her snug downstairs office, and that was where the O'Kanes went to look for her.

Which made finding Ryder standing outside her

bedroom, holding a bottle of wine, a sight unusual enough to momentarily scatter her wits. "Hi."

The smile that curved his lips and lit his eyes didn't do anything for her wits. Or her ability to breathe. "Hi."

"Hi," she echoed again. He made her so stupid that it took a second for the flush of embarrassment to hit her, and she covered it by pulling the door wide in invitation. "I was going to come find you eventually, but I figured you guys would be doing war stuff until late."

"It *is* late." He brushed past her and stopped, surveying her room.

If she'd known he might show up, she would have cleaned—or at least shoved everything into the storage room that passed for a closet. Her table was cluttered with half her nail polish collection and a fresh batch of hair dye Tatiana had put together for her. T-shirts and jeans were strewn over every close-to-flat surface, and she had two baskets of clean clothes stacked near the door, where she'd dropped them after the couple who did laundry for the O'Kanes had delivered them.

And that was just the clutter. Her *life* was on the rows of metal shelves lining the walls, a history that any man with Ryder's super-spy observation skills was no doubt piecing together. The remnants of a dozen abandoned hobbies crowded those shelves—an expensive stash of yarn from the month she became obsessed with knitting, along with the quilt top she'd painstakingly pieced together but forgot to finish. The leather-working tools, stacked next to smaller tools for piecing together jewelry. Three pots she'd thrown on a potter's wheel, only one glazed.

Every single thing she tried, she loved obsessively—until the shine of learning wore off. Then she flitted on to the next thing, because nothing ever managed to hold her interest for long. Nothing but the liquor.

"Sorry for the mess," she said, hurrying to the table. She swept two dozen bottles of nail polish into a basket with her arm, clearing some space. "People don't come up here much."

"And I came unannounced. The apology is mine to offer."

"It's fine." The rest of the bottles clinked into the basket, and she nudged a chair out from the table with a smile, feeling oddly shy, considering she'd had her hand around the man's dick. But that was sex. This was...her *space*. "I'm glad you're here, really."

"Thanks." He held out the wine bottle with a wink. "For you, from the last shipment out of One before Dallas and Gideon halted transport. I figured you might want to enjoy the fruits of someone else's labor for a while."

She accepted the bottle and studied the label. "*Rios*. Does Mad's family make this?"

"Mmm, his cousin, Isabela, has a vineyard near the river." Ryder reached out and brushed his thumb over the curve of her cheek. "Have you been busy? I haven't seen you since the other night."

"A little busy." Warmth crept over her at his gentle touch, and she leaned into his hand. "I oversaw the last batch of raw liquor and then shut down production. First time in eight years all the stills have been quiet."

"Not for long," he soothed.

She gripped the bottle tighter, because there was *something* under his words, something that made her heart beat faster—and not with excitement. "Is shit going down? I saw Lex but I didn't even want to ask—she looks so *tired*."

It took him a moment to answer, and he turned to sit at the chair she'd pulled out for him as he did. "Things can't stay this way forever. Strategically speaking, we wouldn't want them to."

She didn't have wineglasses, but she found two clean tumblers and brought them back to the table. "I want it to be over. But..." Fighting meant bleeding, and hurting, and more people dying.

He held out his arms, his expression full of understanding—and recognition. "Come here."

Nessa eased into his lap, sitting sideways so she could lean against his chest. He cradled her there, not quite holding or trapping her, simply letting her use his strength.

Then he began to speak, his voice low and deep with emotion. "It's not going to be easy, and I wish I could promise you that everyone you love is going to make it through this war. But we all know what the city leaders in Eden are capable of. If we didn't, we wouldn't be at war in the first place."

"I know, but—"

"But," he said, gently. Firmly. "Everyone knows what's at stake. And everyone is going to fight like hell. We may not beat them—that's not defeatist, it's just fact. But if we go down, we go down swinging. That's more than a lot of people get in this life."

The lump in her throat hurt when she tried to swallow. It seemed silly to waste tears on people who hadn't even fallen yet—especially when the days to come would no doubt give her plenty of chances to cry. But it wasn't grief trying to claw its way out—it was sick, terrifying helplessness. "I wish I'd learned how to fight. Bren tried to teach me, and I kept whining about it until he let me off with target practice. And now I can't *help*."

"Hey, that's not fair to you. To a *lot* of people." He cupped her chin and forced her to look at him. "Here's the dirty secret, Nessa. Soldiers with bullets can't win wars, not by themselves."

"Maybe not," she whispered. "Doesn't make being the one waiting at home any easier."

"No." His thumb swept over her knee. "No, I've tried, and I can't imagine anything harder than that."

All her life, words had come so easily to her. Dozens of them, hundreds of them. Sometimes blunt and inappropriate, but a never-ending wave to drown the restlessness inside her that shuddered at silence. But the ones that mattered, the ones that brushed the places inside her that weren't bright and shiny and gleeful—those had always seemed trapped.

Until now. "Dallas and Lex lead us, and everyone else fights and works and keeps the place running, but ever since Pop died..." She laughed hoarsely and closed her eyes. "God, this makes me sound like such an asshole, but I'm used to being the hero. The center of everything we do. I just feel so useless now."

"Ah, I see."

That was all he said for so long that she opened her eyes again. But Ryder wasn't looking at her. His gaze was traveling her shelves again, cataloging all the passions she'd abandoned.

"Do you know what a Molotov cocktail is?" he asked eventually.

"In theory, I guess." She wrinkled her nose. "They're popular in pre-Flare movies. It always seemed like a terrible waste of good booze, to me."

"Or gasoline, kerosene, oil—anything that burns. You bottled more raw alcohol than Jordan and his field medics can use. We could modify some of them in case we run out of grenades," he murmured distractedly, his brows drawing together. "What about the leather?"

"The leather?"

He shifted her weight, then rose with her in his arms and walked toward one of the shelves. "You have tools for working with leather."

"Yeah. I got obsessed with the idea that I could make corsets." In reality, she'd given everyone new belts and bracers for about six months before the appeal had waned—probably because something new and shiny had replaced it. "I can do basic things, I guess."

"Stuart's making some equipment for the fighters—ammo belts, stuff like that. But he's working as fast as he can, and none of the stuff is custom. We could use someone who can make them fit." He looked down at her, and the corner of his mouth tilted up a little. "See? All kinds of things only you can do."

He was just standing there, smiling, cradling her like a princess—but that wasn't why she kissed him. Nessa had been pampered and petted like a princess her whole damn life.

No one had ever invited her to build bombs with them before. *That* was why she kissed him.

She tangled her arms around his neck as her mouth found his. He parted his lips immediately, but it took him only a moment to move beyond the kiss, gliding his open mouth over her cheek and down to her jaw.

She let her head fall back, ignoring the dizzy sway of the room. She usually hated the feeling of being unmoored, adrift from the ground—but she wasn't adrift. Ryder was holding her.

He carried her to her bed, pausing long enough to

snag the bottle of wine from the table, though he left the tumblers behind. "What do you think?" he rumbled. "Drink this in bed?"

"Eventually." She gripped his shirt and dragged it up. "Tell me more about how we're going to make bombs."

"No." He dropped the bottle and set her on her feet. "I don't want to talk about that anymore, not here."

She slid her fingers across his back to trace his spine. "What do you want to talk about?"

He pulled the clip from her hair and let it fall around her shoulders. "You. Me. Everything we can do *right now* to make sure that light stays in your eyes."

Once his shirt was over his head, she tossed it aside and sketched a path down his chest. The med-gel had done its work on his ribs, and the stitches were gone, leaving behind only a thin, mostly healed scar. "I don't know. I know shit about sex that would make hookers blush, but I haven't had a lot of it that was memorable."

His fingers combed through her hair, smoothing the strands. "That's a shame."

She swayed closer, brushing his shoulder with her lips. He still smelled like the woods—his soap or after-shave or *something*—and maybe if she closed her eyes, she could pretend they were locked in his cabin somewhere far away from war. "It is what it is. Sex can't be much more than decent with someone you don't really trust."

"Then it's a good thing you trust me."

Flutters burst to life in her chest, nervous and excited, because it was true. She trusted him so much, *too much*, and she didn't want to stop. She kissed the center of his chest before tilting her head back to meet his warm brown eyes. "I do. So ruin me some more already."

Ryder chuckled under his breath, a rich, low sound that shivered up her spine as he eased her back. Her legs hit the mattress, and he followed her down, catching her just before she hit the plush surface.

Pillows surrounded them. Nessa laughed and swept out her arms, knocking some to the sides and off the edge of the bed. "Sorry. I like pillows."

"I didn't notice," he murmured teasingly.

Her fist closed around one, and she swung it into his side. It bounced right back off, but her laughter dissolved into a gasp when his body settled more firmly over hers. The memory of pleasure tingled through her, and she let go of the pillow and gripped his arms instead.

His breath tickled over her collarbone. "Tell me about all these things. The yarn and the fabric and the paints."

She flexed her fingers on his shoulders and dragged her nails lightly over his skin. "I get...antsy. I like to keep my hands busy."

He guided her shirt up, baring her stomach. "You could do that with one hobby."

"I like to keep my brain busy, too." She sucked in a breath when his skin brushed hers, savoring the heat. As snuggly as her mountain of pillows could be, they hadn't done much to take the edge off winter's bite. "Don't you get that thrill when you learn something new for the first time?"

"No." He eased down, reaching for her belt with one hand while his lips grazed the bottom of her rib cage. "A job well done, yes."

She rose up on her elbows, breathing a little less

steadily as she watched his nimble fingers tug her belt free from its buckle. "So you're saying you like to practice one thing until you get really, really good at it?"

"Focus," he breathed. "It has its rewards."

"I could be persuaded. Maybe."

"Why? You don't have to change." He tugged, and the button on her jeans popped open. "All you have to be is right here, in this moment."

Oh, *fucking hell.*

It was like some too-good-to-be-true fantasy come to life. A handsome, charming man coaxing her jeans down while he told her she was perfect, in all her imperfect, impatient glory. She couldn't even form words as she lifted her hips to help him, too distracted by the soft drag of his touch as he pulled the denim down her legs and over her bare feet.

Then she remembered her bra didn't match her panties—black cotton with cheerful pink skulls on them, of all fucking things—and wanted to melt through the bed again. No sophisticated silk or frilly lace, of course not. That would have required thinking like someone who was used to getting laid.

She still couldn't entirely believe this was happening.

He surged up and shifted the pillows behind her, raising her into a half-sitting position. "All you have to do," he murmured, almost echoing his earlier words, "is watch."

"Okay," she managed. "No touching?"

"Only if you need to hold on."

He disappeared back down her body, and Nessa clutched at the pillows on either side of her. There was some sort of torturous hell in knowing exactly what he intended to do as he worked her underwear off her hips—but still not knowing how to prepare for it.

Knowing all of this shit *in theory* was not nearly as helpful as she'd hoped.

His lips grazed her knee, and she jolted. He pressed a kiss to the top of her thigh, and she gripped the fabric beneath her hands harder, swearing that this time she wouldn't start trembling before he'd even really touched her.

Then he edged her legs apart, and she couldn't help it. She was as naked as she'd ever been in her life, and he was *right fucking there*, his mouth inches from her pussy, staring at her in a way that made her squirm in a confusing mixture of anticipation and nerves.

God, what if this wasn't as good as everyone made it seem?

Fuck, what if it was *better*?

Ryder touched her—smoothing his fingers over her flesh, parting her with his thumbs. And just when she was getting ready to whisper his name, to beg him to put her out of her misery—he bent his head and licked her clit.

The jolt of sensation was immediate, almost too much. A startled noise escaped her before she dug her teeth into her lower lip, holding back a second, more ragged noise as he licked lower. That wasn't as intense, but it still felt *good*, the kind of good that spilled through her in a warm, restless wave. She squirmed when he found another sensitive spot, but he didn't pause there.

No, he was focused. So damn focused. He took his time, like he was making an exhaustive inventory of her reactions. Or maybe this was some super-spy recon shit, because once he'd dragged his tongue over every last vulnerable spot he could reach, he went back to the sensitive ones. The ones that made her hips jerk, the ones that made her toes curl. The spot that built up noises behind the dam of her teeth sunk into her lower lip, until she couldn't hold back a moan anymore.

Then he revisited all those spots again.

And a third time.

"Ryder—" Her hands ached from clenching the pillows. She released one and found the back of his head instead, but that didn't help. He was as immovable as ever, focusing on his mission, and when he meandered his way back up to her clit again, she needed it so badly she rocked her hips up in desperation.

He gripped her hips, but instead of pressing her back down to the bed, he lifted her to his mouth.

"Fuck!" Self-consciousness burned away as she reached for him with her other hand, clutching at him as the trembling started. Not the slow burn of last time, but something hot and messy and intense. "More, more please—"

He sucked her clit between his lips, lashing her with his tongue, and Nessa swore as the tension unraveled without warning. Bliss screamed through her, sending her heels scrabbling for purchase on the bed. But the strong hands on her hips held her in place as his tongue chased each spike of pleasure, wringing every bit of sensation from her until she wanted to start a new religion dedicated to the clearly superior concept of *focus*.

Her body melted, and his attention to detail was absolute. Just as sensation threatened to overwhelm her, he stopped and lifted his head. Nessa gave up and let her eyes drift shut, tracking his movements by the soft, tender kisses he dropped to her skin as he slid back up her body.

The mattress dipped as he stretched out next to

her, and she let the movement roll her boneless body closer to him. His chest was a warm wall of smooth skin over muscle, and she had the drunken thought that if he stuck around after this war, she was going to feed him donuts and candy until she'd softened the edges of the weapon everyone else had honed him to be.

And if he didn't, maybe she'd just trek out to his weird little woodsy cabin once a week to shove cookies in his face.

He stroked the underside of her chin with his knuckles and kissed her, slow and easy. His lips tasted like her, and she smiled against them and snuggled closer. "Focus," she murmured. "I could maybe become a fan."

"To be fair, that's way more fun than knitting." Ryder toyed with the front clasp of her bra before flicking it open with a grin. "Wouldn't you say?"

God, so smug, and she was starting to find it cute. Or at least not irritating, because it was hard to be irritated when he'd earned that satisfied grin. She trailed her fingers down to tug at his belt. "At least as fun as knitting."

"Uh-huh." It was his turn to lean back against the pillows. He tucked both arms behind his head and watched her as she pulled his belt free. "If you tell me a scarf made you come that hard, I'm gonna have some questions."

Nessa tossed the belt over the edge of the bed and then let her bra slip down her arms to follow it. Naked, she straddled his thighs, her fingers hovering just over the erection straining his pants. "Not yet. But since I have about ten of them in the closet, maybe I'll use a few to hold you hostage in my bed until I've perfected *my* focus."

One eyebrow rose in a slow, perfect arch. "You have my attention."

"Do I?" She grazed his cock with the back of her fingers before reaching for the fastening on his pants. "Maybe we should talk about the possibilities. I mean, if you can make smugness hot, God knows what kinky sex games I could develop a sudden, inexplicable appreciation for."

He hissed in a breath, then smiled. "You O'Kanes sure do seem to be into that sort of thing."

"We fight hard, so we play hard." She slid her hands up to his shoulders and leaned over him, her hair cascading forward to form a pink and purple curtain around their faces. "This world's gonna make us feel bad, whether we want it to or not. So why should we leave any possible thing that could make us feel good on the table, just because it's intense?"

"You're preaching to the converted, Nessa." He rubbed his thumb over her side, carefully tracing each rib. "It was an observation, not a complaint."

It soothed an anxiety she hadn't realized she had, that tension that always knotted her shoulders around someone who wasn't an O'Kane. The part of her that was always braced for the snide comment or the preachy moralizing—or, worst of all, the sleazy come-on from some dude who thought a woman who wasn't ashamed of sex had to climb on the dick of any slimeball who wanted her.

If Ryder was like that, he wouldn't be here, because Lex would have stabbed him already. But she still let giddy relief curve her lips as she leaned down to kiss him. His mouth first, and then, breaking away before he could deepen the kiss, his chin. "Tell me," she murmured as she worked her way back down his chest.

"Tell me the games you like."

He didn't answer immediately. "My whole life, I've been playing games," he said finally. "How long can I convince them of this, make them believe that? *Stay in character, Michael, don't ever forget.*"

Nessa paused over his ribs and lifted her head. *Michael*. His first name.

"Every day, different people. Different *me*." Ryder shook his head. "There are things I like, Nessa, things that some people might call kinky. But no, I don't want to play games anymore."

She couldn't wrap her brain around it. Nothing in her life of endless self-expression had equipped her to understand being denied that most basic right. The right to be herself, whoever she turned out to be.

His abdomen trembled under her lips. She traced along the edge of his pants with her tongue before glancing up at him. "No games. Be Michael. Show me what you want."

A taut muscle in his clenched jaw jumped. "Take them off."

She slid down his legs to tackle his boots first, stripping them off one by one and tossing them haphazardly aside. His socks followed, and then his pants. She took her time dragging them down his legs, taking his underwear with them and trailing her fingers over his muscled thighs as she went.

When they'd cleared his feet, she paused at the edge of the bed, marveling that he could look so at ease, so *right*—all his stern control and warrior strength surrounded by the bright, whimsical colors of her pillows and blankets. His secure confidence simply overpowered their silliness, and her heart raced as she crawled back up to kneel between his thighs.

He lifted one hand to beckon her, casual and commanding, all at once. "Come here."

She obeyed, because it felt right. Not because she'd discovered some new appreciation for obedience—she was still pretty sure she'd make a terrible submissive. But maybe they all got this same thrill—the fluttering excitement that flooded her as she straddled Ryder's stomach. The magic of being the one person he could put aside games with. The wonder of seeing him, stripped of everything polite and public.

His hands stroked over her skin, starting at her upper thighs. Up, over her hips, her sides, her shoulders, until he reached her hair. He sank his fingers into it and tugged, not hard enough to hurt, or even to move her, but just enough for her to *feel* it.

She caught her breath as the urge to squirm, to tug against his grip or lean into it or *something* washed over her. But she swallowed it and watched him.

Trusted him.

Ryder paused, then smiled his appreciation as he continued his exploration in reverse, stopping to cup her breasts.

"Oh—" Her head tilted back, and she almost reached for his wrists. Her fingers flexed against her thighs, wanting to move. Sitting still was torment, but so, so sweet. Especially when he pinched his fingers tight around her nipples—and twisted.

It wasn't pain—exactly. It was *sensation*, distilled. The shock of it snapped her head forward again, and she watched him, panting through the clash of heat and hurt buzzing through her.

Just as quickly as he'd introduced the sensation, it vanished, and he leaned up to soothe her nipples with his tongue. Lazy arousal shifted into something more pressing, and she couldn't stop the wiggling this time. "Fuck, Ryder—"

"Now?" he rasped against her skin. "Or can you be patient?"

Nessa had never had patience for anything in her life that didn't involve liquor. Everything had always been *impulse* and *action* with second thoughts trailing a distant third and regret creeping up behind them. She wanted to say *no* because no meant getting him inside her, and she craved that with an ache that doubled with every passing second.

But the rewards for patience had been so *good* last time.

She exhaled shakily and squeezed her eyes shut. "I want to try."

"Good." He lay back on the pillows again, grasped her hips, and moved her back until her pussy ground over his shaft, and that was *so much better* than wiggling against his stomach. His cock was hard and hot and rubbed all the perfect places, even though it wasn't inside her.

She braced her hands on his chest and fought the temptation to fight his grip and rock against him. Instead she held his gaze, trusting he'd read her as easily as he'd been doing from day one, and know when she couldn't take it anymore.

He moved her hips, back and forth, until the grinding turned slick, hot. Until she was gasping every time he worked over her clit, and her fingernails dug into his chest. Until the bright little pulses turned to sharp bursts of pleasure, like the sparks when you tried to start a fire. Frustration surged every time it slipped away, only to vanish with the next roll of her hips, because she was so close, *so close*—

He gripped her hips harder, enhancing the pressure on the final rock, and the spark roared into flames.

It was deeper this time, her body still primed from the first orgasm. She shuddered above him, trusting his grip to keep her steady in a world that seemed unmoored. But the world shifted anyway as he lifted her hips and thrust into her.

He was everything she'd known he'd be—perfect, hard, filling her up until she wondered hazily if he'd be too much. And she didn't care. The stretch twisted with the pleasure into something intense enough to bring tears to her eyes.

She needed more, all of him. Maybe if he fucked her deep enough, he'd break through the noise in her head and she could be like everyone else for a few seconds.

Peaceful.

"Look at me." He drove the last few inches with the command. "Nessa."

She forced her gaze to his, still trembling as she tried to lock her arms to keep herself upright. "I'm okay."

He barked out a rough laugh and flexed his hips. "Just okay?"

Oh God, he stroked *everything* when he did that. Her pussy clenched, and she didn't know if she was still caught in the aftershocks of orgasm or headed there again way too fast. "I'm dying. And I'm perfect. I'm—" She rocked experimentally and shuddered. "I'm never letting you out of this bed."

"Shh." Another quick rock. "Focus, remember?"

"Focus." He made it sound so easy, but her mind couldn't incorporate it all. She could focus on the warm skin under her hands and the way his muscles flexed when he moved—but only until he finished moving. Then it was the friction of his cock inside her, the ever-present fullness contrasting with the jolts every time he rubbed across someplace sensitive. Or his eyes, brown and intent, always there to catch her gaze when she dragged it back to him.

"Help me," she whispered. "Don't let me feel anything else."

He held her gaze, his eyes locked with hers, as he dug his nails into her skin.

The touch grounded her. Slowly at first, she lifted up just far enough to feel the loss of him before grinding back down. "Like this?"

"Like—" The word cut off with a groan, and he nodded. "Like that."

She liked that sound. She loved how it broke his careful, controlled words in pieces. Spreading her fingers wide across his chest, she rolled her hips again, adjusting the speed and angle based on the way his jaw tightened and his muscles clenched beneath her fingers.

This was her kind of focus. The same surety she felt in the distillery, when a hundred little details no one else saw coalesced into knowledge that seemed like magic to everyone else. But she could become an expert in Ryder. She could study all of his miniscule reactions, coax his secrets from him bit by bit, and understand how to make magic happen.

"*Yes*," he hissed. He gripped her ass with one hand, then pressed his other against her stomach, tilting her hips in a way that felt awkward until their bodies met again and something desperate sparked deep inside her.

Gasping, she sat upright, gripping his arms for

balance as the angle sharpened even more. Every thrust felt twice as intense like this, even if she didn't have the same leverage.

Then both of his hands drifted lower, until he was touching her clit and her asshole at the same time, teasing both with the same slow, firm circles.

Too much. It was just too damn much. She lost the rhythm, and whimpered in loss. But then he moved, thrusting up into her, touching her *everywhere*, and she scratched at his arms, begging in broken words for just a little more, a little harder, right there, right—

Fuck.

Orgasm hit her hard, and it was so much better with him filling her up. She shuddered as her body clenched around his dick, shuddered until she wanted to laugh at the sheer joy of it.

Ryder didn't let her come down this time. He flipped her onto her back and drove into her, his arms flexing as he braced himself above her, watching. Watching as she slammed into that peak again, pleasure flooding her body. She tangled her arms around him and clung to his shoulders, helpless to do anything but ride a second orgasm.

And a third.

And then, as he shifted his angle, went deeper and harder, a fourth that built and built until she was half-sobbing at the immensity of the pressure, sure she'd die if he worked her all the way up this impossible hill and didn't manage to tip her over. Her body strained with need, but she was wrung out, hypersensitive, so terrified it would end before this frustration broke.

"Michael—" Her voice broke on his name, but she whimpered it again and again. "Michael, Michael,

Mich—"

He buried his face in her neck, whispered her name against her skin, and bit her.

Maybe the sharp sting of his teeth was what tipped her over the edge, but it was her name rasped in that hoarse, desperate voice that followed her into hazy pleasure and kindled sweet warmth in her chest. She tightened her grip around him as his control finally slipped and he shuddered above her.

When Ryder stilled, he didn't move. He lay above her, covering her, cradling her. "No," he murmured, his breath blowing hot over her flushed skin.

Maybe her brain was shot, because it didn't make any sense. "No?"

He heaved himself up, rolling away with a noise that was half-groan, half-sigh. "*Definitely* more fun than knitting."

It startled her into a giggle—an actual fucking *giggle*, and then before she knew it she was laughing. "Oh God, knitting sucks now. Knitting is the fucking worst."

His laughter joined hers. "Don't hate. It's not supposed to compare."

Still breathless, she curled into his side and rested her cheek on his shoulder. "Holy shit. I hope you're gonna stay in my bed on your own, because I don't think I can move my arms and legs right now."

He cupped her shoulder and pulled her closer. "I'm not going anywhere."

"Oh, good." She hadn't been worried he would roll out of bed and leave—not really—but it was still a relief to relax into him. She slid her hand to his chest, resting it over the place where his heart still beat fast and strong. "Full disclosure, the scarves might not have held you anyway. I wasn't very good at knitting. Too many tiny stitches to count, and when you miss the wrong one everything unravels."

His brows drew together, and he opened one eye to peer over at her. "But you don't mind some things like that, obviously."

"I know." She'd never tried to explain it before, but lazing in his arms made self-consciousness a distant memory. "I was *into* it while I was trying to figure it out. Counting those stitches was fascinating because I wanted to beat it. But then once I had it figured out, it was just tedious. The yarn never did anything new. But making liquor is always exciting. I never know when we get a grain shipment if it's going to be high quality or total trash, but I have to figure out how to make it work. And just when I think I've got it conquered, it changes. New tools, new suppliers, new options…"

"So it's the challenge?"

"Partly." She traced a circle on his chest. "I mean, I don't like it when things go wrong. But I fucking *love* it when I figure out how to make it work anyway. Maybe it's just the adrenaline rush."

"Or maybe it's your connection to it." He covered her hand with his, holding it to his skin. "Your grandfather?"

"Yeah." A tiny icicle of sadness stabbed through her contentment. "Every year, there are fewer of his barrels down there. I'm so proud of what I made of this place, but I'm not looking forward to having to decide when to uncask the last one he barreled."

They fell silent, with only their breathing cutting through the stillness of the room. Finally, Ryder huffed out a quiet, self-conscious laugh. "I think that probably has a lot to do with why I plan to build that cabin. It's not just about seeing my father's wishes come to fruition. It's also a way to hold on to him."

Put that way, she understood. Some things weren't about rational thinking or even wanting. She knew in her heart that there would always be at least one cask down there with her grandfather's illegible scrawl on it, long after she should have let go. "How old were you? When you lost him?"

"Three. Sometimes, I almost think I remember things—his laugh, stuff like that."

She twined their fingers together and closed her eyes. "I was fifteen when my grandfather died. He'd already taken a hard turn, but Dallas scraped together money to get him meds from Five. Something to help with the pain. He took too much by mistake one night and never woke up." She swallowed. "Except I don't think it was a mistake. I think Pop knew Dallas would bankrupt himself to keep him alive, even if he was in so much pain it barely mattered. Dallas was never good at being ruthless when it came to Pop."

Ryder shifted beside her, and when she opened her eyes, he was watching her closely. "There are worse things than going out on your own terms. I know it doesn't make it hurt less, nothing can do that. But it's something."

"I know." Her eyes stung, but she didn't look away. "If he'd hung on, it would have been for me. And I didn't want him hurting. I was okay. I was—" The tears spilled over. "He couldn't have made a safer world for me. It's not his fault I got stupid from missing him."

"What do you mean?"

She trailed her fingers down to the thin scar on his ribs. "That guy you asked about the night I sewed up your ribs. That's how he got to me. I was so lonely, and he made me feel...special. Loved. Like I was the center of someone's world again. And I fell for it so fucking hard."

He didn't speak, simply combed his fingers through her hair—and waited.

Even after years, shame still burned in her gut as she forced out the next words. "He came to meet me one night, and he played the slow seduction just right. I was so ready to climb into his pants."

But then the smell had hit her—nearly masked by too much cologne, but unmistakable. Corn mash reeked so hard it gave most people headaches, but to Nessa it had always smelled like home.

"I was stupid about guys, but I've never been stupid about liquor," she continued in a wavering voice. "He had the operation all set up. All he needed was someone to tell him why the shit he was churning out tasted like gasoline mixed with piss. But they'd had a spill before he came to meet me and he got mash all over his boots. I could smell it on him, and I knew. I fucking *knew*. And I have never in my damn life felt so fucking ridiculous before or since."

Ryder took a deep breath. "Did you kill him, or let Dallas do it?"

She almost laughed. It was watery and weak, but still cathartic. "Bren hadn't taught me how to shoot yet. I was already humiliated, and I didn't *want* to tell Dallas, but I had to. I don't think he told the other guys what had happened, just that someone was making a move. The asshole vanished, and it was years before I let another guy get his mouth near me without having Bren try to scare him off first. And Bren's pretty scary."

"Sounds reasonable." He touched her chin, guiding her to meet his gaze again. "So why do you feel ridiculous?"

"Because I fell for it." God, it was so hard to stare into his eyes and say this. Especially with her heart beating so fast. "I let some asshole with a pretty smile convince me that he wanted me for *me* instead of what I could do for him. And that's all anyone ever seemed to want. To use me for something."

"The guy was an asshole," Ryder agreed. "Got that? *The guy* was an asshole. You didn't do anything wrong or stupid." He snorted. "Jesus, you didn't even let him pull it off before you figured it out. Why aren't you proud of yourself instead?"

"Because too many people depend on me. If it was just me or my heart, whatever. But what if I *had* let him pull it off? My fuckups have repercussions for so many people." Her eyes burned. "A few months before that, I had a bad day. Pop was feeling shitty and I couldn't focus and I got distracted and scorched the hell out of the mash. A whole fucking shipment ruined, and Pop had to drag his aching body out of bed to try and salvage it. We took a huge hit. People didn't get paid, and Dallas had to make the next deal on credit. I don't get to make mistakes."

Ryder's eyes were dark—sympathetic, but that sympathy lay over something hard. Immovable. "That's too bad, because you're human. And humans fuck up. We're pretty much known for it."

It hurt a little, those blunt words. The sharpness of reality smashing through the castle she'd built out of her cross-checks and redundancies, all the ways she'd compensated for her impulsive tendencies. It would have felt better if he'd cuddled her and stroked her hair and told her she could do it. That he believed in her so hard, he knew she could be perfect.

It would have felt amazing—until she fucked up again. And then failing him would have broken her.

She exhaled shakily and shifted closer to him. "It's way too easy to forget you're human when you grow up around Dallas and Lex. They're a little larger-than-life."

"But not perfect."

A smile tugged at her lips. "Blasphemy. You take that back."

"Never."

A loyal O'Kane couldn't let it stand. She tugged her hand free and attacked his ribs, looking for vulnerable ticklish spots. As soon as her fingers slid over the scar on his side, Ryder grimaced and shrank back.

She jerked her fingers away. "I'm sorry—"

Her words cut off as he grabbed her wrists. He flipped her onto her back, then loomed over her, grinning. "Too easy."

Shocked laughter escaped, and she groaned and rolled her eyes, trying and utterly failing to glare at him. "You're such an asshole."

"Whatever." He tightened his grip and bent his head until his lips barely brushed hers.

Kissing him was inevitable. Natural. *Beautiful.* She fell into the sweetness of his lips moving tenderly over hers, feeling safe beneath the shelter of his body.

He was as strong as Dallas and Lex, strong enough to make decisions about war that would lead to people being hurt, maybe even dying. Decisions that might turn out to be mistakes, because he was human, too.

Dallas had avoided those decisions for a long time. He sat on his throne in the Broken Circle, cozy and content. He fought battles with no stakes and fucked women who didn't make him feel too much. He counted his money and shared it generously with the people who helped him make it, but he'd never reached for more. For a notorious criminal with a bloodthirsty reputation, Dallas had led a safe life. Because Dallas felt his mistakes and the hurt that came with them, perhaps more deeply than anyone but those closest to him realized.

Ten years ago, this war would have killed him. Ten years ago, he hadn't had Lex to help carry the burden.

Maybe that was the secret. The reason people groped through the darkness for someone else to cling to. The O'Kanes fucked freely and gleefully, but that wasn't why they fell in love. They found the people who carried them through the fuckups and cherished them even though they were flawed, fallible humans.

Nessa wasn't perfect. Her mistakes rippled out and touched lives, and she always had to be aware of it. That was the price of power.

Maybe, if they survived this war, she wouldn't always have to do it alone.

14

Being back in Sector Five was disconcerting.

It had never really felt like home to Ryder, no more than Four or even Eight had. It wasn't that any of those places were flawed, it was just his nature. For him, the concept of *home* was nebulous, unformed. Something he could almost see, not quite reach. Never touch.

At least, not until this fucking war was over.

Still, something about Five was *different*. Here, he reigned. When people spoke to him, they did so quietly, and they kept their eyes lowered—though he could never figure out whether they did so out of respect or fear. In Four, no one treated him with deference. He could have been anyone, just another guy—

Just another O'Kane.

He snorted at the thought and lifted the binoculars once again. He had an excellent vantage point from the top of the tallest tower on the western side of Five, but the view into Sector Six was dark, still. "I don't see anything. They must be taking their light discipline seriously."

"They are." Hector was grim as he handed over a pair of night-vision goggles in exchange for the binoculars.

The moment Ryder lifted the lenses to his eyes, his blood chilled. Under the shield of darkness, troops were moving into position for an attack, creeping across the burned, fallow plains of Six like locusts. "Jesus Christ."

Dallas grunted next to him. "I don't like the sound of that."

"You shouldn't." Ryder offered him the goggles and stepped back.

After only a moment staring through them, Dallas began to curse. "Jas is bringing the militia over, but even with your men, this is gonna be a close fight."

"At least we won't be bored." Ryder turned to Hector. "You've initiated emergency shutdown?"

Hector nodded.

"Good. Hold off on the final command as long as you can. I want them on top of us before they realize we saw them coming." He glanced back toward Six, but all he saw was inky darkness, and it made his skin crawl. "I'll brief the men."

He headed back down the stairs, keeping one hand on the flashlight on his belt as Dallas's boots thumped behind him. "Your guys are used to brawls and gang shootouts. Are they ready for a large-scale battle?"

"I don't know," Dallas replied. "Closest we've had in years was that shit with the bootleggers your old boss set up. Before that? The fight that won me Four. But that wasn't war."

At least he wasn't telling himself they were all hardened soldiers who could handle anything. Hell, Ryder had been groomed for this war, trained since childhood, and even he had dealt almost entirely in the theoretical, in strategy.

"You have Bren and Cruz," he said finally. "And Jasper seems like he gets it."

"I think he does." Dallas made an amused noise. "I saw that in him from the start, you know. He was this scruffy teenager on a shit-ass illegal farm, underfed and still growing out of his clothes. He looked ridiculous. But men twice his age listened when he spoke. I knew men would follow him, if I could convince him to lead."

"Maybe he was a soldier in a past life."

"Is that what you were?" They hit the bottom step, and Dallas eyed him. "I didn't see it in you at first, but maybe you're too fucking good at hiding it. These men will go any damn where you lead them."

It wasn't a compliment, not exactly, but more of an observation. Ryder shrugged as he pushed through the door to the alley that led toward the staging area. "A soldier can't win a war the way a general can, right?"

Dallas gave him another of those long, appraising looks before snorting. "Soldier or general, just don't get yourself killed. Nessa will murder me."

They hadn't discussed it directly, only in terms of the likely damage to her friends, her family. Her home. "I think she's more worried about you," Ryder shot back. "You're family."

"Yeah, but I'm too contrary to die." Dallas grinned at him. "Plus Lex would follow me down into hell and bring me back so Nessa could kill me again."

Maybe she would, at that.

The men gathered in the staging area were the strongest leaders that had emerged from the remnants of Fleming's men, plus a few factory foremen who had proven themselves tough enough to handle the stress of command. They'd already armed themselves for the battle ahead, though they didn't have much in the way of protective gear. Ryder was pretty sure it didn't matter. This battle couldn't be fought clean and easy, boldly facing their enemy on level ground. It would be rough and it would be dirty.

It was the only way to win.

He stood in front of them as they shifted around, moving into a vague semblance of a line. There was nothing formal about it, but formality was for training, not for the real world. These men were about to bleed and maybe even die together, and that was enough for Ryder.

"We have lots of advantages here," he began, "and the biggest one is pretty fucking big—they're coming up on our western side, right through the factory district. The sons of bitches in the city want those buildings standing when all this is over, no matter what, so they're not going to blast their way through with artillery."

The tense but relieved expressions on their faces told Ryder they understood. With artillery, Eden's troops would roll right over them. Without it, they were left fighting an entrenched enemy force on unfamiliar turf, and that would be Sector Five's saving grace.

He went on. "We'll fight this one on the ground, guns and guts. The blockades are in place, snipers in position. Take these bastards down or drive them to us, just like Hector taught you. Stay in radio contact, and use the codes you learned."

Ryder paused, the heaviness of the moment weighing on him. *He* was giving the orders here, sending these men out to command others. Every death, every potential failure, was a reflection of him. And if he thought about that for too long, the gravity of it would paralyze him. "This is it," he said instead. "This is where we show them what happens when you fuck with Sector Five."

They lifted their fists and rifles in the air, their cheers sounding more like howls of anticipation, and he felt his own adrenaline surge in answer. They headed out to gather their teams, and Ryder turned to Dallas.

He inclined his head. "Good speech."

"Don't blow smoke up my ass, O'Kane."

Dallas barked out a laugh. "Now you sound like Jim."

"He *did* raise me," Ryder reminded him as he reached for his weapons. "Eden will want to send its troops straight up the boulevard—it has the best access, fastest movement. So we have it barricaded off. Their men will funnel into the side streets, and mine will pick them off."

"And any who get past them will end up with no place to go but straight at my men." Dallas made a final check of his sidearm and knives before glancing up at him. "This is gonna get real ugly. You ready for it?"

The first fitful spurts of gunfire had already begun outside, and Ryder struggled to put his overwhelming sense of inevitability into words. He wasn't looking forward to the death and destruction—maybe even his own—but now that it was in front of him, he wasn't afraid. Instead, a strong sense of *fate* gripped him, as if whatever was going to happen had already been written, and they were only fulfilling destiny.

So he didn't answer at all. "Let's go."

Hector must have given the shutdown order, because the only light filtering down into the streets and alleys now came from the moon. Ryder held up a fist to signal Dallas to stop, and they hunkered into the shadows as a team of six men in pristine tactical gear ran past the end of the alley.

At least they wouldn't have any trouble telling friend from foe.

More shots, and Ryder gestured forward. He and Dallas swung out into the cross street just in time to watch the fireteam from Eden cut down a third of the rebel team that met them. Instead of firing—and risking even more of his men—Ryder charged, aiming with the bayonet attached to the end of his rifle.

The soldier in front staggered back from Ryder, surprise overwhelming his training for a critical second before he started to raise his gun. Dallas kicked it out of his hands before swinging around, shoving the man onto Ryder's bayonet.

Rough and dirty, just as Ryder had anticipated. With the added distraction of a flanking attack, the fireteam broke, scattering back toward the safety of the dark alleyways. With a single command, the rebels pursued them, and Ryder tried not to look at the fallen bodies as he kept moving toward the boulevard.

The streets were chaos. Some of the invading troops had already realized they didn't have surprise on their side, after all. Grenades exploded against men and buildings, ripping both apart as screams of pain and bloodlust tore through the night.

They reached the boulevard in time to see a cluster

of Eden soldiers bursting from an alley on the opposite side. Two of the five went down almost at once, as the snipers Ryder had positioned on the roofs took their shots. The other three scattered to be met by Dallas's militia.

Jasper had taken cover behind a steel barricade cut from a reinforced shipping container. Ryder and Dallas joined him, and he nodded as he reloaded his rifle. "Still alive? Good."

Dallas wiped his bloody knife on his pants leg. "How are the boys holding up?"

"Not bad." He paused to peer over the barricade, then leaned up and squeezed off three quick shots before ducking back down. "But I don't think the worst has come yet."

Even as he spoke, more of Eden's troops were streaming into the boulevard, driven by Ryder's men. The two groups clashed, mingling until it was impossible to tell them apart from a distance.

Jasper slung his rifle onto his back and pulled two long, wicked knives from their sheaths. "It looks like this turned into a good, old-fashioned brawl, after all." With that, he dove into the fray with a roar.

Crazy fucking O'Kanes.

Time to embrace it. Ryder followed, channeling his adrenaline and anger into *focus*. Bullets zipped past his head, one so close he swore he could feel the air flowing around it against his cheek, but he ignored them. To his left, a rebel militiaman was grappling with an Eden soldier.

He paused long enough to twist the enemy soldier's arm behind his back. Bone cracked, and the man howled as he dropped his knife. Ryder kept moving, trusting the rebel to finish the rest.

Another man charged at Ryder, the bars on his sleeve marking him as a seasoned soldier. It didn't matter. No one but the Special Tasks soldiers had trained for this as long as he had. Ryder ducked the man's first swing, came in close, and grabbed the back of his neck in a savage grip. With his enemy's movement—and possible retreat—controlled, Ryder jerked him into a vicious elbow strike.

His nose shattered, and Ryder followed him down to the ground, finishing him off with one mercilessly efficient stroke of his blade across the man's throat.

There was no room for mercy here.

Ryder rose and turned in time to see Dallas engaging two soldiers. He ducked blows, and for every one that landed, he hit them back harder. He could hold his own in a fight, even two-on-one, that was for damn sure, and Ryder almost laughed.

Almost.

The hysterical sound died in his throat as a glimmer of movement caught his eye. A third soldier, in half-cover behind one of the electric carts they used to haul freight between warehouses. He held his rifle steady, trained on Dallas, and he'd take the shot, even if it endangered his two comrades.

In a world at war, counting the great Dallas O'Kane amongst your enemy kills was more important than a hundred fellow soldiers.

No time to reach either of them, raise his own gun, even call out a warning. Ironic, since the rest of the world seemed to have slowed to a crawl. Ryder could only watch as the man squeezed the trigger—

"No!" One of Dallas's men hit him hard, taking down one of the Eden soldiers as well. Tank, the others had called him, a giant, smiling brute whose O'Kane ink was still bright and black on his thick wrists.

The shooter's head exploded in a red cloud as one of Five's snipers took him out, and the world snapped back into real, adrenaline-soaked time. Ryder dove for the pile of bodies and pulled away the fallen soldier to reveal lifeless, dead eyes—and Dallas's knife buried to the hilt in his chest.

"Fuck." Dallas shoved the man away and rolled to his knees. "That was fucking—"

His words cut off abruptly as his gaze fell on Tank. The young man sprawled on his back, his breath wheezing out through bloodstained lips. The bullets meant for Dallas had hit him square in the chest, and Ryder knew it was hopeless.

So did Dallas. He clasped Tank's hand and bent over him, his voice roughened by grief but still gentle. "Hey, kid. You saved my ass there. So you rest for a bit and let us mop up, okay? Then we'll have a big party for you, and all the girls will fuss over you, and you'll be a big damn hero."

Tank's lips curved into a smile. His lungs wheezed again as he tried to speak, and the words came out on a fading rasp. "O'Kane...for..."

He never finished.

Dallas leaned forward and pressed his forehead to Tank's. Without looking, he reached out and found the knife still protruding from the dead soldier's chest. His fingers curled around it, and he flowed to his feet.

Anger and grief would have been understandable. But what burned in Dallas's eyes was nothing less than determined *fury*, as if the moment Tank slipped away was all the time he had needed to fully envision the deaths of every Eden soldier left standing, and all he had to do now was make them happen.

"Let's finish this," he snarled, pivoting toward the remaining soldiers.

Then he was gone.

Dallas hit a tight knot of invaders with a roar that served as a rallying cry. Other O'Kanes echoed it, surging toward their leader. But Dallas didn't need any help. He slashed and stabbed like a man possessed. He ripped sidearms out of startled soldiers' hands and turned them on their owners. When he ran out of bullets, he whipped the pistols across terrified faces and took the men apart with his bare fucking hands.

He was a force of nature. Rage personified. Eden's soldiers started to break, scattering back toward the squads of Sector Four's militia, who picked them off easily. With the fight under control—and the enemy fleeing—Hector pulled Ryder off the front lines.

He headed straight for the converted shop they'd designated as their medical aid station. Wounded men lined the walls, with medics rushing between them like bees flitting from flower to flower. Only Dylan Jordan, head of Dallas's secret Sector Three hospital, stood unmoving, his arms crossed over his chest.

Dallas's eyes were still too bright. Dangerous. "Who did we lose?"

"Besides Tank, a few militia members—Crider, Lemieux, and McCutcheon." He hesitated. "Dallas, Stuart took a grenade. He didn't make it."

"Fuck." Dallas's fists tightened. "*Fuck.* Lex is going to murder me."

Hector handed Ryder a list of the known casualties from Five. It was much, much longer, but the names swam together. He wasn't sure he'd recognize any of them, anyway. He didn't know them, even casually. Hell, he'd been better acquainted with Stuart.

So that was the image that stuck with him as field reports continued to roll in, and the combined forces from Four and Five ended the battle with Eden's retreat. Not the dozens of names on Hector's list, but the crinkle-eyed smile of one of Sector Four's artisans, gone in an instant.

15

Nessa didn't want to be here.

There was nothing wrong with the rooftop garden, especially with the early-morning light burnishing everything with warm golds. It caught the shower of water droplets spraying off one of the sprinklers in a rainbow of color that vanished as soon as Nessa noticed it, only to reappear farther down the row of plants.

It was an idyllic setting. No doubt that was why Lex had picked it for the video Markovic was recording. Nessa would bet all the bottles in her safe that no one inside Eden's prissy-ass walls imagined *this* when they thought of the sectors. Dirt and blood, yes. Crime and concrete and death...but not life. And this garden seethed with it, from the plants finally bursting into bloom to the insects that had come from God-knew-where, buzzing from plant to plant doing whatever it was bugs did.

It was pretty as a picture, and Nessa was fucking miserable. Grief was bad enough—Tank had been a new recruit, someone she'd only known for a month or two, but she'd *liked* the impossible meathead. And the way he'd gone down…

Every last O'Kane in Sector Four would put themselves between Dallas and a bullet, if that was what it took to protect him. And the only thing grimmer than imagining how acutely Dallas felt Tank's loss was trying not to think about which O'Kane would be next.

There was plenty of reason to be hurting. But Nessa had her own intensely selfish reason, too.

Ryder hadn't come back from Sector Five. Dallas and Lex had both assured her that he'd come through the battle in one piece—more or less—but that the same couldn't be said for all his men, so she wasn't surprised he stayed. Sector Five was his, and if he abandoned the people who depended on him, he wouldn't be worth all her worry and sleepless nights. He wouldn't be *Ryder*.

Didn't make the sleepless nights easier, though.

"They're almost ready." Jared had shed his jacket for the cause—it barely fit Markovic through the shoulders, but it hung off his large frame. There was nothing they could do about that. The drastic weight loss resulting from months of starvation and torture couldn't be fixed in a few weeks.

Nessa dragged her attention back to the tablet in her hands. The video camera mounted on a trellis beside her displayed its captured image there, showing her Markovic as he quietly endured Lili's final touches.

She smoothed his hair into place with gentle

fingers and smiled. "There we go. Do you need anything else before we start? Water?"

He shook his head, and Lex stepped up in her place, bending over to speak to him.

"This is going to be brutal," Jared whispered.

"I know," Lili replied just as softly. She moved closer to Nessa and peered down at the tablet. "Can you zoom in a little tighter?"

Nessa nodded and slid her finger over the controls along the side of the picture. Markovic filled the frame, perfectly dressed and still utterly out of place in this serene setting. He looked...sharp. Hard. No one watching could doubt that he'd been through hell. Just staring into his eyes was enough—the pain and darkness that stared back left Nessa unsettled.

Which was the point, she supposed. Propaganda wasn't meant to make you feel warm and snuggly.

Markovic took a deep breath and swallowed convulsively. The closer shot hid his shaking leg and fidgety hands, but it couldn't hide his face, not when his face was the whole focus of the video.

"We can do this later," Lex offered.

"No, we can't," he shot back irritably. "It needs to be done by this afternoon. Just in case she says yes."

"All right." Lex bent over again, putting herself on eye level with him. "Then do it."

The noise he made was pure exasperation, but when Lex stepped back out of the frame, his hands were still, his eyes flashing more fire than despair.

Nessa tapped the screen to start recording.

Markovic took another deep breath. "Hello, I'm Councilman Nikolas Markovic. You haven't seen me for a while. Some of you thought I was dead, or that I'd abandoned you. At this point, I almost wish either of those things were true, because the reality is much more dangerous for you all."

Beside her, Jared flinched.

"I was a prisoner in my own city, jailed by my fellow councilmen," Markovic went on. His jaw tightened, but he kept talking. "For ninety-three days, they kept me chained to a wall in a cell at City Center. They gave me dirty water and very little food. There was no trial, no formal charges, because I committed no crime. I was simply in the way.

"Under the direction of Councilman Smith Peterson, MPs beat and tortured me. They interrogated me about my allegiances and activities, and when I didn't give them the answers they wanted, they beat me some more. They cut me, burned me, broke my bones. If they went too far, they called a regen tech to patch me up—and started again the next day."

His voice wavered on the last words, and Nessa couldn't watch him on the screen anymore. It was too close, too *personal*, pain radiating from his eyes as he fought back the memories.

He held it together. "I know some of you are shocked. You don't want to believe that things like this could happen in our city. Others are surprised, but only because it happened to *me*—a councilman, a leader elected by the people. But I think there are probably more of you who aren't shocked at all, because you've seen this. You've seen it happen to a friend or a family member, heard the whispers and the threats. You already know what some of your leaders are capable of."

The fractures in his composure grew. Watching him directly instead of through the camera spared Nessa the close-up of his face, but his leg was shaking harder and his hands curled into tense fists. He looked brittle, strung so tightly that one gentle touch might shatter him.

Markovic paused, and his chest heaved with a single hitching breath. "Peterson came to me with a Council decree—an order to bomb Sector Two. On paper, their goal was to target militant operations and curb the rebellion. In reality, they knew the sector held no strategic value. The bombing was a message, a warning—*oppose us, and we'll murder the most helpless among you*. When I refused to sign off on it, he had me arrested."

Across the rooftop, Lex turned away.

"Put down your arms." It sounded less like a plea and more like a command. "The sector rebellion isn't aggression, it's a *reaction*, and their fight isn't with the people of Eden. Their fight is with the corrupt leaders who hold us all hostage. The men who preach purity in all things while they hide their addictions and underage lovers, who demand integrity and then laugh about the idea behind closed doors. The hypocrites who talk about the sanctity of life...and then wreak destruction on a sector full of children."

He began to stand, and Jared touched Nessa's arm. She widened the shot and followed Markovic, framing him against the backdrop of the garden.

He stood there, tall but on trembling legs, and shook his head. "But it can end here. You have the power to say *no more*. You deserve leaders who will lead, public servants who will serve, who care about more than wealth and unchecked power. You deserve to take back your city from the *real* threat here. You're the only ones who can."

Nessa held her breath as he stood there, his words

a powerful call to action. Something sparked hot and bright beneath the pain in his eyes, the same thing Dallas had. Charisma or power of will or whatever it took to inspire people, to make them loyal. To make them believe.

Jared reached over and cut the recording. "It's off."

The moment he said the words, Markovic stumbled away from the chair and around the side of the greenhouse. A second later, the sound of retching filled the still morning air.

Lili exhaled softly. "We need to get him back to Three. Let Doc look him over."

"No," Lex said firmly. "He's not going back to the hospital. I promised."

Jared rubbed one hand over his face. "Lex—"

"The man's weak, not dying." She turned around, her eyes dry but red. "He still needs care, but he can get it here. No more hospitals."

Lili nodded. "All right. He can have my room. We'll get him settled in."

Lex didn't move. "Tell him..." But she never finished. "Never mind. I'm sure he knows."

They helped Markovic down the stairs, and Nessa set the tablet aside and crossed the roof to stand beside Lex. "You okay?"

"No, I'm not." She turned her red-rimmed gaze on Nessa. "You have no idea how many times I said I wanted to watch Sector Two burn."

"Lex." Nessa wrapped her arms around the older woman. "C'mon. We say shit we don't mean. I do it fifteen times a day. I told Ace *this morning* that I hoped he got his dick caught in his zipper."

"That's the problem, Nessa. I did fucking mean it." She closed her eyes and shook her head. "I didn't make it happen, I know that. But I didn't stop it, either."

Nessa held on tighter. "You couldn't have stopped it. Hell, if you'd tried, maybe you just would have been there when it happened."

"Maybe." Silence. "Cerys is dead."

Maybe she was growing up, because Nessa bit back the words that wanted to come flying out. *Good fucking riddance.* Cerys had fucked with Lex and Dallas for years, but she'd been a force in Lex's life, for good or ill. "When did you find out?"

"I didn't," Lex admitted. "But she must be. It's the only thing that makes sense."

They'd just listened to Markovic discuss ninety-three days of torment at the hands of the men in Eden. Was it better to agree with Lex, or to point out that Cerys could be in one of those cells, rotting away? There were no soothing answers. Nothing easy to say. "It's okay to feel shitty about that, you know. Even if you hated her."

"I did worse than hate her. I understood her." She kissed the top of Nessa's head and patted her back. "I'm fine, honey. Just...ready for this war to be over so we can get back to doing what O'Kanes do best."

"Fuck and drink and fuck some more?" Nessa asked, trying to make her tone light. "Or sleeping until noon."

"Something like that." Lex reached for the tablet. "Did Dallas give you Ryder's message?"

"He grumbled at me that Ryder would be back as soon as he could and not to worry because he was more-or-less intact." Nessa wrinkled her nose. "I don't know what you said to him, but that's better than I expected. He hasn't threatened to kill him in front of me, not even once."

"Dallas likes him. I don't think he expected to, but there it is."

Warmth flooded her cheeks. "I like him too, Lex. I mean *like him*, like him. More than the hot making out."

Lex stared down at her, the last of her melancholy slipping into humor and something fiercer, something almost like pride. "You've been an O'Kane even longer than I have, Nessa. You should have known you'd never be happy with anyone who couldn't stand toe-to-toe with your brothers."

She smiled, but after only a few seconds her smile wobbled. "I don't think he's planning on staying around if we win, though."

Lex seemed to consider that for a moment. "Does knowing that change anything?"

"I—" For once, no words came. Nessa missed Ryder already. Missing him was a symptom, and more of them kept popping up. Daydreaming. Wanting. Fantasizing. He was in her head and under her skin, seeping into parts of her she'd barely realized were there.

She could end it before he got to her heart. It might protect her a little. Or it might make her miserable for the final days of her life. If they lost, if she *died*—she'd regret every second she hadn't spent living as hard as she could.

And if they won, and he broke her heart... Well, she'd be alive. Work had filled the void in her life before. She'd find more of it, enough to fill whatever space he left behind. "No. It doesn't."

"Mmm." Lex tilted her head and smiled softly. "My advice? Just let it be. Sometimes life surprises you."

"Let's hope." She gave Lex a plaintive look. "Do you think he'll be back soon?"

"Oh, I think the odds are pretty goddamn good."

Then she'd wait for him. If the end was coming for her, she was going to face it like an O'Kane—fighting to squeeze the joy out of every damn second she had left.

And if it wasn't, she'd face that like an O'Kane, too. And fight for what she wanted.

penny

Everyone knew Penny was lying when she poked her head into the NetSec hub and told them she was running out for some decent coffee.

Eden had been under heavy rationing for weeks, and the only thing close to approaching real coffee was seven floors down, in the executive suite, where tense, wary assistants prepared beverages and food for what was left of the Council. Outside their glass tower, people were reusing grinds for weeks or mixing them with the synthetic coffee from Sector Eight that tasted like burnt dirt.

No one thought Penny was really going out for coffee, but no one murmured a word of protest, either. Twelve of the nineteen men and women who worked under her supervision were bent over their tablets and computer screens, as drawn and haggard as she felt, scrambling anxiously for some tiny victory that would deflect Council displeasure for one more day.

She'd started with twenty-five employees. Council displeasure was taking its toll.

She tried not to think about it as she stepped into the elevator. Trying not to think was how she bridged the sparse minutes between work and sleep—the latter of which she hadn't been getting nearly often enough. Maybe that was why the elevator's swift descent made her dizzy.

Penny steadied herself in the tense seconds before the doors opened. Then she strode into the lobby, ignoring the way people skittered out of her path when they recognized the insignia on her jacket. No one wanted to attract the attention of a NetSec officer and risk a digital investigation that might uncover evidence of treasonous activity. Penny could have told them not to worry. If the Council wanted treasonous activity uncovered, nothing would stop them, including innocence. Manufacturing evidence had been back in vogue since the start of the insurrection.

Another thing Penny was trying not to think about.

She pushed through the glass doors and into the harsh sunlight. The steps down to the street were usually cluttered with people going about their business, but today only a few people scurried nervously past under the assessing gazes of a Special Tasks squad. Penny doubted most of them realized that was what the four men were—even now, Special Tasks was more legend than reality to the citizens of Eden—but the dangerous menace apparent in their heavy armor and deadly rifles was unmistakable.

Things got grimmer on the main street. Rationing lines snaked around buildings, cluttering sidewalks with tired, blank-eyed people waiting for their chance at enough food to get their family through the next few days. MPs were posted at checkpoints between neighborhoods, scanning bar codes and turning away people who didn't have a travel pass. Shorter lines trailed out of the recruitment stations, men with trembling hands and fear in their eyes.

They would make for terrible soldiers, but the Council didn't care. They would serve their intended purpose—as warm bodies to throw at the sectors, cannon fodder to tire out the enemy before the real soldiers swept in. After the defeat in Five, they needed all the warm bodies they could get.

Penny ducked into what had once been the most popular coffee shop in the heart of City Center. All the cute little tables were abandoned now. The glass jars that usually held bright sprays of flowers were empty, and the digital displays in the center of the room where you ordered your drinks had gone dark. Even the owner was missing. His daughter had taken his place behind the counter, looking drawn and terrified as her gaze fixed on Penny's jacket.

That was why Penny wore it. She deserved the constant reminder that she was a monster.

She didn't bother trying to put the girl at ease. It would be futile. Instead, she ordered the most expensive coffee on the menu and swiped her wrist over the scanner to pay. The smell from the cup turned her stomach, but she left a generous tip to compensate for the woman's fear and her own guilt before leaving the shop.

Crumpled-up trash and torn recruitment posters

littered the streets—actual *garbage* on Eden's shining roads, the clearest sign of their current desperate state. Eden had always been rotten on the inside, but maintaining the pristine exterior had always been everyone's top priority.

Penny wasn't sure *what* their priority was anymore. Survival, maybe. It certainly was hers.

A man in a black sweatshirt with a hat pulled down over his ears appeared from between two buildings, startling Penny. She tried to step out of his path, but he bumped into her hard enough to knock the coffee from her hand. She bit back a curse as the hot liquid scalded her fingers, but the man was already disappearing down another side street.

Chasing him down wasn't worth it. And it wasn't like she wanted to *drink* the damn coffee. She recovered the cup and tossed it into the nearest recycling bin, the habit too ingrained to allow her to leave it in the street. Cradling her stinging hand, she hurried back to the building that headquartered the Council.

It wasn't until she was leaning against the side of the elevator as it whisked her skyward that she felt the odd crinkle in her jacket pocket. She slid her hand in and pulled out a folded piece of paper.

Nothing on the outside, not even her name. But when she opened it, her heart began to race. The ground felt unsteady beneath her feet. Her stomach swooped up into her throat as hope and denial chased each other in a dizzy loop that only broke when the elevator door *dinged.*

Panicked, she shoved the paper back into her pocket. Then she took a deep, steadying breath and flattened her features.

She stopped by the NetSec hub first and stuck her

head in. "Any updates on the Riley situation?"

Her best surveillance tech, a sixty-year-old woman with hair so blonde the silver barely showed, looked up from her station. "No. I caught Liam Riley on a camera over by the docks, but it's only about ten seconds of footage, and I can't pick him up on any of the nearby feeds. It's like he vanished."

Or he knew exactly what the angle of surveillance was for every camera Eden had in play. Penny could change the angles, add new ones, but the hackers worming their way through the system would map them and report back to Liam Riley every time. "Keep trying, Leigh. Pull Simon and John in to spec out new equipment by the docks, if you catch him there again."

The woman nodded, and Penny retreated across the hallway to her office. As the head of Network Security, she had a cozy corner space with vast windows that made her feel exposed. She usually kept the curtains closed, but today she walked over and pressed the button to open them.

This high up, Eden stretched out below her like a model of a city. She was higher than any of the other buildings, higher than the walls. To the southeast, she could see Sector Four, the buildings squat and dark, made of concrete and brick instead of the shining steel and glass favored in the city.

Her hands trembling, she pulled the piece of paper out of her pocket again and carefully unfolded it. It was just one line and a string of numbers—an unfinished quote, an IP address and a time. But the *words*—

Life shrinks or expands in proportion to one's...

She heard the final word in the sentence as if Nikolas Markovic was standing behind her, his warm voice full of the good humor and kindness that had first pierced her wary armor. *Life shrinks or expands in proportion to one's courage.*

It was either a message from a ghost or a trap.

She checked the time on the paper against the clock in her workstation. Seventeen minutes. Not nearly long enough to figure out a safe way to approach this. Nikolas had vanished in the middle of the night months ago, plagued by accusations of treason. No one had ever told her that he'd been executed, but no orders had come down from the man running the Council now to find him, either. If Markovic had been alive and on the run, Smith Peterson would have had every resource in NetSec searching for him around the clock.

Penny had assumed Peterson's lack of concern meant he knew exactly where Markovic was, and she'd done her grieving in private. Nikolas would have understood, she told herself. He knew what she was when he plucked her out of detention. Not a noble hero like him, not a fighter.

He'd done his best to make her better, but you couldn't change the core of a person. And Penelope Mathieu was a survivor.

This note was almost certainly a trap. Peterson had been enraged at her inability to protect Eden against every digital attack from the sectors. Even though she'd gotten the power grid back up within two days, it didn't matter. As far as the Council was concerned, there was no excuse for some uneducated sector trash hacker to be able to compete with Eden's elite, much less beat them, however momentarily, unless she wasn't trying hard enough.

And she of all people knew surveillance was everywhere. Someone could have recorded Markovic saying this to her. Someone could have tortured him until he spilled everything. They wanted to see if she'd reach out to a traitor. They wanted proof of her guilt.

Except...Peterson didn't need proof. If he wanted her dead, he'd walk into her office and pull the trigger himself. He'd probably enjoy it, too—the rumor was that Peterson had taken more than one torture and extrajudicial execution into his own hands lately.

And if it *was* a trap, she could cover. Claim she'd been setting a trap of her own to lure Markovic into the open. She could spin it. That was what survivors did.

And if it wasn't...

Her heart still beating erratically, she took her chair and engaged her anti-surveillance tech to scramble the signals of anyone trying to listen in. Then she watched the minutes count down. At the appointed time, she opened a window and entered the IP address. She got a password prompt back immediately, and stared at it for a few seconds before looking down at the scrap of paper again.

Life shrinks or expands in proportion to one's...

Slowly, she typed in COURAGE.

A video connection opened up, and she choked back an unexpected sob when Nikolas's face filled the screen.

He was alive. He looked *terrible*—his face was drawn, his cheekbones so sharp it hurt to look at them. His skin had a sickly pallor, and there were deep creases around his eyes and between his brows that hadn't been there before.

But he was alive.

He looked like he'd aged ten years in the weeks since she'd seen him. She felt like she'd aged a hundred. And she didn't know what to say to a ghost.

"Hi, Pen," he rasped finally. "I'm glad you could

make it."

"Nikolas—" Her voice cracked. Even though her antibugging device was running, she couldn't bring herself to speak above a whisper. "Where are—no, don't tell me. You're okay?"

"For some definitions of the word." He tugged on the tie knotted around his throat to loosen it. "What about you?"

There was no answer she could give that wouldn't deepen the stress lines around his eyes. Nikolas cared. That was his most powerful asset and his greatest vulnerability, how very much he cared. "I'm okay. I'd say I wish you were here, but...you know. I like you too much for that, even if you're an annoying do-gooder."

He closed his eyes and jerked—not quite a wince, but close enough to make her fingers twitch on her lap, as if she could reach through the screen to soothe him. "I need you to broadcast something for me."

If it had been anyone else in the world—living or dead—she would have disconnected the call. Talking to him was treason, an offense severe enough to earn her an immediate bullet between the eyes. *Helping* him—

That would earn her a trip to the empty white room beneath the tower. The place where they broke you and healed you just to break you again, over and over until you begged for them to stop fixing the parts of you they'd ripped away.

She'd had a taste of it once, when she'd been brought in for hacking the City Center network and refused to tell them where she'd hidden the datacard with the dirt she'd stolen. They broke her fingers one by one, then left her there with a threat hanging over her head—give them the data, or they'd let her fingers heal like that and start breaking other parts of her.

Nikolas pulled her out of that hellhole. He arranged for the regen tech to restore her fingers so perfectly that her knuckles only ached a little when it rained—but the nightmares never went away completely.

If it had been anyone else…

She tightened her fists until her fingers turned white and wet her lips. "What is it?"

"I've recorded something—a message for the people." He tugged at the tie until the knot unraveled, then pulled it free and opened the top button of his collar. "The truth about what happened to me, and what's happening to them."

"Propaganda," she whispered.

"If you wish." He leaned forward, his eyes intense, and she could just make out an angry scar peeking out of the top of his collar. "My words are only part of the picture, and they need to see it all. Do you understand?"

See it all.

Penny had seen it all—an ironic feat for a girl who had once been tortured for stealing a few secrets. As the head of NetSec, she had them all at her fingertips—the foibles of councilmen, the indiscretions of their families, the hypocrisies of the wealthy men who formed the power structure directly beneath the Council.

Most she'd been tasked with deleting, covering their tracks even as she exposed the less privileged. But a few bits of choice blackmail material had always found their way into Nikolas's possession as insurance. Just in case.

He might be a hero, but he was a pragmatic one. And Penny had never cared much for laws or commands. Her loyalty began and ended with the man staring up at her from the vidscreen. She'd fight to protect her staff, but if she had to choose…

There had never been a choice. She'd been his since the day he saved her.

The doorknob rattled, and Penny jumped in her chair. When no knock followed, she knew it was Peterson before the soft *beep* of him overriding her lock sounded. She caught one last glimpse of Nikolas's worried expression before she shut the connection and pulled up the surveillance footage Leigh had sent her.

Smith Peterson was an objectively handsome man, but it had been years since Penny had been able to look at him and see anything but *danger*. He strolled in, hands in his pockets, his sharp, assessing gaze at odds with his casual demeanor. "Good morning, Penelope."

"Mr. Peterson." He enjoyed subservience and respect, two things he'd never earned and didn't deserve. Penny offered them anyway, rising from her chair and doing her best to look pleasant and accommodating, even if she couldn't manage a smile. "I was just reviewing the techs' work from last night. We might have a lead on Liam Riley."

"Might," he repeated. His expression didn't change, but something in his tone raised the hair on the back of her neck.

She spun the screen around and played Leigh's footage. "We know where he's been seen recently. We're going to deploy additional surveillance tech and narrow the blind spots—"

"Five people," he interrupted.

Penny stared. "Five people?"

"I'm reassigning five people from your staff." He straightened the shirt cuff that extended below the sleeve of his jacket. "I think their infantry enlistments would be a better allocation of city resources."

No one on her staff was remotely equipped for the

infantry—and very few people left in Eden were qualified to replace them. It was petty cruelty, venting his frustration and disappointment on her, because she made an easy target—and fear would make the others work harder.

She swallowed the pain, because she had no other choice. "Whatever you think is best."

"Yes. Remember that, Penelope." He turned for the door. "Have their names on my desk by the end of the day."

"Have—" Her composure cracked. "You want me to choose them?"

Peterson didn't even pause. "It's your staff." He reached the door and flashed her a warm smile, though his eyes remained as cold as ever. "Your responsibility."

She heard the warning beneath his pleasant words as he left her office. *When you fail, they pay the price.*

She sank back into her chair and stared at her screen. Her own face reflected back at her—light brown skin, light brown hair, light brown eyes. Her uniform jacket was light brown, too. She was nondescript. Nameless. A cog in this machine she'd never wanted to be a part of, a machine she wanted to destroy until Nikolas brought her inside and promised her a chance to change the future with him.

Hope had died with him. For weeks, Penny had been putting one foot in front of the other, doing things that turned her stomach to protect herself and the people who reported to her.

Still not enough.

Moving slowly at first, then with increased confidence, Penny navigated through the network until she found the hidden stash of files she'd set up for Markovic. She pulled them all down to her private network and decrypted them one by one before playing the first.

Peterson filled the screen, as handsome as ever, but his eyes were as cold as his words as he leaned across his desk toward the camera—a clever device that had been hidden in Markovic's tiepin. "*Fuck* those lazy freeloaders. They're the ones who got us into this mess, with their incessant whining about wanting *more more more.* If they didn't want their illegal brats requisitioned and sent to the communes, they shouldn't have bred without authorization."

The next video was at a different angle, not in Markovic's office. Peterson was pacing back and forth, a Special Tasks Lieutenant listening attentively. "The farms need more workers. They're threatening a fifty percent shortfall without five hundred new bodies to get crops into the fields. So you take your men, and you find them five hundred bodies. The first grubby peasants you can lay your hands on. And take their families, too, so there's no one left behind to sob about it."

There were more videos, fifteen in all. A thoughtfully curated, carefully preserved collection of all the disdain, hatred, and loathing for Eden's residents that Peterson hid behind his fancy suits and polished smiles. The silver bullet Markovic had never gotten the chance to fire.

Doing it for him would get her killed. And it might not change anything.

She dithered about it for the rest of the afternoon while she performed routine tasks and added and removed names from her list.

He just had a kid.

Her mother depends on her income.

She's taking care of her three younger siblings.

He's seventy-five—he'll die in the first battle.

She's seventeen—she'll die in the first battle.

Before Markovic had dragged her into his ridiculous circle of heroism, she wouldn't have known their stories. She wouldn't have cared. She would have picked the five she needed the least and shipped their names off, knowing she couldn't stop it, couldn't help them.

Frustrated, she deleted the list and went back to the IP address. It took her forty-five minutes to figure out where Markovic had been calling her from. The first forty, she wasted tracking and backtracking, digging through ridiculous layers of rerouting. It had to be that mysterious hacker in Sector Four, the one who seemed to know more about Eden's network than she did.

He was good, very good. Maybe better than her. But she had better tools and more processing power. She could hand all this proof over to Peterson now and maybe spare herself.

Instead, she typed out seven words and sent a message that had nothing to do with survival.

Send me your video. I'll do it.

16

Ryder told himself he had things to do in Four. It was a lie.

He had things to do, but they were all solidly centered on Sector Five. The battle there had taken its toll not only on the men who had fought in it, but on the sector as a whole. The factories were still standing and operational, but some of them had been damaged. And even the citizens who had refused to involve themselves with the rebellion were now facing the realities of death and war—cleanup efforts, rebuilding.

Burial detail.

Sharp, stinging guilt raked him. They had won the battle, successfully defeated the largest invading force of troops from the city that anyone had seen so far, but at great cost, and he couldn't help but wonder whether they might have fared better with more training, more preparation. More of his attention.

Dallas had insisted that Ryder's presence in Four was necessary to their success, and he didn't doubt it. Dallas didn't seem like the sort of man who would ever admit he needed something, even if he did, unless it was a matter of life or death. But Ryder hadn't exactly fought him on it either. He could have offered other solutions, like visits or encrypted video calls or traveling back and forth on a daily basis. But he hadn't, and that reason was now tangled up with his guilt and recrimination.

Nessa.

He had promised her he would come back. Not right away—he had too much shit to do to even think about it—but as soon as he could. And the fact that he'd been able to think of little else for days, even as he worked in the dirt and dust and blood alongside the frightened people of Sector Five, was almost enough to make him turn around and stay out of Four for good.

He'd always excelled at self-sacrifice. But not this time.

She wasn't in her office, or in the aging room, or the distillery, or any of the other places he could think of, and he almost took it as a divine sign that he should haul his ass back to Five. But weariness drove him to the apartment above the Broken Circle instead.

Nessa was sprawled on his couch, her boots on the floor next to her and a tablet resting on her stomach. Sound spilled out of it—the crash of metallic sound effects while music worked toward a crescendo—but she was oblivious. Her chin was tilted down toward her shoulder, and strands of pink and purple hair had slipped over her cheek.

Something lurched in his chest, twisting free a tightness that had been building for three long days—and even longer nights.

He knelt by the couch, moving as carefully and quietly as possible, and smoothed the hair from her cheek.

She jolted awake, her hands scrabbling for the tablet as it started to slide off her stomach. Then her eyes met his, and her lips curved up in a sweet, sleepy smile. "You're back."

It took him a moment to find his voice. "Yeah, I'm back."

"I broke in," she confessed in a low whisper. "I wanted to be waiting for you."

"I'm glad." He saw the heaviness in his heart reflected in her eyes. "I'm sorry about Tank and Stuart."

She swallowed and sat up before shutting off the tablet and tossing it aside. "It sucks. All of it sucks. All of it—"

"Hey." He sank onto the couch beside her, but he couldn't think of anything reassuring to say. There *wasn't* anything. Later, maybe, they'd be able to say that Tank's sacrifice had helped win the war. For now, the only thing they had was senseless loss.

"I know." She crawled into his lap, straddling his knees with her own resting on either side of his thighs. Tears glistened in her eyes and on her lashes, but she blinked them away as she cupped his face. Then she ran her hands down his neck and over his shoulders. "Dallas just told me you were in one piece, more or less. He didn't tell me if you'd gotten hurt."

"Scrapes and bruises, nothing a little med-gel couldn't fix." He covered her hands with his. "If I'd needed stitches, I would have waited for you."

She huffed before continuing her determined exploration across his chest. "I'd stitch you up crooked to teach you to take better care of yourself."

Worry and fear tinged her voice, not irritation. "I didn't take unnecessary chances."

"I know." Her hands stilled, one pressed over his heart. "I worry about the necessary ones. Then I remember you're a super-spy with a murder book. You got this."

As much as anyone could—his mother and Jim had made sure of that—but life rarely offered guarantees. He couldn't bring himself to say as much, so he took a deep breath. "I may have to start spending more time back in Five."

For the first time since he'd met her, Nessa's open expression shut down. Her fingers tensed under his, but it was the only physical clue she gave him. Her expression was so carefully, studiously blank, and when she finally spoke, it wasn't a cheerful babble. Just two precise words. "I understand."

"No, you don't. I don't *want* to, but the damage—" He bit off the words. "How many people did Dallas lose from the militia?"

Nessa tugged her hand free and touched his lips. "Ryder. I *understand*—"

"How many?"

"I don't know, nine or ten?"

"Ten," he repeated, "including Tank. Sector Five lost forty-seven men."

Her hand dropped to her lap. She wasn't good at holding that blank expression, and it cracked as he watched. First, she caught her lower lip between her teeth. Then her brows pulled down as sympathy and pain filled her eyes. "You have responsibilities," she said softly. "People depend on you. I'm trying not to be another burden, okay? So don't worry about explaining it to me. You have important shit going on."

"You're not a burden." Not quite a lie, and not for the reasons she thought. For the first time in as long as he could remember, he wanted something—wanted *her*—as much as he wanted to tear down Eden, and it was dragging him in two different directions. "Just... don't act like it means I'm shutting you out. I'm not."

"We didn't make any promises." Her right hand still rested under his, pinned against his chest, and she curled her fingers into his shirt. "I'll miss you when you're not here. I'll be sad. I'd hide it if I could, but I'm shit at hiding things, so I'll be here when you come back, every time. And I understand."

He tightened his fingers around hers. "Do you really believe that?"

"Do I believe what?"

"That we haven't made any promises."

She exhaled shakily. "It would be stupid. This isn't a good time for promises."

"Selfish," he agreed. But some things couldn't be stopped. "I've never been selfish before. I think it might be time."

She eased closer, until her chest pressed against his. She smelled like cinnamon and cloves today, with a sweet undertone of vanilla. Her lashes were thick and black, spiky with unshed tears. "You can be selfish with me."

No, he couldn't. It was a luxury none of them could afford, not with Eden pressing in on them, becoming more and more desperate with each thwarted advance.

But here, tonight, he would take it. The stolen moments, the chance to stop thinking about whether he'd done enough, or whether he was making the right decisions. With Nessa, she'd tell him if he did something wrong, and his focus was crystalline. Absolute.

He touched her chin, lifting her face to his. "I missed you."

"I missed you, too." She wrapped her arms around his neck. "I thought about crashing in your bed, but it felt weird. You haven't invited me there yet."

"I can fix that." He slipped one arm beneath her legs, rose with her in his arms, and regarded her solemnly. "Will you stay with me tonight?"

"Yes." Her voice was equally solemn, but her eyes ruined it. They glinted with uncontainable mischief as she gravely told him, "But only if you promise to do some really filthy stuff with me."

"Count on it." He walked into the bedroom and stood her beside the bed. He wanted her naked before she touched the mattress, nothing between them but open space—empty, and yet full of possibilities.

He started with her shirt, tugging the tight purple fabric up until it bared just the lower curves of her breasts. He paused, slipping his fingers beneath the cotton to stroke her nipples. She arched into his touch with a moan, swaying on her feet. He steadied her, then stripped the shirt over her head.

It left her hair in disarray, and Ryder took a moment to smooth it around her shoulders, combing the silken strands with his fingers. He brushed the hollow of her throat, and her pounding pulse made his blood throb in answer.

"Ryder." She tilted her head back, her eyes drifting shut, trust evident in every line of her body. In the way she whispered his name. "Michael."

"Just that look." Her belt buckle clicked under his

fingers. "That's all I want you wearing tonight."

"I can't control my looks." She traced up his arms to his shoulders. "Whenever you put your hands on me, I can't control much of anything. I think I have nerve endings that only exist when you're touching me."

"Shh." He slid her patched jeans and her black lace underwear off her hips and down her legs, leaving her naked when she stepped free of the fabric.

He tore off his own clothes in record time. There was nothing sensual in undressing himself, just a means to an end—flesh against flesh, feeling her skin heat against his as he captured her mouth in an open, hungry kiss.

She went up on her toes, pushing as close to him as she could as her arms tangled around his neck. Her kiss was desperate, her noises needy. He spilled her back to the bed, never relinquishing the contact that felt like a lifeline.

Even with the world crashing down around them, he could be this for her—safety, shelter. Protection.

No waiting. He thrust inside her, then stilled with a low groan as she shuddered beneath him. Her fingernails dug into his shoulders, almost hard enough to break the skin, and she panted against his lips. "Oh God, oh *fuck*—"

Ryder steeled himself against the delicious pain and soothed her with soft, grazing kisses across her jaw and down to her collarbone. He braced one arm beside her head and lifted his upper body, gritting his teeth when the movement drove his cock deeper into her grasping heat.

But he didn't move, not yet. He touched her instead—tracing patterns on her skin with his palm, his fingertips, the back of his hand. Each one offered a different sensation, a new revelation of reaction. Nessa liked the softer caresses on her throat and shoulders, and a firmer pressure on her breasts. So he gave her those things, watching her intently as her face flushed and her body heated.

She squirmed beneath him, spreading one thigh wider and wrapping the other leg around his hips. “I don’t know how you do this.”

“Do what?”

“Make it so *hot* to be this frustrated…” She dug her head back into the bed with a soft moan. “One second I want you to pound me through the mattress, and the next I just want you to play with me all night.”

“You want it all.” He rolled her nipple between his fingers. “Say it.”

“I want it—” Her voice broke, and she clutched at him. “Fuck, I want it all. I want more. Harder, please, just a little—”

He clenched her hair in his fist. “Wait for it, Nessa. Trust me.”

She whimpered her protest before her gaze found his. Something in his eyes stilled her impatient wriggling, and she stared up at him as her rapid breaths lifted her breasts. “Is this what you meant? The things you like that aren’t a game?”

“I don’t know.” He’d never really thought about it, and he damn sure couldn’t right now, with her trembling beneath him. He only knew that he needed her trust, needed for her to believe that he would give her anything she desired. “Let me take care of you.”

Nessa cupped his face again and smoothed her thumbs over his lower lip. “I trust you, maybe more than I trust myself. I’m just made of impulses and impatience, all wanting and doing, and people get tired of trying to stop me."

Another promise he could make. "I'll always stop you, if that's what it takes."

She kissed him softly and then let her hands fall away. Her arms settled on either side of her head, the backs of her fingers brushing the hand he had tangled in her hair. "Make me wait for it."

He wrapped his fingers around her wrist—not to trap her there, but to ground her, so there would be one steady, fixed point, no matter what—and started fucking her.

Slowly, carefully. It had to last forever, through each quickening heartbeat and gasping breath. It had to be enough to earn the trust she'd offered him, to pay it back a thousand times over.

It had to be enough.

Her body heated for him, as eagerly as always. She was shameless, showing him every response, rewarding him with moans and whimpers, and guiding him inexorably to the perfect spots, the perfect rhythm. And through it all she stared up at him, the wonder of it still fresh and bright in her eyes.

Pure honesty. Unbridled truth. Nessa shared the deepest parts of herself with an ease that humbled him even as it strengthened his resolve to shield her from harm, sorrow. From the world.

He caught her mouth again and told her so without words, and she melted beneath him, around him, the sweet clasp of her body growing hotter around his with every thrust.

And tighter. She tensed beneath him, already trembling on the edge of an orgasm. Her teeth sank into his lower lip as she arched her body, straining upward. Ryder narrowed his focus to her reactions, keeping her balanced on the precipice with short strokes and soft whispers.

And when she tumbled over that edge, he kept her there too, coming and coming until her voice was hoarse and hands were back on his shoulders, on his arms, her nails raking over his skin and then just clinging, like he was the only truth in her world.

And when it was too much, she didn't beg him to stop. She turned her face into his cheek and panted. "Michael."

His name on her lips sounded like a broken prayer, and he gave in to it. He followed her into a shuddering bliss that seemed to go on and on, until it could only be measured in the spaces between her hammering heartbeat and his.

When he regained the sense to shift his weight off her, she wrapped her arms and legs around him and dragged him back, holding him against her and inside her. "No. Don't leave me."

"I wouldn't." He rolled them both instead, so that he was lying with her draped over him, their bodies still joined. "Better?"

"Mmm." Her hair cascaded across his shoulder and tickled at his neck as she snuggled her cheek against his chest. "It's almost quiet in my head."

Almost. "Tell me the parts that aren't quiet?"

She pressed her lips to his skin, and he felt her smile. "The part wondering how fast you can do it again. The part wondering how fast *I* can do it again. The part wondering if I can reach a blanket or if moving my arms might actually be too much. Just three parts. Almost quiet."

An answering smile curved his lips as he hauled the corner of the blanket up and over them, shielding Nessa against the slight chill. "I'll take it."

17

"C'mon, Nessa."

It was hard for a man with a voice as low and rumbling as Flash's to sound wheedling, but Nessa had long ago recognized his supernatural ability to be a pain in the ass when he put his mind to it. "Go away," she told him again, struggling to keep her lips from curving up.

It wasn't like the numbers on her tablet were resolving into sense anyway—she'd read the same page of this spreadsheet three times—but she'd promised herself she wouldn't mope once Ryder was gone, and catching up on the tedious parts of her job that she kind of hated wasn't the worst way to carry on. If she was making herself look at crop projections, it meant she believed in a world where people would be harvesting crops this fall, and she'd be turning that grain into liquor.

Not exactly hope, but close enough that she'd given herself a mental high-five before Flash showed up.

"Just one bottle," he said again, leaning against the doorframe to her office. "That stuff you gave us the night I marked Amira. The bourbon that was kinda sweet, like vanilla? I want a present for her birthday, and she loved that."

"I'm sure she did." Nessa glanced up at him with a teasing smile. "You could trade a bottle like that for six months' rent on an Eden penthouse."

He waved a big hand, dismissing the value. "I'll make it up to you."

"Oh, you will, will you?" She was already doing mental inventory, guessing how many bottles she had left in her safe. But needling Flash was *fun*. "You know that means doing my shopping for, like, a year. Minimum."

"Fine."

"And you have to pick up my laundry."

His eyebrows drew together.

Nessa bit the inside of her mouth to keep her expression stern. "And take a dive in the cage next time the betting gets hot. Maybe against one of the Armstrong brothers."

"*Nessa.*"

She burst out laughing at his outraged expression and tossed the tablet aside. "Yes, you dumbass. I'll find you something—"

The screech of the alarm drowned out her voice, and Flash reached for her before she could fully process the meaning of the loud blare. "*Move.*"

He'd dragged her out of her office and halfway

down the hall before her wits caught up to her shock. She wrenched her arm free to keep him from lifting her off the ground entirely and half-ran to keep up with him.

They spilled out into the bright afternoon sunlight, and Nessa put her hands over her ears to dampen the wail of the siren. Customers were starting to trickle out of the Broken Circle, mostly grizzled old men too old to join the militia, along with one worried-looking dancer.

Flash was already turning toward the staging area when a flash of light reflecting off a shiny surface caught Nessa's attention. Something silver streaked out of the sky and crashed into the warehouse where they held fight night. The shriek of ripping metal almost drowned out a muffled explosion that shattered the high windows of the warehouse, and Nessa covered her head as glass rained down on the courtyard.

"Get back inside!" Flash waved his massive arms at the gathering crowd. "Head to the basement—"

Another wicked glint, and a second object flew into the courtyard and slammed into the cracked asphalt. For a split second, Nessa stared at it in horror—it was a drone, the kind they used for surveillance in the city. It had something taped to the bottom of it, something that looked like a wad of modeling clay attached to a black box.

Flash was still hauling her behind a stack of reclaimed tires when the drone exploded, and there was nothing muffled about it this time. Nessa's ears ached not only with the volume of it, but the sheer force.

Flash gripped her upper arms. "You okay?"

His lips moved. The words vibrated through a few layers of cotton before she heard them past the ringing.

She jerked her head in a nod and raised her voice. "We need to get them all inside!"

His jaw clenched, and when he pulled her from behind the tires, she understood his grim expression.

There was no one left standing in the courtyard. It looked like almost everyone had made it back into the club—almost. A man she didn't know lay still near the exit, a splintered piece of wood from a shipping pallet piercing the left side of his chest. Beyond him, the brick wall was splattered with blood, and another man she *did* recognize—Fuller, who only drank his tequila with salt, never limes—was slumped against it.

They were dead. No one could look at them and wonder, not for a goddamn second.

It still felt wrong to run past them without trying to help, or *look*, or just take a fucking moment to process their deaths. But Flash didn't give her the option. One massive arm across her back hustled her toward the back door and through it, into the kitchen with all its cool steel and carefully stacked crates of liquor.

Oh God, if a bomb hit that—

The rise of panicked shouts dragged her across the kitchen and out the swinging doors, Flash close on her heels. The main room of the Broken Circle was chaos, with a harried dancer still in her robe trying to usher customers through the staff door and down the hallway that led to the basement. A bottleneck had formed, and people were shoving to get through.

Someone caught the dancer with an elbow, and Flash waded into the mess, his voice rising above the ruckus. "Settle the *fuck* down! The next person who shoves someone is getting their ass thrown to the back of the line."

The shouts reduced to mutters, but no one else

pushed. Nessa caught the dancer's eye and jabbed her finger toward the door in a silent command. She didn't know the woman, had never talked to her outside of the occasional cordial nod—but the employees were O'Kane responsibility.

And the ink on Nessa's wrists put her in charge.

The dancer nodded and slipped through the door. Nessa moved toward the stage to check for stragglers but stopped when a gravelly voice groaned her name. "Nessa—"

One of the old-timers who usually held down the table near the door was slumped in the shadow of the stage, one gnarled hand clutching his left shoulder. Lewis was pushing eighty years that he'd admit, and probably another ten or fifteen that he kept shaving off the back end. He'd been one of Pop's drinking and poker buddies, sitting up with her grandfather late into the night, swapping increasingly wistful stories of the world before the Flares.

Lewis was sweating. His face was pale and his breathing came shallow and raspy. The hand clutching his chest and shoulder was a bad sign—stress and hard living had run rampant on the ranch, and Nessa had watched too many of the older ranch hands slump to the ground and not get back up.

Lewis had to get the fuck back up.

She wedged her shoulder under his arm and hauled him to his feet, terrified at how fragile he felt. She could hear Flash in the hallway, yelling for someone to move his ass, so she shouted at a few men jostling for position near the front of the line. "Hey!"

One turned, but he didn't abandon his spot until she raised her voice. "Get over here and help him or I will *stab you myself.*"

She didn't know if it was the ink or the threat or if she just had murder in her eyes, but he scrambled over. She passed Lewis off to him with a final order for the old man. "You stay alive until I get down there, you hear me?"

"Yes, ma'am," he wheezed.

As soon as they were moving, Nessa exhaled and made one last sweep of the room. Once Lewis and his helper made it through the door, there were only about five people between her and the hallway.

When the next drone crashed into the Broken Circle, it was five too many.

The sound hit her first. Crashing and cracking from above, and the shattering of glass. Her mind spun with dizzy panic. She couldn't remember if the sector leaders had been meeting in the upstairs office. Surely they would have come down at the first alarm. Surely—

Her body moved. Instinct. Those impulses she usually hated. She dove for the nearest table, crawling under it as the secondary explosion hit, and if the first one was loud, this one was like the end of her world.

The end of the O'Kanes.

Her ears couldn't process the sound because they were still ringing. It was the vibrations that heralded it, the wooden floor trembling beneath her outspread fingers, shaking beneath her knees. Then the groaning—and if she could hear *that* over the ringing, it had to be a like a howl of doom.

The stage crashed in first. Just collapsed, because the beams of the ceiling were falling into it. Nessa closed her eyes and covered her head with her arms, as if flesh and skin and bone would be able to stop it when the three stories above her crashed into the table and flattened her.

Ryder wouldn't be here to see it. She'd said goodbye early that morning with a kiss that prompted him to fall back into the bed with her for a stolen minute that had turned to ten. Fast and still so good, because everything was good when he touched her, and she was *so glad* he'd touched her. So glad she'd let him ruin her.

And so glad he was gone. He wouldn't be standing outside, wondering if he could have gotten inside to save her. He'd be sad, because he cared about her, but it wouldn't be his fault. Wouldn't be anyone's fault.

Something thudded hard on the table above her, and she choked back a shriek. God, if she was going to get flattened, she hoped it would just fucking happen, already. Now, before fear caught up with the adrenaline throbbing so hard she wanted to puke.

Something heavy shifted—not the uncontrolled, chaotic smash of falling debris, but like someone searching through wreckage, and a voice called out, "Nessa?"

Her name—muffled, but sailing through the chaos like a lifeline. She forced herself to drop her arms from her head. "Flash?" Her voice broke on the sound, and she lifted it higher, until the volume shredded her throat. "Flash!"

"I've got you." His dust-covered boots crunched on glass as he stopped by the table and reached down for her. "Corner booth, huh?"

Hysterical laughter fought its way into her throat as she grasped his big hand and tried to make herself move. It took two tries to crawl out from under the shelter of the table, and when she did…

Any urge to laugh died.

The Broken Circle—the heart of the O'Kane empire, the symbol of everything Dallas had tried to build—was in shambles. The back part of the bar had collapsed, bringing the meeting rooms above down onto the stage. The giant conference table where Dallas had been planning the war had spilled down from a gaping hole in the ceiling and now balanced precariously on a pile of wood and steel. Leather chairs and glass screens and shattered pieces of tech formed a barricade, blocking their corner off from the rest of the club.

The hallway had caved in, as had the space directly in front of it. Her brain couldn't make sense of the tangle of limbs and bodies—pieces of the people who'd been waiting to get downstairs, and she turned her back before any of it came into focus. She couldn't think about it. Couldn't think about how many people—*Lewis*—had been struggling to make their way into the basement.

Couldn't think about who might have been upstairs.

Just. Couldn't. Think.

She blinked at Flash instead, a bright spot in the middle of a nightmare leached of color. Dust coated his shirt and arms even more thickly than his boots, and her stomach lurched.

He looked like a ghost. "Flash—"

"Everyone in the hall made it downstairs." He patted her hand. "The front door's blocked, but I think I can move some of this shit. Just don't freak out on me, okay?"

Oh God, she *was* freaking out. So much for being an O'Kane badass. A few little bombs and one building falling in on her, and she'd melted into uselessness. Just because she was trapped and might never get out—

The familiar panic rose, the terror she'd hidden so assiduously from the other O'Kanes. Her deep, dark secret...

Nessa bent over and braced her hands on her knees. Dragging in a deep breath didn't help much—with all the dust, she started coughing. Flash put a hand on her shoulder, but she shook her head. "Give me a second."

She didn't think about that root cellar and the dirt and the fear. She thought about the elevator. Ryder's hands on her arms. The warm, soothing cadence of his voice. The sparks and the butterflies, all the good things worth living for, because he would be on his way here. He'd come back for her. So would Dallas and Lex, and Jasper and Zan and Finn. Ace and Cruz. Six and Bren.

She was never going to be that lonely little girl in the root cellar again, because she had a whole fucking army who would come to save her.

Not that she needed them. She would fucking well save herself. But knowing she had backup was what let her push herself upright and square her shoulders. "Okay. Let's do this."

"Watch out." Flash gripped the edge of the conference table. The muscles in his arms bunched and strained as he slowly lifted it, then tipped it at an angle and set it down more firmly, forming a makeshift ramp toward the front of the building. "Come on, I got you."

Scrambling up the table wasn't graceful. Nessa muttered a few unpleasant words at whoever had polished the damn thing so smooth, but Flash steadied her and followed behind as she maneuvered down the other side. Rubble shifted beneath her boots with every careful step, but Flash had it harder, with his greater weight displacing the precarious pile more easily.

By the time they were on semi-firm ground again,

Flash's face was contorted into a grimace. Nessa's worry spiked as he clutched his side with one hand. "Are you okay, man?"

"What? Shit yeah, I'm fine. I just got knocked around a little when the top floors went, that's all." His pained grimace eased, but he was moving more slowly now. "I think I cracked a rib."

His casual words didn't soothe her spike of worry. If anything, it grew worse as she helped him with the painstaking, dangerous task of shifting broken boards and heavy stone and steel bars away from the tangle blocking the door. The ghostlike illusion wasn't just the dust anymore—Flash was getting *pale.*

And sweaty. He grunted softly as he reached for a board, and sweat cut a line through the dust at his temple and down his cheek. "Flash—"

He ignored her and lifted, his muscles bulging. And maybe she was overreacting, because *she* was sweating, too, and the shit she could move on her own was half the size of what he was dragging around. Her fingers were cut and raw, and she had a splinter embedded under one nail that spiked pain every time she braced her tired muscles to lift the next piece.

But when Flash staggered a few minutes later, she knew something was wrong.

"Hey." She caught his shoulder before he could lift the next piece of debris. "Let's sit down for a second and catch our breath."

He turned, and her blood ran cold through her veins. Along with the sweat and dust, there was blood on his face now—a trickle of it at the corner of his mouth.

But enough.

"What?" Flash stared down at her, his brows drawn

together, then swiped the back of his hand across the edge of his mouth. "Aw hell, Nessa, this is nothing."

But she knew it couldn't be *nothing*, another legacy of her life on Quinn O'Kane's ranch. Men fell from haylofts. They got kicked by horses or crushed by equipment or trampled by bulls who didn't take kindly to being wrangled. Nessa had seen enough internal bleeding to understand that Flash was full of shit when he said he got knocked around a little.

And he was full of shit now.

"Sit," she commanded, pointing to a clear spot of space. "I'm not fucking around, Flash. Do not lift another fucking thing."

He didn't argue, just did as she said, his upper lip beaded with sweat. "Okay. Okay, I'm sitting."

The fact that he'd obeyed was the scariest part yet. How much pain must he be in? How much had he ignored to do what he had to do? Enough that Nessa turned back to the door with renewed stubbornness, ignoring the burn in her muscles and the raw flesh on her hands. She ignored the glass that cut into her skin and the bruises where she slammed her legs and arms into hard edges.

She dug, and she did the math. Some men on the farm went slow. Quinn never could do anything for them, but Quinn hadn't had Doc. Or regeneration tech. Or access to all the drugs Sector Five could produce, not to mention a state-of-the-art hospital. If Nessa could get Flash out—

And people would be digging from the other side. Dylan would already be on his way, with the squads of helpers Jyoti had trained and all of the medicine they'd been stockpiling. They just had to meet in the middle. Clear enough of a space to get Flash through to the help waiting on the other side.

The metal bar she was trying to lift slipped in her hands. She blinked down at the blood smears and stopped long enough to wipe her hands on her jeans. The cut on the heel of her hand kept bleeding sluggishly, and she didn't remember getting it. Couldn't take time to bandage it. She lifted again, dragging the bar out of place and wincing as rubble began to shift dangerously.

Stop. Think. The last thing that would help Flash was bringing even more debris down on top of them both. So she took a step back and tried to use the edge of her shirt to staunch the bleeding. "You hanging in there with me, Flash?"

He was leaning his head back against a busted booth, eyes closed, torn vinyl curling against his cheek.

Fuck. She abandoned the rubble and sank to her knees next to him, clasping one clammy hand between both of hers. "Hey, dumbass. Look at me. Come on."

Slowly, he complied. "When did you get so fucking *bossy*?"

"I don't know, when I was twelve or something?" His gaze was glassy and unfocused, and when she put a hand to his cheek, it was clammy too. More blood trickled from the corner of his mouth, and she wiped it away gently. "You have to stay focused, though. We gotta decide which bottle of booze you're giving Amira for her birthday."

"Oh, fuck." His chest heaved in a deep breath that turned into a rattling cough. "*Fuck*. I'm gonna miss her fucking birthday."

Nessa wanted to deny the truth. She wanted to open her mouth and let a reassuring avalanche of babbled denial wash over him, enough hope to erase the last hour. They could be back in her office. She'd give him his bottle of liquor, and he'd leave and be somewhere else when the world caved in around her.

And then he'd be there for Amira's birthday. He'd be there for Hana's next birthday. He'd be there to give her a little brother or sister, to watch the next generation of O'Kanes grow up in a world that was a little less cruel, a little less hard. A little more hopeful.

She built that alternate timeline in her head, parted her lips...and nothing came out. No words of reassurance. No protest.

Flash was dying. And they both knew it.

"Tell me," she whispered instead. "What you want to give her for her birthday. For all of them. Tell me all of it."

"The bourbon," he rasped. "And make—make her go see the ocean. She has to take Hana—" His eyes squeezed shut. "They have to see it, at least once. I promised."

"I'll go with them." She tightened her grip on his hand. "I love you, meathead. You're the most annoying, exasperating, awesome big brother I have. I'll do anything for them. We all will."

He didn't answer.

"Flash." She patted his cheek, softly at first and then harder. He didn't stir, and tears formed an impossible lump in her throat as she pressed her ear to his chest.

His heart was still beating. Weakly. There was nothing she could do but cling to his hand and choke on tears as the erratic thumps slowed. Her brain scrambled for something, *anything*, but even CPR wouldn't help now. His blood just wasn't where it was supposed to be.

All the money and tech and medicine in the world, and sometimes death was still inevitable.

Flash's heart stopped long before she heard the crash of debris shifting and the shouts of rescuers, but she couldn't bring herself to move. She just stayed there, her cheek pressed to his chest, listening to all that emptiness. She let the silence expand until it pushed everything else from her mind.

No thoughts. No grief. Nothing but numbness.

When Lex finally came to pry her away from Flash's dead body, she still hadn't cried.

18

Ryder had never known real fear before.

He thought he had, plenty of times. He'd certainly been in situations that called for it. Back when he was a kid, he'd run messages in and out of the city. His mother never wanted him to go, but Jim had insisted that no one could understand true evil without seeing it with their own eyes.

So Ryder would go on his runs. One day, a confused older woman stopped him in the market square—and called him by his father's name. Between sobs and apologies about not trying harder to save him, she managed to draw the attention of a few MPs. Ryder talked his way out of it, but not before a special kind of horror had gripped him. Fifteen years old, and that was the first time he truly understood that his life could *end*—over, forever, just like that. All because of a sad old woman, choking on memories and regret.

That day, he learned that terror had a taste, suffocating and metallic, and that he never wanted to feel it again.

So he learned to ignore it, and then to master it. He almost compromised his cover in Sector Five on at least a dozen occasions by refusing to follow Mac Fleming's orders. Every single time, he'd stare into Fleming's flat, cruel eyes and wonder if that would be the end of it, one step too far. And every single time, Fleming would break with a laugh and a remark about his backbone or cunning or balls of steel, leaving Ryder to wonder what kind of hell Fleming saw in those moments, staring back at him.

He wasn't scared of dying, not anymore. But when he heard the explosions and one of the scouts radioed in to say Sector Four was under attack, that copper-penny terror came rushing back. Because the only place to strike at Dallas O'Kane was in the heart of his compound—the jewel of his empire, the Broken Circle.

And Ryder had left Nessa sleeping in his bed.

He always walked to Four, but bikes were faster, so he took Hector's. The drive was a blur that turned into a tangle of frustration three blocks away from the club, where debris and people clogged the streets. He abandoned the bike and worked his way through the crowd, ignoring the confusion and anger and desperation.

Ignoring everything but the hard knot in his throat.

The street in front of the Broken Circle looked like a war zone—*because it is, you idiot*—bustling with medics assessing the injured and rescuers digging through rubble. Ryder stopped at the edge of the chaos and tried to find a familiar face, anyone he recognized.

Instead, his gaze snagged on a line of cloth-draped bodies close to where the front door had been. Some were covered in dark fabric, but others in light-colored shrouds soaked through with blood.

He had to go look. He knew he had to look, he just couldn't make his feet move.

"Ryder." It was Finn's voice at his shoulder, a moment before a hand gripped his shoulder. "When did you get here?"

At least his voice still worked. "Where is she?"

"Nessa?" Finn waved toward the far side of the parking lot. "Lex took her to get checked over—"

He kept talking, but Ryder didn't listen. There would be time for the other shit later—status reports and casualties, strategy and rebuilding—but right now all he cared about was seeing Nessa, feeling her strong, steady pulse thump beneath his fingers.

His gaze finally locked on her. She was at the edge of the makeshift first-aid station, seated on a folding table with a blanket wrapped around her shoulders. Her hair was disheveled and coated with dust, and her expression remained blank as Jyoti bent over her hands, dressing angry welts and jagged scrapes with med-gel.

She looked like she'd been through hell—and he'd never seen anything more beautiful in his life.

Even when he walked toward her, she didn't see him. She just stared into the distance, shock painting her features with a distant sort of pain that made his stomach clench. "Nessa? Nessa, sweetheart, I'm here."

Nothing. So Ryder glanced at Jyoti, who nodded and handed him the gauze and gel applicator. He took over dressing Nessa's wounds, talking softly as he cared for her. "You scared the hell out of me. I couldn't get here fast enough. I stole Hector's bike, and he's gonna be so mad when he finds out that I don't even remember where I left it."

She blinked slowly. Didn't look at him. "Flash is dead."

He thought about those bodies lined up outside the Broken Circle. "What? How?"

"Surveillance drones." She wet her lips. "They had...something attached to them. Like clay. Explosives? They—" She blinked again, her gaze suddenly fixing on him. "I was in the bar with him."

Part of his brain went to work immediately, cataloguing the information and analyzing what it told him about Eden's resources, their strategy, their desperation. But the rest of him—*most* of him—could only focus on dressing Nessa's hands with waterproof bandages and pulling her against his chest. "I'm sorry."

"I couldn't save him." Her words were small and muffled. For the first time, she sounded *fragile*. "He must have gotten hit hard—I think he was bleeding internally. And I couldn't get us out fast enough. I tried..."

"Nessa, stop." He tilted her face up. "This isn't your fault. The city leaders—*they* did this. They killed him."

Her eyes filled with tears. "They killed him."

It was so much worse than the situation in Five. After the thwarted invasion, there were surely people just like Nessa—shocked, but slowly slipping out of their numbness to face devastating grief and pain. But he hadn't had to *look* at them. They'd been locked away in their homes, facing the emptiness of their losses, while he'd been preoccupied with assessing the casualties in a purely tactical way. No faces, not even names, just numbers. Assets. The only way to make it through a war without losing your mind.

But at what cost?

Nessa's pain was tangible. It flowed from her in pulsing waves, dragging at him every time she hauled in a ragged breath. This was how the people in Five—*his* people—must have felt, and he'd missed it. He'd ignored it.

In that moment, Ryder hated himself.

"Come on." He lifted her off the table, supporting most of her weight, but keeping her feet on the ground. Something solid in a mad whirl of confusion. "Where should we go?"

People were watching them. Nessa seemed to notice, and her back stiffened. She stood straighter, drawing her O'Kane pride around her like armor. "I need to get out of here. To my office or my room."

"Someplace safe," he qualified. "Have the other buildings been checked yet?"

"I don't know." She swallowed and looked around, but when her gaze reached the wreckage of the Broken Circle, she shuddered. "Dallas would know. Or Jas..."

The first person he saw when he turned around was Lex. Only the bloody, ripped edge of one sleeve remained on her shirt, and beneath it, a stark white bandage wrapped around her upper arm. Dirt streaked her face in odd patterns, and Ryder realized with a start that the cleaner lines on her cheeks were dried tear tracks.

Her eyes burned when they fixed on Ryder, then softened when she glanced at Nessa. "Jasper and Ace checked out the secondary warehouse. It wasn't hit."

All this carnage, and Eden didn't even manage

to take out the place where the O'Kanes stored their weapons. *Their intelligence is shit*, the small voice in the back of his head whispered.

He shoved that detail back with the others and pulled Nessa's arm around his neck. "Thanks, Lex."

"Don't go too far." She brushed a stray lock of hair back from Nessa's forehead. "Dallas wants everyone to stick close for now."

Just in case. She didn't say it, but it was there all the same, flaming in her dark, red-rimmed eyes.

Noelle had already taken charge inside the warehouse. Her eyes were as red as Lex's, but there was steel in her usually sweet expression. She stood just inside the door, directing dancers and bouncers as they carried stacks of blankets and crates of bottled water into the center of the newly cleared space.

Her easy rhythm faltered when she caught sight of them. "Nessa—"

"I'm okay," Nessa said quickly.

Noelle didn't believe her any more than Ryder did, that much was clear. But she nodded and squeezed Nessa's shoulder gently before looking at him. "If you can help her up the stairs at the back, there's a suite with a shower at the end of the hallway. I'll find some clothes for her and have someone leave them outside the door. Maybe some food, too—"

"No food." Nessa's complexion was sickly pale. "I just want to be clean."

She had to eat eventually, but there would be time. Too *much* time, maybe, once her haze had worn off and she was left with her pain cast in sharp relief.

Ryder took her upstairs instead. The suite was small, just two bare, undecorated rooms with exposed block walls, a utilitarian bath, and a narrow bed on a scarred iron frame. The shower barely had room for both of them, but Ryder stripped down and climbed in with Nessa anyway.

She was bruised underneath her clothes, covered with bumps and tiny cuts and bright red spots that would deepen to purple by morning. And it wasn't just dust in her hair. She stood silently, her hands braced on his chest, as he carefully worked the wood splinters and tiny shards of glass from her tangled strands.

She stood like that until he'd rinsed the last of the soap from her hair, then tilted her head forward until her forehead rested on his collarbone. Her first sob was silent, lost beneath the sound of the water cascading over them, but her shoulders shook violently beneath his stroking hands.

There were no words to break the heavy silence. Nothing to be said.

The water started to go cold before she cried herself out. Shivering a little, she lifted bleak eyes to him. "I don't want to feel this anymore."

"I know." He cut off the water and cupped her face between his hands. "You're not alone. I'm here, and so are all the other O'Kanes. People who loved Flash, too."

"They'd been through *so much*," she whispered. "All the danger of building the O'Kanes, and then when Hana got sick—" Her voice broke. "Tank was hard. He made winning bittersweet. But now winning can't feel like winning, because even if we take down Eden, he won't get to see it. And I know that's so fucking *selfish* because other people have died, too…"

A painful echo of his earlier guilt, but falling from Nessa's lips, it seemed unfair. "Of course it hurts, Nessa. But you can't stick this next to winning the war and say it's not worth it, because it's never really been about winning. It's about having a chance to *live*." He swallowed hard. "Flash won't have that chance, but Amira will. *Hana* will."

"I know." She wrapped her arms around his neck and went up on her toes, and the agony in her eyes made her words a lie. When she kissed him, it was hard and desperate, more pain than passion.

She was hurt, spiraling, and sex might make her forget for a while, but it couldn't last. So Ryder gentled the kiss, soothing her with his lips as much as his hands smoothing over her back.

When she broke away, he reached for a towel and wrapped it around her. She didn't fight as he lifted her out of the shower, tucking her face against his throat with a soft sigh. "Tell me about your cabin."

He considered it as he grabbed a towel for himself, then guided her to the bed and stretched out behind her. "What do you want to know?"

Her voice came out small and soft. "Is there room for me in it?"

He hadn't thought about the cabin in a while. Too long, perhaps, but he'd been so busy with planning and fighting and *Nessa* that it hadn't even crossed his mind. "If you want."

"I'd go with you." Her body trembled until he pulled her closer. Her hand slid to cover his, as if she was holding his arm around her. "That's what I want to dream about tonight. A cabin in the woods. I'm trying to imagine it."

She'd hate it—being in the middle of nowhere, cut off from her friends and family and the bustling activity of the O'Kane compound. But maybe that was the whole point. This sounded like her idea of escape, and Ryder couldn't bring himself to argue. "Okay."

"How many rooms were you going to build?"

The question startled him, though he couldn't quite put his finger on *why*. "I don't know. As many as I need, I guess."

"A kitchen. A bathroom, I hope." She traced her fingers lightly over the back of his hand, building his cabin with words that seemed to pick up speed. "A bedroom and a living room, one with a fireplace. And chairs close enough that you can curl up next to it when it's cold. Some kind of barn or something, too, to keep your tools in. And animals. Hawk's sisters keep chickens, but those things scare the shit out of me."

"I don't know anything about farm animals," he admitted.

"Were you going to hunt instead?"

Unease prickled up his spine. "Sure. Hunt, fish, that kind of thing."

"Oh." After a moment she squirmed onto her back to stare up at him. "It's okay, you know. If that's not what you want. Me, in the cabin with you."

"*No*, that's not it." Her words painted the picture so clearly, so readily, that he felt ashamed to confess that it was the first time he'd ever tried to really imagine that cabin. "We have to get there first, and that's..."

"We're going to get there." She cupped his cheek, eyes feverishly intent. "We have to get there. You're coming back to me after this."

The unease exploded, and Ryder bit back the easy reassurance that rose to his lips. He'd spent so much of his life lying, and he never wanted to do it again. Especially with her. "It's not that simple—"

"It *is*," she interrupted. "You're coming back to me, and we're going to live in a cabin in the woods and probably starve to death because I don't know if either of us can cook, but I won't care because I'll be there with you."

It was a reckless promise, one none of them could make right now, and Flash was proof. "Nessa, don't."

The silence lasted for five of her breaths before she simply...deflated, like a balloon with the air rushing out. She sank over onto her back and stared up at the ceiling. "I know," she said finally. "I'm sorry. It's stupid anyway. I'd be a mess in your cabin. I'd drive you crazy within a week, and you'd throw me out to sleep in the barn. It was just...a dream."

He was a complete bastard. "Nessa, you can ask me for anything else—*anything*. But don't ask me to say that I know I'll survive this, because I can't do that."

"I know," she said again, swiftly, like she could silence his explanations if she agreed hard enough. "Forget it. I'm just—I'm fucked up right now." She rolled upright to sit on the edge of the bed, her back to him. Her damp hair stuck to her shoulders, barely obscuring a rising bruise. "Don't listen to anything I'm saying."

He touched her back, just below the perimeter of that angry bruise. "I'll try," he offered quietly. "That's all I can do."

She nodded shakily. It took forever for her to sink back to the bed, and it wasn't the same. She was quiet and stiff against him, her eyes tightly shut and her lips pressed together.

He'd never seen her closed off before.

Anything he said now would be consolation in the worst sense of the word, careful half-truths with none of the certainty she craved. So he held his tongue, wrapping an arm around her in an effort to bridge the distance between them.

It didn't work.

19

The end was starting to feel a lot like the beginning.

The O'Kanes had started in a warehouse like this. The years since had brought enough luxury to soften the starkness of their surroundings, but this was where they'd come from. Hard cement floors, unadorned steel beams, people perched on wooden crates and stacks of pallets, passing around too many bottles of liquor and not enough bags of food from the market.

At thirteen, it had felt like an adventure. Tonight, Nessa could only see how far they'd fallen.

Dallas's voice rose and fell a few feet away, a cadence so familiar it was hypnotic. Nessa kept trying to focus on his words, but her brain could only hold two or three words in a row before their meaning slipped away. Too bad, because she had no doubt he was being properly inspiring. Dallas always rallied when things felt bleakest, and she couldn't tell if it was faith and belief, or if he was just too fucking contrary to stay down when someone kicked him.

Nessa had always thought she had that personality quirk in spades, but one kick had laid her out on the floor, reeling.

On the opposite side of the room, Hana fussed quietly. Nessa shouldn't have been able to hear her over the murmur of voices, but she felt hyperaware of the kid's voice now. The guilt would come either way, so Nessa leaned into it and glanced over to where Amira sat between Noelle and Trix.

Shock still dulled her reddened eyes. She moved on instinct, soothing Hana with a gentle hand between her daughter's shoulder blades. Noelle wrapped her arm around Amira's back and murmured something, but Amira didn't even blink in response.

Nessa's throat burned. Grief overcame guilt, and she looked away, her eyes stinging. The marks around Amira's throat lingered behind her eyelids like an after-image—a permanent reminder of what Amira had had...and what she'd lost. Nessa wanted to crawl across the warehouse floor and beg forgiveness, but the urge was purely selfish. Amira deserved time and space to grieve.

They all did. And none of them would get it.

Forcing her eyes open again, Nessa sought out Ryder's familiar profile. He was seated next to Finn, close to Lex and Dallas and Mad. His expression was serious and his gaze alert—*he* had no trouble focusing on Dallas's words. This was the moment he'd been trained for, the culmination of his life's mission. The reason he had all those super-spy skills and perfect muscles and all that endless patience.

This was Ryder's war, and he'd die to see it through, if he had to. She didn't think he wanted to die, but she didn't think the notion scared him, either. He didn't share her need to fight back against terror by building a fantasy where death was impossible. To him, it was another fact in a long list of facts. Eden was corrupt. Water was wet. He might die. To promise otherwise would be to lie.

And Ryder didn't lie the way she did.

Oh, she never *meant* them to be lies. In the moment, she meant every goddamn thing she said. Lying there, cradled against him, her mind had been alive with the potential of that cabin in the woods. She could see the grain of the wooden floors. The rocking chair in the corner. The colorful quilts on the huge, hand-carved bed, and all the pillows he tolerated because he knew she loved them. She'd seen the table where they would have their coffee and the little garden plot where they'd grow vegetables and the chickens she made him deal with because they would always scare the shit out of her.

For thirty seconds, she had wanted to live in that cabin more than she'd ever wanted anything in her life. Because that was how Nessa had always fallen in love with things. Swiftly, irrationally, recklessly…

And temporarily.

She loved Ryder. She was addicted to him, obsessed with him, desperate to spend every waking second drowning in him—and she didn't know if it was real. Was it the kind that would outlast the giddy rush of a new infatuation, or would her need for him fade when the shiny wore off?

She didn't know if he was the liquor or the knitting.

And *God*, she hated herself for not knowing. She hated that she might never find out. Most of all, she hated that their last moments together had been awkward and lonely, because they hadn't had enough time to learn how to reach across the gulf between his caution and her enthusiasm. They hadn't had enough time to figure out if it was even possible.

Time. She'd wasted so fucking much of it, and now that every hour was precious, that every *minute* mattered—she was running out.

"Fuck it." Zan's harsh, angry words cut through her reverie. "I say we drive right through the fucking gate." A few gathered voices rose in murmurs of assent, so he went on. "We have reinforced trucks big enough to do it, so let's do it."

Lex shook her head. "It's not enough to breach the gate into the city. It's a ready-made bottleneck. They'll cut us down the second we march—or drive—through. We need *access*."

Jasper studied the map spread across a stack of pallets. "We could position trucks and forces at every city gate and hit them from all sides at once. But it would take time."

"No more time," Dallas said, his tone brooking no argument. "We're going in at dawn, one way or another. And we're driving a path straight to the City Center and taking the Council down."

"Smith Peterson." Markovic had been leaning against the far wall behind Dallas, but he stepped away from it as he spoke, bracing his weight on the carved wooden cane in his hand instead. "He's the one you're after. The Council follows the strongest leader, like a snake trailing after its own head. Cut off that head, and you kill the Council."

"I'll start with Peterson," Dallas agreed. "But if you can't make them fall in line behind *you* after that, I'll keep cutting off heads until we're knee-deep in them."

Markovic inclined his head. "Fair enough."

Lex worried her lower lip with her teeth. "We have to get in there first."

"I think I can help with that." Bren walked up with a huge duffel bag slung over his beefy shoulder. He swung it up onto the pallets, where it landed with a heavy thud right on top of the maps. He tugged open the heavy zipper, revealing dozens of black-wrapped bricks.

Jasper's eyebrows rose. "Is that—?"

"Enough C-4 to blow a hole in the world." Bren ran one hand through his hair. "I've been collecting it ever since that shit with Trent went down in Three. Some from Five, some from Eight. Figured we might need it one day."

For several tense moments, everyone simply stared at the duffel. Something inside Nessa wrenched, as if the import of all the words and all the planning had crystallized into reality. *War* had been a vague concept, even after they started fighting it. *After* had been a nebulous time, some future she could see past but couldn't bring into focus.

They weren't talking about fighting petty little battles anymore. They were talking about bringing down the wall that defined life for everyone on both sides of it.

Tomorrow.

Dallas touched the side of the bag. "How big a stretch can you bring down with this?"

Bren grabbed a marker from Ace and shoved the

bag aside until he revealed the area of the map that covered Sector Four. "We blow the south gate and the central gate." He marked them on the map, then added several more Xs along the curving edge of the border between Four and the city. "Breach a few more places along the wall, and they won't be able to cover all of them."

Nodding, Dallas glanced up at Mad. "ETA on your cousin?"

"The Riders and most of the Temple guards should be here in a couple hours." Mad jabbed his finger down on the entry point that left the clearest shot toward the City Center. "The guards can hold whatever ground we take. They're solid fighters, but mostly trained in defense. The Riders? They're your best bet of cutting a path to the Council."

"All right." Dallas reached out, and Ace handed him a second marker. "So the Riders—"

"Dallas!"

Nessa turned toward the sound of Noah's voice. People melted out of his path as he jogged across the warehouse, and for the first time in weeks he didn't look like someone had run him over with a delivery truck. His hair was as wild as ever, standing up in red spikes that seemed to defy gravity at this point, but his eyes flashed with excitement.

"You've got to see what just came over the vid network." He dropped a tablet on top of the map and reached into his pocket for a slim projector. Turning toward the distant wall, he waved his arms, ushering people out of the way. "Fuck, it's on *every* network, in every sector, on every device. It's probably streaming on people's watches and desks and shower walls and refrigerators."

Both of Dallas's eyebrows shot up. "The propaganda?"

"Worse." Noah set the projector down and swiped his fingers over the tablet. "Or better, if you're us."

At the final flick of his fingers, the bare cement wall lit up with bright white light. A figure appeared on it, blown up to three times the size of a normal person. Nessa had never paid much attention to the news broadcasts out of Eden, but shocked recognition rippled through the crowd. Hawk first, and Jeni. Jared and Lili. Markovic and Dallas and Lex and even Ryder.

Noelle was the one who named him. "Smith Peterson," she said, her voice raw, and it clicked into place.

Smith Peterson. The man who'd arrested and tortured Markovic, kidnapped Hawk and Jeni, and murdered Noelle's father.

Such a pleasant, average-looking man. He was almost handsome, smooth in all the ways Nessa had always liked in spite of herself, with a fancy suit and an elegance that seemed to come with paying for people to do all the hard shit in life.

He didn't look like a monster. Not until he opened his mouth.

"Get video of all of it," he commanded someone sitting at a workstation. "Make it bloodier, if you have to. Convince them the sectors are coming to rape their wives and eat their babies. And double—no, triple the enlistment bonuses."

"Triple, sir?"

"We need three thousand bodies minimum to wear them down before we send in the real soldiers. Promise whatever you have to so we don't need to conscript. Most of them won't survive to complain about what we actually give them."

The screen went black for a moment, then faded into Markovic's face. The video Nessa had recorded played through, but someone had tweaked it slightly. The colors of the garden were more vibrant. Markovic's words echoed deep and strong. Beside Peterson's oily contempt, Markovic sounded like the voice of salvation, calling out from someplace beautiful.

Noah cut the sound as Markovic finished, but another, different image of Peterson had flickered onto the wall already. "There are almost a dozen of them," he told Dallas, waving at the video. "It's alternating on a loop between Markovic and leaked clips of Peterson saying some pretty crazy fucking shit."

"There," Markovic said heavily. "Penny came through. Now you can hold off on your invasion, give it time to—"

"Tomorrow," Dallas interrupted. "At dawn. This is as much for them as it is for us, Markovic. You think Peterson's gonna go any easier on his own people if they get in his way?"

"Of course not," he snapped, his eyes blazing. "Are you really so arrogant that you think he reserves his cruelty for you? Everything he's willing to do to the sectors, he's willing to visit first on every goddamn person locked inside those walls."

"I know. That's why we're putting him down. *Now*."

Markovic slammed his hand down on a crate beside him, the sound thundering through the warehouse. "*Why*, then? I had to relive the worst weeks of my life, then put someone I care about in mortal danger, and for what? Tell me why any of this matters."

Dallas braced both hands on the pallets and leaned forward, eyes intense. "It matters because tomorrow, we won't have to kill as many people who don't have it coming just to get to Peterson. It matters because instead of fighting against us, all the people you've been trying to protect all these years might stand up and fight *with* us."

"Might," Markovic echoed. "And you can't wait long enough to know for certain because the great Dallas O'Kane has to get his vengeance, his pound of flesh—"

Ryder had been silent and still during the whole exchange, but he flowed out of his chair to stand between the two men. "You want yours, too," he noted bluntly. "You're a lot of things, Markovic, but you're not a hypocrite. Don't fault O'Kane for being human."

Lex toyed with the strap of the duffel bag. "It's not about vengeance." Her voice carried through the warehouse, low but loud, like she needed them all to hear her words. "If it was, we'd find our own drones, load them with this shit, and fly them straight into the city."

She turned to face the crowd, her gaze tracking over each of their faces. "We've been holding off on invading the city because we didn't want innocent people to die. But now Peterson is sending them out *here* to die. It sounds fucked up, but the only way we can protect them now is to get in there. We can't fight this from a distance, not anymore."

Over the years, Nessa had gotten to known Lex well. Better than most, because in the beginning it had been just the two of them in a world that was all about men. She'd seen Lex's strength of will, her steely stubbornness, and the ice-cold streak of pragmatism that surfaced when someone Lex loved was in danger.

Lex cared about people. *All* people. It was there, underscoring everything she did, but the only one who ever got to see her naked sincerity was Dallas. The rest of them had to settle for glimpses, the moments when her guard slipped and Alexa shined through. Tiny sparks of hope in the night.

Right now, she was glowing with it. She was radiant. She *believed*, and the force of that belief tugged at the places inside Nessa that were built on a foundation of O'Kane pride.

"We never wanted this fight," Lex went on. "Never asked for it. The only thing we ever asked for was to be left alone, in peace, to live our lives on our terms, the way *we* fucking want. But the things that have happened in those Council offices—" Her voice broke. "It has to stop. Not just for our sakes, but for all those people in there. They don't deserve this. No one does."

"No one," Noelle said loudly, her words drowned out by Ace shouting, "Fuck, yeah!" Then it was a jumble of sound, voices rising in agreement, in defiance, in *cheers*.

Nessa met Ryder's eyes. He stared back at her for an endless heartbeat, then the corner of his mouth ticked up in a smile.

Her heart lurched. The butterflies—those beautiful, terrifying butterflies—danced. If she lost him tomorrow…

"Okay, Bren." Dallas thumped his hand on the map to silence the room. "What do you need to set this up?"

"Anyone with demolitions experience to help with the charges. Cruz?"

Cruz nodded. "I'm in."

"So am I." Ryder shrugged. "No sweat, right?"

Of course Ryder knew how to blow shit up. His endless childhood training wouldn't have neglected something so vital. Funny, how many emotions churned through her as Bren nodded to accept his assistance. Pride at his skill. Anger at the people who'd taught him so many ways to kill and so little else. Worry at the risk he was about to take.

Selfish disappointment that she wouldn't even get one last night with him.

Their voices drifted back into wordless sounds as she pulled into herself. But instead of grief, something else was building. Something dark and angry that fed off Amira's pain and Lex's hope equally, something stubborn and proud and vast enough to swallow Eden itself.

Looking down, Nessa rubbed her thumb over her wrist. Her O'Kane cuffs had been a part of her for so long, she barely noticed them. She'd grown to adulthood on a steady diet of fuck-the-world and protect-the-weak, as heady a cocktail as anything they served in the bar.

And you needed both parts. Just the former, and you were nothing but an asshole. Some idiot swinging your fists around just because you could, without giving a shit who you hit. Just the latter, and you were too scared to stand up to the bullies. They'd run you over, and drive the people you were trying to save down into the dirt.

Eden was the biggest fucking bully around. They were used to swinging their fists at people too hurt or fragile to swing back. And that was all tomorrow was, in the end. A big damn *fuck you* aimed directly at the most corrupt of them. The same kind of thing the gang had been doing since they'd formed up, only on a bigger scale.

Nessa was a fucking O'Kane. She'd never been

too scared to come back swinging. She'd never doubted they would win.

So tomorrow she was going to do her part. Plant her steel-toed boot in Eden's metaphorical junk. She'd do it for Flash and Amira and Hana. For Tank. For Stuart. For the forty-seven people Ryder had lost. For Hawk's sister and for Shipp. Fuck, even for Noelle's asshole father.

When it was over, she'd deal with Michael Ryder like an O'Kane. They'd end up crashing together or they'd crash and burn, but she'd face it head-on, either way.

And he wouldn't know what hit him.

20

Sometimes, Ryder almost forgot that Bren Donnelly and Lorenzo Cruz had once been soldiers in Eden, mission-oriented and meticulously trained. But after staying up all night, watching them confidently assemble directed charges with the plastic explosives and detonators, he wasn't sure he'd ever forget again.

They might be ink-wearing O'Kanes now, through and through, but the past was still a part of them. It informed every moment of their lives, and Ryder understood that. More than any of Dallas's other people, he felt a kinship with these two.

Not that they'd thrown some kind of demolition-themed slumber party. They'd barely talked, all three intent on their shared task, as well as the battle ahead. When they had spoken, Cruz and Bren had told stories about Flash—funny and poignant and sometimes painful stories that filled Ryder with regret that he'd never had a chance to climb into the cage with the hulking man.

Ryder finished placing the last of the charges in the spots Bren had marked along the wall. They'd saved the gates for last, simply because there was no way to hide their activities there from the assigned guards. Not that it would matter soon, anyway—with every able fighter in five different sectors gathering near the wall, it would take negligence on a criminal level not to notice that shit was about to go down.

Gideon was the most impressive—and the least subtle. He'd left his Royal Guard back at the O'Kane compound to protect the noncombatants gathered there, but close to a hundred of his Temple guards were gathered in the open space between the wall and the buildings. And in front of them…

The Riders. Forty-five in total, once Gideon and Mad joined them. They'd arrived on sleek, perfectly maintained motorcycles, all clad in black leather and carrying enough weapons to stock an arsenal. They stood easily, patiently, showing none of the fear of the Temple guards behind them.

Nearly four dozen men who weren't afraid to die.

Beside them, Six had gathered with her girls, every one armed to the teeth and decked out in even more leather and spikes than the Riders. They wore expressions Ryder recognized easily—they weren't eager to fight, not exactly, but they were *ready*. Battling for survival was second nature to them, a daily, never-ending struggle, and they weren't about to lose that fight now.

Finn stood with the men from Five. They had always looked to him as a leader, and his defection to O'Kane's gang hadn't changed that. He spoke to them, even laughed with them, relaxing their worried, shell-shocked faces. Hector had brought in every last fighter who hadn't been killed or wounded in the sector battle, and an ache splintered in Ryder's chest at their diminished numbers.

He embraced it. The best way to honor the fallen was to hit Eden hard. To *win*.

Sector Six had even fewer people. Hawk stood with his mother, who had her long hair pulled back in a tight braid and an impressive rifle resting on one shoulder. A massive bear of a man stood just behind her, making final checks on his crew of smugglers as they waited with eyes burning with vengeance. A few dozen farmers huddled behind them, grim refugees armed with shotguns and desperation. But they straightened with purpose when Hawk walked into their midst.

Every group counted at least one O'Kane amongst their ranks. That wasn't news—Jim had spoken of Dallas's recruitment strategy, noting with almost envious admiration how he seemed to be drawing powerful leaders from every sector into the fold, people who could rally those sectors to O'Kane's cause when the time was right.

Ryder understood the truth now—Dallas simply attracted strong followers, and he didn't give a flaming shit where they were from. Far from being a calculated strategy, it was a bit of accidental brilliance, nothing he could have truly planned, and one of the many things that had elevated him to the point of leading this rebellion.

Given the fact that Ryder had always been told

that it was *his* job to lead the sectors—and the city—to freedom, he was surprisingly okay with it. Dallas had earned this, not through subterfuge and careful groundwork, but by sheer strength of character.

Dallas stepped away from where Jas had gathered with the O'Kanes and their militia and strode into the open space between Ryder and the amassing army. He hopped up onto an overturned food cart and stood in silence, one arm raised.

The murmur of voices faded. Heads swiveled, gazes shifted. Effortlessly, Dallas drew all focus, and held it through three long, slow breaths.

"They started this war," he said, his voice loud and clear enough that the guards were probably listening from inside the gate. "They started it years ago, when they bombed the shit out of the factories in Three to teach us not to ask for fair treatment. They kept it going every time they hurt you just to prove they could, or took more than they needed just to keep you from having enough."

There was a rhythm to his words. A cadence. He was gathering them along with him as he got louder, faster. Angrier. "But they *never* have enough. They wanted more from Sector Two. More money, more lives. And when the leader said *no*, they murdered helpless women and children. Because if they can't have something, they'll destroy it."

The crowd murmured. One of the farmers from Six shouted in angry agreement, then another. Dallas's voice rang out over them. "But they made a *fucking mistake* this time. They got so busy taking, they forgot to keep us fighting with each other. And do you know what we can do when we work together?"

He flung an arm out, pointing toward the city.

"We're gonna tear down their fucking wall and *end their fucking war.*"

The noise that answered his words couldn't even be described as a cheer. It was something deeper, primal. Dangerous.

Ryder arched one eyebrow at Dallas as he jumped off the overturned cart. "Nice speech."

Dallas grinned, feral and furious. "I've had a few years to come up with it."

"And everyone thought you were an impulsive caveman."

"I am." He turned to stare up at the wall. "That's their real mistake, you know. I'd pretty much reached a point where I liked my life just like it was. Fighting and fucking and not worrying about what happened beyond my sector. I was content, and they could have let me be content."

But they hadn't, and now it was too late. Bren joined them, a sleek trigger switch in one hand, which he offered to Dallas. "Want to do the honors?"

Dallas took the detonator in one hand and cradled it. Then he looked back at Lex. She returned his stare, her eyes full of so much emotion that Ryder couldn't begin to untangle it, and nodded shortly.

Dallas smiled slightly as he turned back to face Eden's pristine wall. "If we pull this off," he murmured, "I'm gonna sleep for a fucking week."

Then he hit the trigger.

For a moment, stillness. Then the silence exploded painfully, and the ground shook beneath them. The solid surface of the wall seemed to shudder, then cracks splintered across it in every direction.

Another sound rose in the sharp morning light—alarm sirens, nearly drowned out by the rumbling roar as the wall broke apart and crumbled, raising smoke and dust in its place.

A second roar rose, drowning out the sound of the collapsing wall. The Riders didn't wait for the dust to settle. They were already moving, charging toward the destruction without fear or hesitation.

That didn't surprise Ryder. What did, even though maybe it shouldn't have, was the sight of everyone else charging just as readily, from the farmers who'd fled Sector Six to the merchants who ran stalls in Four's marketplace. In this moment, they were one, united in anger and wrath and mourning. There were no lives in the sectors that hadn't been damaged by the greed and hypocrisy of the city leaders.

And they were ready to strike back.

jas

Jas had thought that the greatest challenge in their initial invasion of the city was bound to be the perimeter guards near the wall. They'd raise the alarm, then hit the rebel forces straight on.

He'd been really fucking wrong. The bastards ran. They flipped on the goddamn sirens and then they *ran*.

What the hell are they playing at? He motioned for the rest of his men to halt while he strained to listen for the sound of marching feet, shouted orders, anything to give him a clue as to whether the guards were cowards—or leading them into a fucking ambush.

He got his answer when small projectiles sailed over the buildings in front of them, silhouetted against the morning sky.

"Grenades!"

Jasper didn't know who yelled out the warning, but everyone scattered for cover, including him. He vaulted over the half-wall that closed off the small courtyard of a building—

And came face-to-face with a man and two small children.

He pulled his young daughters behind him, facing Jas with bleak eyes. "Just let them go. Please."

The words were so helpless, so hopeless, so *rage-inducing* that Jasper almost forgot why he'd ducked into the courtyard to begin with. Then the first of the grenades exploded out in the street. Neither child screamed, though the older one did clap her hand over the younger one's mouth.

The heartbreaking sight of it startled him out of his silence. "Do you have a basement?"

The man stared at him.

"A *basement*," he repeated firmly. "Do you have one?"

A second explosion jolted the man out of his shock. "The building has three maintenance sublevels—"

"Go there. Now." Jasper grabbed his shoulder and turned him around. One of the kids uttered her first sound, a frightened whimper, and he tried to soften his voice. "If it's locked, get to an interior room, one with no windows. Stay there and don't come out."

The younger girl pried her sister's hand away and stared up at Jasper. "Are you gonna come and kill us?"

"Hush, Evie." The man prodded his daughters toward the door to the building, casting one wary look back over his shoulder, as if half-expecting Jas to put a bullet in his back.

Fuck.

Jasper popped up over the half-wall. The wave of

incoming grenades had slowed, but people had started spilling out of their homes, drawn by the noise.

He rushed out, keeping an eye on the sky, and grabbed the nearest fighter—one of Hawk's friends from Sector Six. "Watch their trajectory, and you'll see where they're gonna fall," he shouted. "We need to get these people back inside. Go!"

The man hurried off, and Jas turned and waved his arms at a cluster of onlookers who were staring at him. Where was their fucking sense of self-preservation?

Out of the corner of his eye, he saw one of the grenades hit the edge of a roof and bounce toward him. There wasn't enough time to run, so he ducked around a narrow ledge of brick lining a shop window and covered his ears. The pressure of the blast made his teeth ache anyway, and hot prickles of pain shot up his unprotected side.

He looked down. The frag from the grenade had ripped through his pants and jacket, leaving angry, burning scores in his flesh. Gingerly, he prodded the wounds, but every single one was a scrape, not a hole filled with hot metal.

He'd take it.

Hawk appeared around the corner, his gun gripped in both hands. Blood streaked his temple and cheek, but he ignored it as he assessed Jas's side. "You okay, man?"

"Yeah, I'm good." He almost followed it up with a snarky remark about how the bastards would have to try harder than that to kill him, but it felt like tempting fate, so he bit his tongue.

If he came back dead, Noelle would kill him.

He slapped Hawk on the shoulder. "Come on. Let's go."

ace

Once upon a time, Ace had enjoyed the adrenaline of battle. For all of his jokes about how he was a lover and not a fighter, he'd taken to the occasional violence of life as a member of the O'Kane gang easily and joyfully.

That enjoyment faded after Rachel and Cruz had come into his life. Not that he couldn't still get shit done when the occasion required it—and he wasn't *bothered* by the need to kill—but the risk-reward math had skewed way out of control once he had something to live for back at home.

And once Rachel turned up pregnant…

This is the last fucking time, he promised as he shot out the knees of a soldier rushing toward him. Their body armor was pretty solid across the chest and protected the bulk of their heads, but the idiots had left their *knees* exposed, and no one could run with his knees blown out. He reached the man while he was still howling in pain and put a third bullet between his eyes, then abandoned his empty pistol and swept up the dead man's sidearm.

The streets of Eden were fucking chaos. Ace had lost sight of Cruz seven dead soldiers ago, which meant the push toward the center of the city was working. Mopping up the strays was less dangerous work, but *less* was relative in a melee where bullets were flying as fast as fists and knives and clubs.

And explosions.

Ace lit the last of Nessa's Molotov cocktails and slung it toward a trio of guards peeking around a wall. The glass shattered, and the liquor splashed onto the pavement at their feet and splattered their pants with flames as the fireball erupted. They dropped their weapons and started slapping at their burning clothes, and Ace had all the time in the world to draw his gun and put them out of their misery.

The dozen Molotovs he'd brought with him had proven effective at scattering Eden's resistance every time they managed to rally it. Something about a wildly laughing sector soldier chucking burning liquor at them fed all the nightmares they'd grown up on, the scary stories about demons and hell and the fire that awaited them if they thought bad things or touched themselves in places that felt good.

Raining down literal hellfire was totally worth setting Nessa's precious liquor on fire—but he wouldn't tell her that.

A soldier popped out from between two buildings, and Ace cursed and barely got his gun up in time. This one he shot at point-blank range, right in the face, and blood splattered back at him. *The absolute last fucking time.*

"Nice shot!" Finn jogged toward Ace, a dozen militia fighters trailing behind him. He had a rough bandage tied around his upper arm and blood smeared across his face, and he swooped down to steal the soldier's rifle. "We need to push—"

The shuffling of multiple footsteps around the corner tickled the edge of Ace's hearing, and he grabbed Finn's uninjured arm and pointed with the other hand.

Finn nodded and gestured to the men behind him. They spread out, covering the space between the buildings, ready to deal with the dead soldier's backup. When no one appeared, Ace took a deep breath, whispered a silent apology to Cruz and Rachel, and whirled around the corner.

Twenty terrified men stared back at him, their weapons gripped in shaking hands. They didn't even have half-decent body armor, just drab gray uniforms that wouldn't protect them from a stiff breeze.

Conscripts.

As soon as Ace thought the word, the man in front dropped his weapon and held up both hands. "We don't want to fight. We only came out because *he*—" the man gestured to the dead soldier, "—threatened to shoot us if we didn't."

Finn stepped out next to Ace as more weapons clattered to the ground, every clack a credit to Markovic's pretty face—or Peterson's ugly words. Either the propaganda had worked, or the people of Eden were as miserable as their sector cousins.

"If you want to surrender, kick over your guns—" Finn started.

"Fuck that shit," Ace interrupted. "If you want to surrender, pick your guns the hell back up and come kill these motherfuckers with us. Take back your damn city."

Finn only hesitated a second before nodding. "And take off those jackets so people know you're on our side."

Fabric rustled as the men complied, stripping off their jackets to reveal threadbare clothing with patched holes. They looked hungry and scared, these people who lived inside the walls of paradise but had never tasted its riches.

Time to change that.

This is the last fucking time—but it's worth it.

mad

The Riders were dying.

They were good deaths. Righteous deaths. *Eager* deaths. Each one of his cousin's men took down dozens of enemies before they fell, and Mad wouldn't disrespect their sacrifice by crying for them. Back in Sector One, in a temple at the heart of his family's land, the outlines of their portraits had already been sketched onto a memorial wall. When a man joined the Riders, he accepted death. He faced it on that wall, knowing the priestess would paint in his portrait on the day he fell.

Mad had been a teenager the day they sketched his portrait onto the wall. An orphan. He'd imagined joining his mother and father someday, dying the way they had—as heroes.

That hadn't been his dream in a while.

So Mad didn't grieve for Riders who went down clearing a path to the City Center, but he didn't take the same risks, either. He had three very good reasons to live waiting for him back at the aid station—three people whose hearts would break if he came back broken into pieces they couldn't mend.

His caution didn't blunt the advance. Eden's soldiers couldn't hold in the face of wild-eyed warriors who feared neither pain nor death. Zeke shot one of the Special Tasks soldiers trying to hold the line, and when the wounded man staggered back, Deacon snapped his neck. Exhilarated, Zeke spun around to find his next target with a laugh. Fighting the city that had tossed him out all those years ago energized him, and more than one soldier broke ranks and ran in the face of his laughter.

Deacon wasn't laughing. Neither was Ivan, a second-generation Rider whose father had died protecting Mad's mother. Mad took down a second Special Tasks soldier with a head shot, then grunted when Ivan smashed into him, knocking him to the ground. A bullet dug into the road next to their heads—one that would have gone through Mad's heart.

Maybe caution didn't matter if you were a Rios surrounded by Riders. They'd all die before they let him take a scratch.

The soldier who'd fired on him was lifting his gun for a second shot when a blur of brown skin and black hair slammed into him. Reyes, the eldest son of Sector One's wealthiest family after Mad's own. He dispatched the soldier with a knife across the throat, then turned and threw the same knife into the neck of a second soldier.

By the time Mad made it back to his feet, Zeke had broken through the ragged line of defenders. Three more Riders followed him, chasing the undisciplined soldiers back into alleys and side streets. Eden had always relied on the power of a bully—bigger guns, bigger bombs, bigger armies. The military police were accustomed to scared citizens who had never learned how to fight back.

Now, faced with hardened fighters who'd grown up tough and mean in the sectors, the soft, spoiled bullies of Eden scattered like terrified children.

"Come on!" Mad slapped Ivan's arm and gestured to Deacon. "The O'Kanes are right behind us. We're almost to the City Center."

They fell in behind him, obeying him as readily as they would have obeyed Gideon. And as they pushed toward the center of the city, Mad spared one moment of grief. Not for the Riders who had fallen so willingly, but for the man who had sent them to die.

Against his will, Gideon was confined to the aid station by lingering injuries from the assassination attempt that had almost killed him. They'd had a brief, vicious fight over the matter—for the first time in his life, Mad had lost his temper and screamed at his more powerful cousin. A man who still got breathless after a few minutes of strenuous activity didn't belong on a battlefield. So Gideon had stayed behind with part of his Royal Guard to coordinate the protection of the medical staff.

And he'd sent his men to die without him.

Gideon would be frantic. He'd grieve for every life lost. He'd cry for the men who had died willingly, righteously, even eagerly. He'd mourn, and he'd take more blame onto his shoulders than any mere mortal could carry.

After they took down Eden, Mad would have to find a way to help his cousin forgive himself.

lex

Pushing through to the center of the city was the hardest thing Lex had ever done.

It wasn't just the fighting—she'd been prepared for that, for the danger and the carnage and the adrenaline. For the strange blankness that came from being so fucking riled up, but also having to detach yourself from the possibility of death in order to simply function. She'd been ready for all of those things.

But leaving the wounded behind *killed* her. It didn't matter that every single one had been handed off to Dylan's well-trained medics, or that they were headed back to the best field care you could hope for in a situation like this. She didn't *know* whether they were going to be okay or whether they were drawing their last breaths, and it hurt. It hurt so goddamn bad.

Finn took a bullet in the thigh three blocks out. Ace took his place in the advance, leading a ragtag collection of defectors. Twenty yards from the City Center, he jammed into her, knocking her out of the path of a bullet that hit his shoulder hard enough to spin him around.

No. "Ace!"

"I'm fine," he snarled. Lied. He smashed to his knees on the pavement and waved his uninjured arm at her. "*Go.*"

"Don't snap at me, Santana." She lifted his good arm around her shoulder. "I've got you."

His fingers dug into her shoulder. "No, you've got to finish this. Nothing else matters, not even my glorious ass. So *move it*, sister."

He was right. He was *right*, and that only made it worse. "Get back to the aid station," she told him. "I'll find you when it's over."

She ran to catch up with Dallas, who fired his last bullet into an MP's shoulder. When his gun clicked empty, he whipped it across the man's face, driving him to the ground. "The Riders cut a path for Bren, Cruz, and Ryder," he told her as he stripped the man of his weapon and straightened. He fired absently at another man rushing them. "Reinforcements are coming now, though. I think the Council must have scared the cowards into running back at us."

"We'll have to find cover and deal with them." They couldn't risk having enemy soldiers regroup—or, worse, surround them and cut them off from the others.

"Right. Flag down Mad—"

It was as far as he got. A man wearing the sleek uniform of a Special Tasks soldier whipped around the corner of a statue, a wicked-looking automatic rifle in his hand.

Aimed at Dallas.

She didn't have time to reach him. She didn't even have time to scream as the soldier squeezed off a burst of rounds, and Hawk slammed into her, driving her to the ground. She caught Six out of the corner of her eye, a blur of brown hair and leather followed by rapid gunfire.

Then Six's voice, rough with worry. "*Fuck*—find a team with a doctor. *Now*."

Lex didn't try to get up. She dragged herself from beneath Hawk, kicking when his weight held her pinned, and crawled across the smooth pavement, which was now littered with glass and spent shell casings and blood.

Dallas's blood.

Six had already torn open his shirt, and the world went gray around the edges when Lex saw the holes in his chest and stomach. She pressed her hands to them, but blood seeped sluggishly through her fingers and she couldn't do this.

She couldn't do this.

"Alexa."

She met his eyes, and the world stopped. Everything ceased to exist but the way he was looking at her—like she was life, breath, all the things he'd always known he needed plus a few he'd never considered.

It didn't hurt. This was something beyond agony, unthinkable and unlivable. But she managed to drag in a breath that turned into a sob. "Don't do this."

His hand shook as he reached for her face, and his fingers slipped on her tear-slicked cheeks. "Everything good I am, everything good I've ever done... It's all you."

He'd said it before, but she'd never told him that

it went both ways. If she hadn't chosen *him* as a mark, if he'd gone out instead of staying in that night, if he'd never caught her stealing shit out of his personal safe, then she would have carried on with her sad excuse for a life—drifting from sector to sector, closed off from everyone around her. A thief with nothing and no one.

That life stretched out before her again now, like a flickering image from Noah's fancy wall projector. She shrank away from it and buried her face in the hollow of Dallas's neck instead. "You can't leave me."

"Never." His hand sank into her hair, but his grip was weak. "Always with you, Lexie. Love you."

"I love you, too." It felt too much like goodbye, but she couldn't *not* say it, just in case this was it, the end of *Dallas and Lex.* Of Declan and Alexa.

Of everything.

His hand fell away, limp and unmoving. Lex gripped him tighter, as if she could hold him to her through sheer need and force of will. She fought the hands that tried to pull her away, until a familiar voice murmured in her ear.

"You have to let them work, Lex." Mad wrapped his arms around her and hauled her back against his chest. Dallas's fingers slipped from between hers, but Mad caught her hand before she could reach for him again. "This is Kora. She's the one who saved Gideon."

"No." This wasn't real—all the desperate moments, the worry, the *death.* In her worst nightmares, she'd never imagined this, because this was impossible. Dallas couldn't die. Without him, she didn't exist.

She clung to that as fiercely as she clung to Mad. As long as she was breathing, that meant Dallas was, too. Because surely the moment he stopped, everything else would, too.

ashwin

The only thing Ashwin could still trust was the impersonal truth of numbers, so that was how he ordered his life.

One hundred and thirty seven: the number of hours since he'd last slept. Even for a Makhai soldier, he knew he was pushing the outer edges of his stamina. If necessary, he could stay on his feet for another few days, but his ability to analyze and react to situations would become increasingly compromised.

Two: the number of hours he'd spent watching Cruz, Bren, and the man from Sector Five as they quietly, efficiently rigged the wall around Eden with explosives.

Fifty-seven: the embarrassing number of minutes it had taken him to extrapolate their plan and force his own fractured thoughts into a semblance of order and purpose.

Three: the number of minutes it had taken him to find a weak spot in Eden's defenses to slip over the wall just before dawn.

Eighty-three: the number of Special Tasks soldiers he estimated still survived, many of them men Ashwin had trained, whose skills he had honed while undercover in the city.

Forty-eight: the number of Special Tasks soldiers he'd killed that morning. They'd been laughably easy to find, because Eden was predictable. Six of the seven remaining council members had retreated to their individual penthouses, and each one had requisitioned a Special Tasks squad for their personal protection. That was their fatal error. If they'd gathered in a single place, they could have set a nominal guard and charged the rest of the squads with halting the sector advance. But the remaining councilmen didn't trust each other, and they didn't trust Smith Peterson. So they scattered instead, and Ashwin had no trouble picking off their protectors, one squad at a time.

Thirty-five: the number of Special Tasks soldiers O'Kanes' men might have to get through before they reached Peterson.

That was the number that brought Ashwin to City Center. It suited Peterson's arrogance—instead of taking refuge in his own home, he'd chosen the center of government as the spot of his final stand. The government building thrust into the sky, towering above all of the other structures in the heart of Eden.

It sparkled in the clear morning sunlight, beams dancing off glass and steel, too bright and clean for the slaughter taking place at its base.

The sector forces were close to surrounded. They'd formed a wide, tight circle several people deep, and the outer ring fired on the Special Tasks squads closing in from all sides.

It was irrational for them to stand their ground in the open when there were innumerable options for cover only a dozen yards away. Even as he thought it, he watched a blonde woman in leather take a hit to the gut and go down. Before another fighter surged to fill her place, he caught a glimpse of the center of the circle.

A glimpse was enough.

One: the number of seconds it took for him to process the sight of Dallas O'Kane on his back. Bleeding out under the hands of—

He didn't count the men he shot as he surged out of the alley and crashed into the first soldier. He didn't count their deaths. He didn't count the number of bullets that grazed him, or even the ones that sank into his flesh.

They were firing toward Kora.

They had to stop.

Now.

After so many weeks of conflict, it was invigorating for his life to be so starkly, wonderfully simple. Ashwin glided from kill to kill, ignoring the blood on his hands and skin, reveling in the reduction of noise that followed each execution. Fewer gunshots meant decreased risk.

It was the kind of math he could do without numbers.

The final Special Tasks soldiers ran from him. It made them easier targets. When they slumped to the ground, the square went silent.

Ashwin turned toward the circle, which seemed to draw together in front of him. The faces staring back at him were tight with terror, and they didn't shift aside as he approached them.

One lifted a rifle.

A part of him, a part buried so deep it felt like the echo of someone else's memory, knew he didn't want to kill the people in front of him. But he could *feel* Kora's presence beyond them, a tingle of awareness beneath his skin. It short-circuited the pain receptors pumping feedback about his various wounds, overlaying them with the agony of recalibration drugs.

It hurt to think about Kora. And it hurt not to see her.

"Ashwin."

The clump of women in front of him parted to reveal a brunette with blood staining her hands and cheek. *Six*, the echo supplied. The leader of Sector Three, a member of Dallas's gang. She was watching him warily, her hand still gripping her pistol, but she gestured with one hand and the circle broke in front of him.

Kora was covered with blood. A swift appraisal of her visible skin revealed no wounds, and her clothing showed no tears or bullet holes. *Not her blood.* Of course, it wouldn't need to be—Dallas O'Kane lay beneath her busy hands, pale as death.

That mattered, somewhere. The echoes were even more distant now. All he could hear was *her*.

"Kora."

She glanced up, did a double take, and nearly smiled with relief as she turned her attention back to her task. "Lieutenant." She held out her hand, and one of the medics beside her placed a clamp into it. "I was wondering when you'd show up."

A sickly discomfort crawled up his spine, and he wasn't capable of processing it. Unease? Dread? He didn't know what a normal human would call this feeling. All he knew was the action it demanded. Reinforcements could be arriving at any moment, and Kora was exposed.

Unacceptable.

"Come on." He stepped over Dallas's sprawled legs and reached for her. "You need to get to a secure location."

She shrugged him off with another glance, this one incredulous. "I'm a little busy here."

Kora wasn't capable of protecting herself. Because of what she was, and how they'd shaped her. She would stay here, in the face of certain death, driven to heal, to ease pain, no matter how hopeless. No matter how much it hurt her.

She couldn't make the hard decision, so Ashwin did.

He hauled her to her feet, his hands gentle but implacable around her upper arms. "Now, Kora. It isn't safe here."

The sound of a pistol's safety disengaging drew his attention. He'd anticipated bluster from the O'Kanes, but time slowed to nothing when he turned toward the noise and found a wild-eyed Lex holding the weapon in one steady hand.

Pointed at Kora's head.

"I don't want to do this." Lex's voice wavered, but her aim didn't. "Don't make me do this."

On any other day, he would have called her bluff. Alexa Parrino didn't have the cruelty inside her to shoot an innocent woman for the sins of a man. But the look in her dark eyes—

Ashwin couldn't name the sick feeling churning inside him, but he recognized it. With Dallas bleeding out on the ground, Lex was capable of doing anything.

Right now, so was Ashwin.

It was a tragedy in the making, worse because he knew he could shoot her. It would be unnecessary and inefficient, and he disliked both of those things. But not enough to stop his hand from sliding toward the gun strapped to his thigh.

Kora's blood-slicked hand covered his. "Stop. Please, Ashwin."

She was shaking. Trembling in his grip, with terror filling her sweet, gentle face—and she wasn't even looking at Lex. Her fear slammed into his gut, more painful than all his bullet wounds combined, more agonizing than the drugs he'd pumped into his veins to wipe her from his psyche.

Because it was *him*. He was hurting her, just like Cruz had sworn he would.

His hands spasmed once on her arms and then opened. He stumbled back, and Six stepped between them, bristling with fury as she pointed her pistol at the center of his forehead. "Keep moving."

He did, because two steps was far enough to afford him a glimpse past her, a last look at Kora's pale face. "I'm sorry," he whispered. But she was already sinking back to her knees, her focus on the man she was trying to save.

They were both what their creators had intended. Perfectly formed tools meant for a single purpose. Trying to change that was a futile act that led to malfunction. He was proof of that.

He was a weapon, meant for only one thing. It was

time for him to go back to the Base and let them reforge him. A few months at the nonexistent mercies of the recalibration team would break him down into parts so small, nothing inside him would remember how good it had been just to be near her.

He'd forget how to feel again. And she'd be safer without him.

21

The administration building at City Center was a marvel of engineering. Ryder had never seen it this close before, but he'd studied the blueprints until his eyes burned. He'd memorized the layout, along with every point of access, every security feature, even the ventilation system.

And, now, here he was.

"Fuck," Cruz murmured, gripping his weapon tighter. "I hate this place. I always hated this place."

"That's because you have a brain." Bren quickly cleared the alley that led around the side of the building. "Peterson has to be here. What's our approach?"

"We could stick together and clear the floors one by one..." Cruz let his gaze slide up the endless side of the building. "But it'll take a long time."

"So we split up." Ryder checked his rifle and tried not to think about Nessa.

She'd be waiting for him, back behind the front lines. He'd tried to convince himself she was too smart for that, but it was no use. It wasn't about being smart, or realistic, or even about understanding how lucky they all were to have made it this far.

It was about hope.

But hope was a dangerous thing. It introduced fear into the equation, made you think about all the things you stood to lose if your day went south fast. So Ryder shoved it down, locked it away.

This was his mission. It always had been. And that was why he knew exactly where he'd find Smith Peterson. "Cruz, you search the lower floors. Bren can handle the middle. I'll take the top." Because where else would a douchebag like Peterson go but the penthouse?

Cruz studied him for a silent moment, as if he knew exactly what Ryder was thinking, but he only nodded. "You'll need someone with security clearance to get you to the top few floors—or just their bar code. Anyone in Special Tasks can do it."

Ryder grinned. "By the time I get there, I'm sure I'll find a spare arm or two the original owners don't need anymore."

"Probably." As they reached the empty lobby, Cruz broke away toward a bank of elevators. He swiped a hand between a sensor in the doors of one, then a second, setting off a smooth mechanical hum. "Don't get reckless. There are about ten O'Kanes who want to haze you a little in the cage before they give their blessing for you to go chasing Nessa."

It hit Ryder like a blow, and he closed his eyes against the pain.

When he opened them again, Bren was staring at him. “Be careful,” was all he said.

“Yeah.” Ryder turned for the south stairwell. His boots thumped on the cement stairs, keeping time with his heart but not his racing thoughts as he climbed floor after floor.

He made it to the twenty-first floor before meeting any resistance. A soldier stood on the landing, propping open the door with one foot. Ryder slammed the butt of his rifle into the man’s jaw, then slung him over the railing to tumble through the stairwell. His prolonged scream brought his comrades running, and Ryder dispatched them with quick, clean shots.

He didn’t have time to waste.

He exited at the top of the stairwell, four floors beneath the penthouse. Most of the lights were out, and the few that were still on flickered ominously, casting the long, interminable hallways in eerie shadow.

Ryder carefully pulled the stairwell door shut and paused in the darkness of an alcove. He could rush the halls, shooting the place up, but it would bring the rest of the soldiers running. He had no idea how many Peterson had standing guard in this one spot—Christ, probably more than the whole rest of the goddamn building. Men like Peterson never left their own safety to chance. They’d risk anyone else, sure, but not their own sorry asses.

Discretion is the better part of valor. Jim’s voice, echoing in his memory, and Ryder listened. He wouldn’t do anyone any good if he got himself killed now, here, so close to victory he could almost taste it.

He slung his rifle over his shoulder, drew his knife, and crept toward the first intersection, ready to fight quick and dirty. But the intersecting hall was deserted in both directions. Not a soul, dead or alive.

For a moment, confusion gripped him. Had he miscalculated? Was Peterson holed up somewhere else in the building, well-protected by a heavy guard that Bren or Cruz would have to handle all alone?

No. Ryder's instincts told him he was right, goddammit. Which left another, even more baffling possibility—that the soldiers guarding Peterson had fled.

Ryder pressed on.

On the other side of the building, voices echoed in the empty corridor. He stopped short, straining to make out the words.

"You saw him, Sawyer." The man's voice was low, urgent. "It was Donnelly down there. Forget all the rest of it, that motherfucker *cannot* be trusted. He'll shoot you in the face and laugh about it."

"I never worked with him," the second voice replied, just as low. "But I grew up on the Base with Cruz. I trusted him a hell of a lot more than I ever trusted anyone giving us orders."

"Maybe back in the day, sure, but not anymore."

"He hasn't been gone *that* long. Not even two years. And tell me you never thought about walking off the job and never coming back when Miller was calling the shots."

"Of course I did. We all did." Silence. "But we never did it."

Sawyer sighed. "Maybe that doesn't make *us* the trustworthy ones."

Ryder's recall of the building's layout was absolute, etched into his brain from dozens of hours of study. If he wanted to get to the elevator, to *Peterson*, he had to go through these men.

He crept closer as the first man launched into

another story about just how evil Bren was. He'd almost made it to the end of the wall when the voice cut off abruptly, mid-sentence.

Like his buddy had signaled for him to shut the fuck up.

Dammit. Ryder shouldered his weapon and swung around the corner, but there was only one man standing in front of the elevator, glaring down the barrel of his high-tech rifle.

A door *whooshed* open behind Ryder, followed by the quiet scrape of boots on carpet. "Drop your weapon."

Just like that, he was fifteen again, cornered by MPs in the city square and facing death. But what flooded him this time wasn't fear—it was certainty. He tightened his grip on his rifle and shook his head slowly. "I'm not here for you."

The man in front of the elevator sneered. "I know why you're—"

"Shut up," Sawyer said from behind Ryder, and there was something in his voice. A vulnerability.

Ryder had heard that tremor before. Every time he'd taken on a new persona, he'd run into men worn down by working for powerful, corrupt assholes. Every day brought new horrors to batter their consciences but, for most of them, there never seemed to be a good way out.

Part of his job had been to figure out who needed a nudge in the right direction and then make it happen. He'd been working up to it with Finn in Sector Five, back before Trix had shown up to give him a shove of her own.

Sometimes, all it took were the right words.

"There's still time," he murmured, pitching his voice low.

The soldier guarding the elevator frowned in confusion. But the one behind him sighed again, exhausted and resigned. "Is Markovic really alive?"

"Yeah." Ryder watched the man in front of him shift his grip on his weapon, his finger tightening slightly on the trigger, and fought the urge to squeeze his eyes shut. "Yeah, he is."

"Sawyer, what the fu—"

Gunfire exploded in the narrow hallway, and Ryder steeled himself against flinching. The die was cast, and whatever was going to happen would happen.

But when the smoke cleared, Ryder was unhurt. The soldier named Sawyer stood there, stone-faced and silent, but with bleak eyes. He stared at his fallen comrade for five seconds before lowering his weapon. "He was a son of a bitch," he said quietly. "A real asshole. That's all they let us be."

There was only one question to ask, one thing that mattered. "What do you *want* to be?"

"Gone." He strode past Ryder and stepped over the man he'd shot. The elevator doors had a flat panel embedded next to them, and he swiped his wrist across it. A moment later, they whirred open. "Go. He's in the penthouse."

He didn't need to be told twice. Ryder stepped into the elevator, then turned. "You should find Dallas O'Kane and—"

But the man was already walking away, his gun lying discarded in the hallway.

The doors slid shut, and Ryder pressed the button for the top floor. There would be no more guards—if Peterson didn't trust them to patrol the upper floors, no fucking way would he trust them right at his back. There was nothing left between Ryder and his target.

Nothing, it turned out, except one woman with a gun pointed at her head.

She was seated in a chair in front of Peterson, her hands gripping the arms so tight her knuckles stood out white against her light brown skin. A bruise was rising on one cheek, and her ponytail was disheveled and falling down, as if Peterson had used it to drag her somewhere.

As Ryder stepped out of the elevator, Peterson's triumphant smile faltered. He stared past him, his gaze sweeping the empty car, and his brow furrowed. "Where is he?"

"Who?" Ryder kept the barrel of his rifle pointed down, but ready. "Your guard?"

"My…?" His gaze swung back to Ryder, and he spaced out his words, as if speaking to a child. "I don't give a shit about my guard. Where the fuck is Markovic?"

In another time or place—and without a frightened hostage between them—Ryder would have laughed. "That's what you think this is, a coup d'état? You think Markovic busted out of your torture chamber and decided to take over the city?"

"And what would you have me believe?" Peterson waved the gun at Ryder before returning it to his hostage. "That Jim Jernigan's little orphaned pet and *Dallas O'Kane* executed a plan of this magnitude? Besides…" This time he jabbed the pistol into the back of the woman's head, provoking a choked whimper. "Penelope is *his* pet."

The hacker. Ryder took another step, then stopped when she whimpered again. "Don't know what to tell you, Peterson. Markovic isn't here. *I'm* here."

"Well, that's disappointing." He grabbed Penelope

by the hair and hauled her head back. "You were supposed to be useful for something other than offering excuses for why your work is so inferior. How does it feel, knowing he asked you to throw away your life and didn't even come to save you?"

She clenched her jaw and said nothing.

He sneered and shoved her. The chair toppled sideways, spilling her to the ground with enough force to send her skidding across the carpet. She came to her knees immediately and scrambled back against a desk, silent and wary.

Peterson ignored her as he righted the chair and gestured to it. "I suppose this is better. Nikolas Markovic is tiresome. For years, all he's done is bleat the same naïve sentimentality. Jim Jernigan, though..." He met Ryder's gaze and smiled. "That was a man who understood the value of pragmatism."

Ryder shrugged. "Sure, he did. Until you had him killed. It *was* you, right?"

"An unfortunate necessity." Peterson strolled around the desk and dropped his gun on it with a clatter. A thumb pressed to the edge of the surface triggered a drawer that slid smoothly open. From it, he pulled a box of the finest cigarettes manufactured in Sector Eight. "Though, in all honesty, I was surprised he died. Especially when so many inferior men survived."

As if taking a bullet to the heart was a test of character instead of something that would kill a king as quickly as it would a peasant. It spoke volumes about Peterson—instead of viewing his power as a construct, something he'd taken from others through manipulation and force, he saw it as something intrinsically *his*. A God-given right to rule.

Disgusting.

Peterson lit a cigarette before laughing at him. "Oh, don't look at me like that. I can't believe Jim raised you to be a fool. Jim and I go way, way back. We found a way to work together through all the years of disagreements. He wouldn't want you to waste the opportunity in front of you. Think about it—all eight sectors could be yours."

He wasn't entirely wrong. Jim Jernigan was a hard man. Ruthlessly practical, willing to make deals with the devil himself—*if* it furthered his cause, and that was the part this grandstanding jackass would never understand. Every compromise, every backroom deal he'd ever made, had all been in preparation for this.

The only opportunity Jim wouldn't want him to squander was the chance to put a bullet right between Peterson's eyes. But something stilled his hands.

Peterson gestured toward the window. The view was breathtaking from this high up, offering a clear sight of the rolling orchards and distant farmland of the northern edges of Sector One. "If you don't want the bother of running all of them, you can have your pick. I've heard that Gideon's estate is quite nice, if you don't mind being cut off from civilization. All you have to do is take care of him. And O'Kane, of course."

Anger sizzled through Ryder's veins, most of it directed at himself. He had a clear shot, and he was hesitating. Why, goddammit? He'd met blessedly few people in his life who deserved to die as much as Smith Peterson. Hell, he deserved *worse* than death—

And then it hit him, the answer that Jim had always been too filled with cold rage to consider—this man's fate wasn't theirs to decide. He belonged to the people of Eden, and they would have to figure out what to do with him.

This shot belonged to someone else.

"You're under arrest." Simply saying the words aloud made Ryder feel like the weight of the world had lifted from his shoulders. It wasn't clean and easy, but it was fair, and it was just.

Peterson laughed and crushed out his cigarette on the smooth, expensive surface of the desk. "What a disappointment you're turning out to be," he murmured, shaking his head. "At least Jim's not here to see it."

He honestly didn't know what Jim would think. Would he be angry that he'd made all these plans, and Ryder was ignoring them? Hell, maybe he'd be proud of him for forging his own path. For all his faults, Jim had never wanted him to be a puppet.

His mother, that was easier. She would have been glad to see him rise above the easy satisfaction of death and vengeance to look ahead to his future. And his father—

His father never would have wanted his death to consume anyone, much less the three people who'd meant the most to him.

"Hands up, Peterson. Behind your head."

Instead of complying, the man snatched up the gun he'd abandoned on his desk and fired.

22

Nessa had always assumed she had a handle on the whole *waiting at home to stitch up the wounded* gig. She'd been doing it for most of her life, first on the ranch under Quinn's guidance, and then at the warehouse as the men went out and fought the battles that won Dallas control over Sector Four.

She was always the calm one, soothing the people left behind as they fretted over their loved ones who had gone off to fight. They were *all* loved ones to her, from the first men to sign up to the rawest recruit.

But *love* was a word with shades now, and her heart didn't seem to care whether Ryder was the knitting or the liquor—it just cared that he was gone. Fighting. Maybe dying.

And all she could do was wait.

Well, that wasn't *all* she could do. She could free up the more experienced doctors and nurses by dealing with the basic injuries. She sewed up shopkeepers from Sector Three and farmers from Six, guards from Sector One and former pleasure house trainees from Two.

She babbled at them. Reassurances she barely believed and promises they all knew she couldn't keep. When she discovered one of the Armstrong brothers sprawled on a pallet, nursing a nasty slash on his thigh and another across his cheek, she teased him about being a war hero and told him his brother would be the handsome one now.

Pain tightened his features for the first time. "Ike got hit just inside the wall," he rumbled, then jerked his head toward the side of the parking lot where the dead were stretched out, covered with whatever fabric they'd been able to scrounge up.

"I'm sorry." It was all she could manage. She finished stitching his wound, applied med-gel, and moved on to her next patient in silence.

She couldn't find the reassurances anymore. Even the empty ones.

"Nessa!" Trix's voice cut through the noise, quick and panicked. "Help me! Finn's been hit."

Oh *fuck*. She throttled down panic as she smoothed a bandage into place and snatched up her kit. Trix's red hair stood out in the jumble, and Nessa threaded her way through the crowd to where Finn was sitting on a stack of pallets, his teeth gritted in pain.

"Okay, deep breaths," she said first, grabbing Trix's shoulder and squeezing until the woman looked at her. Then she shoved her kit into Trix's hands. "He's upright and he made it back here, that's good. Find the painkillers."

Trix obeyed, and Nessa crouched next to Finn and touched his wrist. His pulse beat steadily beneath her fingertips, but his jeans were a bloody mess. At least the bullet had gone straight through, and the fact that he hadn't bled to death already meant it *probably* hadn't hit anything too vital.

Probably.

Bullet wounds were above her paygrade. She flagged down one of the medics before taking the injector from Trix's hand. Finn opened his mouth—undoubtedly with some dumbass argument about how he didn't *need* drugs—and Nessa jabbed him in the arm. "No displays of manly ego allowed today."

Finn grunted, but his expression softened when he looked at Trix. "I'm fine, doll. You know it takes more than a bullet to knock me down."

She dragged his hand to her cheek. "I wish you didn't feel the need to keep reminding me by getting shot."

"Men," Nessa huffed, reaching for the adhesive gauze. Staunching the bleeding until a real doctor showed up wasn't much, but it was all she could do. "You ask them to show up naked with dinner, and they go get shot like heroes instead. They're fucking impossible."

Finn stroked Trix's jaw. "I may come home a little banged up, but I'll always come home."

Nessa's chest collapsed. Trix and Finn didn't seem to notice, so maybe she was successful at hiding the sudden appearance of a black hole of sadness right where her heart was supposed to be. God, what she would have given to hear Ryder murmur those words, or anything close to them…

Or anything, right now. At all.

She finished wrapping Finn's thigh and rose, prepared to bluff her way out. But she didn't need to. Trix and Finn were in their own perfect world, gazing into each other's eyes like they were going to fall in and swim around for the rest of the day. Nessa gathered her supplies and started across the lot again, only to stop cold when two teenage boys ran by her with a stretcher.

"Ace!"

Nessa raced after them, reaching their side just as they set him down. He grunted softly and squinted up at her. "Thought I heard you, glitter-bug."

"Shit, Ace." She sank to her knees beside him, panicked by the amount of blood soaking his shirt. She groped for her kit as she glanced up at one of the boys. "Go find Doc. *Now*."

The boy took off, and Nessa reloaded the injector with shaking hands. "You better not argue with me about this."

"Fuck, no," he groaned. "Dope me up. Hell, give me double. Do you have any idea how much this *hurts*?"

"No, you idiot. Because I don't get shot." She was gentler with him than she'd been with Finn, and the relief that slid over his face as the drugs took effect soothed her. She reached for the gauze next and pressed it to his wound. "What's happening in there?"

"We're kicking their asses." Ace's grin was already a little stoned, and when he tried to pat her cheek with his good hand, he got more of her hair than anything else. "Don't look so worried, darling. Ryder's with Cruz. Cruz won't let anything happen to him."

"I know," she soothed, guiding his hand back down to his chest. "Just rest, Ace. Rachel will be waiting for you back at the compound. We just gotta get you patched up first."

Dylan and Jyoti finally arrived, and Nessa relinquished her spot to him. Jyoti touched her arm as she rose, studying her with worried eyes. "If you need to take a few moments—"

Nessa swiped at her cheeks and told herself the burning in her eyes was exhaustion, not tears. "I'm fine. I just need—"

"Out of the way!" The pretty blonde doctor who'd arrived with Gideon's people hurried in, her soft voice hard as steel. "Clear some space, and someone get me a surgical tray. *Now.*"

Nessa started to move, but her entire body seized in denial as two of the Riders rushed behind her, carrying a stretcher between them. Nessa didn't have a good angle to see who was on it, but it didn't matter.

Lex was with them, wild-eyed and distraught. And covered—*covered*—with blood.

Oh God, not Dallas.

One of the nurses slammed past Nessa, knocking her out of the way. She stumbled a step and barely caught her balance. The ground didn't feel entirely solid anymore, because Dallas had been the foundation for so many years, the strong stone on which she'd built her pretty little tower. He was *family.*

And he was Lex's world.

That got her feet moving. The first two steps were jerky, but then she was running. She caught Lex around the shoulders, holding her tight. At first, Lex didn't move. Then she gripped Nessa's arm so hard that her nails bit into her skin.

"He'll be okay," Nessa whispered. Not empty reassurance or a lie. A prayer. She needed to believe it, as if her belief could shape reality. "He's too stubborn to die if it means leaving you."

"I'm breathing," Lex answered blankly. "I'm breathing, and so is he."

She held Lex tighter, knowing words were useless. The blonde doctor had plenty of help now, and Nessa couldn't watch the bloody, gruesome process of trying to piece him back together. She fixed her gaze on his temple instead, and wondered when the hair there had begun to silver. When the crinkle lines next to his eye had gotten so deep.

He'd seemed so powerful and strong her whole life, it was unsettling to think about him growing old. But it was better that than the alternative.

It was only then—standing by in helpless horror as she watched a city doctor struggle to rebuild Dallas's body from broken pieces—that she realized she hadn't heard gunfire in a while.

The constant patter of it had become white noise. The lack of it echoed in her mind, looming large until something rose to replace it.

It sounded like a murmur at first, then like music—like the club did from a block away some nights, snatches of louder sound coming whenever someone opened the door. As it rose, the people closest to the opening in the wall began to drift closer.

Nessa hovered, torn between loyalty to Dallas and the need to *know*. But when the sound resolved itself into cheers, she released Lex and pushed through the growing crowd, using her elbows and her scowl and her O'Kane ink to make it to the front.

The view inside Eden was...apocalyptic. Rubble filled the streets. So did bodies. The wide road where the old gate had been led straight toward the heart of the city, and that was where the poorest residents of

Eden were gathering. Some of them looked like they'd fought. Some looked like they'd just been swept up in the moment. But they were all screaming their support of the cluster of people coming toward Nessa.

Mad was in the front, flanked by a handful of his cousin's Riders. She caught sight of Cruz behind them, and then Bren. And in the middle…

Ryder half-pushed, half-dragged a man with a broken nose bleeding all over his pristine gray suit. Smith Peterson, his once objectively handsome face ruined—not by the broken nose, but by the contempt he no longer bothered to hide.

The citizens he was supposed to represent had gathered along the street to curse and jeer at him, and he *still* thought he was better than all of them.

He'd learn better. Lex would teach him, if no one else got to him first—and if Dallas didn't pull through the other side in perfect health, Peterson would beg for someone to grant him the mercy of death.

Right now, Nessa didn't feel very merciful.

Someone had brought Markovic over from the O'Kane compound. He stepped forward—without his cane—and stood in the center of the ruined street, hands clasped behind his back, waiting for the procession to reach him. When it did, he eyed the men silently, his throat working.

Then he spoke, his voice booming out over the crowd. "Smith Peterson. The people of Eden trusted you, and you betrayed that trust."

Peterson lifted his chin, still haughty. "Yes, Markovic. Soothe yourself with all the formalities and legalities before you hand me over to your tame barbarian. I underestimated you. Clever of you to get sector trash to do your dirty work."

"No remorse," Markovic observed. "You're not even sorry you got caught, are you? You're still completely convinced you had the right to use your office for nothing more than your own comfort and wealth."

"I *earned* that comfort," he replied, his voice full of such conviction that it made Nessa's skin crawl. "Who do you think has kept us safe all these years? Idealists who would throw open the doors and let the sectors overrun us? Bleeding hearts who let the useless idiots hold out their hands for *more more more* instead of forcing them to earn their place in our city?" He sneered. "Someone has to be the adult. You never had the stomach for the hard choices."

"Hard choices." Markovic echoed the words, his expression a mixture of disgust and vague pity. Then he nodded to the Riders accompanying Peterson. "Take him away."

The Riders gripped his arms and fell in behind Mad as he led them down the street, beyond the ruined city walls. Markovic's gaze followed them, the disgust and pity never diminishing. But Nessa was close enough to see the hands gripped behind his back so tightly his knuckles had gone white.

That wasn't just revulsion in his eyes. It was death, and Nikolas Markovic wouldn't need Dallas or Lex or anyone else to pull the trigger for him. When the time came, he would exact justice himself.

It was no less than Peterson deserved.

The man vanished from Nessa's mind as she turned her attention back to Ryder. He stood close to Markovic, talking in a low voice that only reached her in murmurs. Nessa swayed, fighting the urge to launch herself into the middle of whatever important political thing was happening—and into his arms.

Ryder was alive. His left sleeve was torn, revealing an angry red furrow across his upper arm that could only have come from a bullet. A medic swooped in, blocking him from view, and the numbness she'd been wrapped in for the last twenty-four hours cracked.

This time when she swayed, Trix caught her. She clasped Nessa's hand, steadying her, but it was her words that held Nessa up. "See? Ryder came home, too."

"He did." And she was relieved, so relieved. She should be floating on clouds with how fucking relieved she was.

But Amira wouldn't get this moment. Fuck, Lex might not, either. Neither would all the people who'd loved anyone stretched out in that sad, endless line of silent bodies.

The numbness she'd been wrapped in for the last twenty-four hours cracked, and Nessa turned into Trix's shoulder and muffled a sob. Of relief. Of grief. Of sheer, overwhelmed exhaustion.

They'd won, but Nessa had been right. It didn't feel like victory yet.

23

Even if half the O'Kane compound hadn't been compromised by Eden's drone attacks, Ryder would have known where to find Nessa.

Her distillery had escaped the carnage. The warehouse had some superficial damage, but the structure itself was solid. Even the bottles on the shelves inside were still upright, unbroken, and his relief knew no bounds.

Of all the loss she'd suffered, this wouldn't be part of it.

She wasn't in the distillery, or the storeroom, or her office—not that he'd suspected she would be. Instead, he headed for the aging room.

It was silent down here, insulated from the bustle of activity above, with just the soft hum of a generator and the echo of Nessa's footsteps. He followed the sound and found her running her fingers over the top of one of the heavy casks.

Her fingertips lingered over the messy scrawl, and she didn't look up even as she spoke to him. "These are his barrels. My grandfather's. I've always known I'd have to bottle and sell them someday, but it was *so close*..."

"They made it through the war." He reached for her shoulder but stopped just shy of touching her. "Nessa, we made it through the war."

She turned, staring up at him with big, tear-filled eyes for half a heartbeat. Then she lunged, colliding with his body and tangling her arms around his neck. "You made it through the war."

He closed his eyes, inhaling the scents of wood and spices and Nessa. "*We* made it. I stopped by the hospital before I came here."

Her body stiffened in his arms. "Is—is Dallas...?"

"He's gonna be fine. Dr. Bellamy has to do his regeneration therapy in stages, but he's stable. He's good."

"Oh, thank God." All of the tension seemed to rush out of her at once, and he tightened his arms to steady her. "Did you hear anything about Ace and Finn?"

"Finn's already healed up. Trix brought him home a little while ago." Ace's condition was trickier. "Santana snuck over to the children's ward. He's been drawing cartoons and decorating casts. I think he's planning a mural."

She pulled back far enough to look up at him, her shaky smile shadowed by the worry lingering in her eyes. "Is he going to be okay, though?"

She deserved the truth. "The bullet did a lot of

nerve damage. They're going to try regen, but it's iffy. He may not regain full use of his arm."

"Oh." Her smile wobbled, then came back. "Well, if he's already doing art for the kids, he'll be fine. That's what all this shit was about, right? Maybe we don't all have to be ready to fight all the time anymore."

No, hopefully they'd never have to fight again. Then, instead of going back to their old lives, they could move on to something better. "I'm sorry. About the way I left things."

"Me too." Her thumb traced up and down the back of his neck. "You're so careful. And I'm impulsive. Crashing into each other and getting hurt was kind of inevitable."

"No. You asked fair questions, reasonable ones." It wasn't her fault that he couldn't answer them. But explaining meant starting at the beginning. "Can we sit down?"

Nessa stepped back and caught his hand. Silently, she led him back down the aisle, past dozens of casks of liquor, to the table where Lex had caught them kissing.

It seemed like a lifetime ago. Even under the threat of open war, they hadn't understood. *He* hadn't understood, after decades of being schooled on the dangers, the sacrifices. The loss. It wasn't something you could fathom, not until you were in it. And then, there was no time to process it. Battles were won or lost, people were hurt or died, but the war stopped for no one. You just had to carry on.

And now it was over. And Ryder didn't know what to do with himself.

He leaned on the table, avoiding her eyes. "They asked me—the other sector leaders, I mean—what my plans are for Five. And I don't know what to tell them, because I don't know."

She hopped up on the table next to him, her shoulder so close to his they brushed as she swung one leg. "That was never really your plan, was it? Running Five?"

"Taking over Five wasn't a goal. It was a means to an end." He finally met her gaze. "To *the* end, Nessa. Winning the war, that was all that mattered. It was all Jim talked about, all he seemed to care about. All he said my father cared about. And I listened. I listened so hard that I never thought about what would come after winning."

"But the cabin—"

"Was my father's dream," he finished. "I took it. I figured I would do that for him, honor his memory with it, the same way I would with the war. I didn't even realize what I was really doing."

She nodded slowly. "I get it, I think. I mean... this?" She waved an arm at the aging room. "It started off as my grandfather's dream. And, you know, I never let myself wonder if it was my dream, too. I couldn't. Too many people were depending on me."

"No." He straightened and took a few steps, trying to order his thoughts. How could she understand when he wasn't making any sense? Finally, he turned to face her. "No one shoved the cabin thing at me, because we never discussed the future past the war. It's like it didn't exist. When I called winning *the end*, I meant it literally. Everything I was told, everything I was *taught*, it all stopped there."

"Oh." Sympathy softened her gaze. "That really sucks."

"I'm so angry," he whispered. It was the first time he'd let himself think the words, much less say them aloud. "Jim spent *years* turning me into the perfect rebel leader, but he couldn't spare five goddamn minutes to teach me anything else."

"It's okay, you know," she said gently. "To be pissed off about it."

No, it wasn't. Because it wasn't something Jim had ever done on purpose, and now he was dead. "My mother never liked any of it. I used to think it was because she was afraid I'd die. But now..." He stepped closer to Nessa, almost close enough to touch. "I think she was afraid I'd wind up alone."

She tilted her head back to face him. "You don't have to be. But you do have to figure out what you want. Not all the details, just enough to get you started. Close your eyes and dream, Ryder."

"I don't know how," he confessed. "I tried once, and not only did I just steal my father's dream, I fucked it all up, too." He knelt in front of her. "It wasn't about the cabin. He wanted what it represented—a safe, peaceful place where he could be with the people he loved."

She touched his cheek. "I'm good at dreaming. I can come up with ten dreams right now, and I'll forget half of them by tomorrow. I don't know if life with me could ever be peaceful. Makes me feel kind of like an asshole for hoping you want to try."

"What happens when you forget them?"

"I dream up more." She smiled at him. "I'm an O'Kane princess. I never run out of dreams."

An O'Kane princess—who belonged in Sector Four. "You need to be here, don't you? This may be your grandfather's legacy, but it's *your* future. O'Kane Liquor."

"Maybe." She shrugged and looked away, her gaze sweeping the aging room. "Most of the time, I love it.

I'm really fucking good at it. But I never got to *choose* it." When she looked back at him, her thumb touched the corner of his mouth. "And if it gets in the way of choosing you… I don't know. I might be a mess in your cabin, but I'd find a way to love it. Because you'd be there."

Warmth flooded him, a relief that made winning the war pale in comparison. Because he'd survived the fighting—but with Nessa, he could do more than survive. He could *live*. "It's not about the cabin, remember?"

"I remember." She brushed his lips again. "Close your eyes."

He obeyed as he rose. "What?"

"I'm going to dream for you." She pulled him closer, until he was standing between her knees, and framed his face with her hands. "For the next week, we're going to take care of each other, because it's going to be a hard week. And I know that even if you don't want to run Five forever, you feel responsible for the people there. So you'll go and help them start to move on. And I'll be here, helping my people do the same."

She tugged him down gently, until his forehead rested on hers. "But some nights, you'll come back here, and we'll eat dinner and talk about our days and then we'll shove all the pillows off my bed and do crazy hot dirty stuff to each other. And some nights, I'll come over to Five, and you can show me where you live. And there probably won't be nearly as many pillows on the bed, but the dirty hot stuff will still be awesome. And when we make it to the end of the week…"

She was so close that her breath blew against his mouth. "The end of the week," he echoed. "What then?"

"Then we dream up the next week." She kissed him, sweet and soft and gone too fast. "Together."

Ryder licked his lips, and he could still taste her. The reality of it opened his eyes, in every way. "Just like that?"

"Why not?" She stared at him from barely an inch away. "Everything's unsettled, Ryder. I'm impulsive enough to promise I'll run away to a cabin, or ask you to move in with me and become an O'Kane...but that's not you. And that's okay. Maybe we don't have to crash into each other and get hurt. Maybe I can learn to move a little slower, and you can learn to dream selfish dreams. And we'll be better together."

He traced the bow of her mouth. "I don't want to show you where I live in Five. It's Fleming's old penthouse, and it's horrible. I want to show you my old place instead. And maybe...we can go to Eight, too."

"We can go anywhere," she promised. "That's why we fought, right?"

He fought because he'd been raised to, because it was the right thing to do. He never did it for *himself*—but maybe that was the first step. "Can I see the barrels?"

"Pop's?" She edged him back and slid off the table. Row after row of casks bore her neat block letters, but toward the back of the room, the writing changed. She led him back to where he'd found her and smiled as she touched the messy scrawl. "Dallas and I are the only ones who can read these. Pop wasn't a big fan of writing stuff down. He liked to keep it all in his head. He was paranoid because of how the law was cracking down before the Flares. It was illegal to do what he was doing."

"I know." At her questioning look, he had to smile. "My father was a police officer. That's how he knew Jim—they were partners."

"Oh God, he was a cop?" She leaned against the cask and laughed. "This is Pop's worst nightmare. But I bet he would have liked you anyway. All the super-spy skills. Pop appreciated resourcefulness."

Ryder ran his hand around the rough edge of the cask. "Why don't you buy them?"

"Because…" The word faded away as she stared at him. "I don't know. I guess I never really thought about it. It's always been about how I can maximize profits, and my feelings didn't get a lot of input."

"The wall is coming down." And, with it, the trade restrictions Eden's former Council had imposed on the sectors. "I don't think you have to worry about Dallas's profits anymore."

"Maybe I will buy them, then." She touched her grandfather's handwriting again. "I wish I had more of him. I think about Hana, and I…" Her voice wavered. "Our parents were just trying to survive. They didn't have time to think about preserving our history. I know my other grandfather was Vietnamese, but I don't know what that *means*. I've never seen a picture of him, and my parents died before they could tell me stories. And I want Hana to have more than that. And Rachel and Cruz and Ace's kid. We need pictures and vids and *stories*. For whoever comes after us."

Somewhere, hidden away in Sector Eight, his mother had placed a lockbox full of memories for him. He didn't even know what was in it, but he cherished the fact that it was *there*, that it existed. That his parents weren't lost to him forever, not completely.

"That doesn't have to be a dream," he whispered. "All you have to do is start taking pictures, asking questions. Writing."

Her nose scrunched up. "Maybe I'll recruit Noelle

to do the writing. She's a bookworm. But pictures, I can do pictures. And vids." She stepped closer, leaning into his chest. "Just promise me that you want me in your future, even if you can't see it clearly yet."

"I've always been able to see you." Even when the future had been some unthinkable mystery, the single void in a lifetime of focus and study. "Sometimes, you're all I can see. I should have told you that already."

"Oh." A single syllable, but it was more a sound. It was discovery, relief. "Yeah, that would have been nice to hear. But I know it can be hard to get a word in edgewise when I—"

He cut her off with a kiss. Not because he didn't want to hear what she had to say, not exactly.

He wanted to taste it instead.

Her lips parted, and her arms slid around his neck. She moaned against his mouth, and he had to catch her as she jumped up and wrapped her legs around his hips. Her kiss was everything she was—open, fearless, *eager*.

"Another dream." He murmured the words against her mouth. "Tell me."

"This," she replied, laughing softly. "This is what I wanted to do that first day I found you in here with Jas. Climb right up your body and have glorious, inappropriate sex on the tasting table."

"We'll break something," he told her approvingly.

"That's the point." She nipped at his lower lip. "C'mon, Ryder. Be reckless with me."

"Well…" Her belt fastened with a hook instead of a buckle, and he flicked it open with one hand. "Since we're dreaming, and all."

She gave a little wiggle. "Dream big?"

"Something like that." It was the final lesson Jim

had neglected, the one Ryder's mother, lost in her grief, hadn't had the words to convey.

His future wasn't a time, or a place, or a thing. His future was a woman, and that woman was in his arms.

24

Someone had upgraded the party room.

Nessa put her money on Noelle, especially since the biggest addition was a shiny new couch. The leather was supple and pristine, as if servants had been tasked with conditioning it weekly. Dallas had resisted the temptation to pillage Eden—baffling the surviving council members more than a little—but Noelle hadn't been shy about claiming her share of her inheritance.

And she spent it on Dallas's comfort.

Nessa knew she wasn't the only one who kept glancing up at the dais to reassure herself that he was really there. Lex hadn't left his side from the moment he lowered himself onto his new throne with a sigh of relief and a scowl for her hovering.

They were all hovering. But Dallas was alive, and

getting stronger every day. And the O'Kanes had gathered to celebrate.

If Nessa unfocused her eyes a little, she could almost believe it was just like old times. Music throbbed through the room, loud enough for people to dance but not too loud for the conversations happening around the edges of the room. Laughter rung out and liquor flowed, and she'd missed this. God, how she'd missed this.

Her O'Kane family had turned out in style. Leather and denim. Lace and silk. Skin—Nessa had never realized how soothing nakedness could be. But the first time Ace slid his hand under Cruz's shirt and bit his shoulder teasingly, she wanted to laugh and cry at the same time.

Things had gotten so bleak, she'd wondered if they'd ever find their way back here, to the slow, easy parties filled with brotherhood and sisterhood and joy. To teasing and joking. To sex that wasn't tangled with desperation, that didn't feel like clutching at every moment until time tore it through your fingertips.

Even tinged with sadness, this was what victory felt like. A glimpse of the life they'd had before, and proof that they could have it again.

Or maybe even something better.

Ryder's arm slid around her waist. He didn't speak, but when she craned her neck to look up at him, he was eyeing her with concern.

Probably because her eyes were misty. She smiled and rested her hand over his, pulling his arm more tightly around her. "I'm okay. It's a good kind of pretending-not-to-cry."

"How about pretending-to-drink?" He pressed a bottle into her hand. "Rachel's latest batch. Maybe the last one for a while."

"Probably." Nessa supposed it was inevitable, once shit got back to normal and Cruz had enough time to ponder the idea of a pregnant Rachel climbing up ladders to mess with giant vats of boiling liquids. Not that *she'd* forgive herself if Rachel got woozy and hurt herself.

She didn't look woozy now—just blissful. Ace had his left arm in a sling, but he'd never needed more than one hand to be all over her. And even Cruz's stern expression eased a little when Jared sat down next to them and tugged Lili into his lap.

At one time, the sight would have made her jealous—not that she'd ever really admitted it, even to herself. To confess to jealousy, she would have had to own up to being discontented with her cushy life, and that was a door she'd always kept firmly locked.

Until Ryder had wandered along and kicked it right the hell in.

She sipped the beer and leaned back against him. "You know this party's gonna get wild, right?"

"Jas already warned me." He snorted. "For that matter, so did Bren, Trix, and Zan. I think they expect me to faint when people start fucking."

"That would be pretty cute." Of course, since her concept of how good sex could be had gotten upended since the last time she'd watched them all fall on each other in a pile, *she* might be the one who swooned. That would be embarrassing as fuck. "You should have seen Hawk's eyes the first time they brought him to a party. He didn't know where to look once people started getting freaky, so he mostly stared at his boots or the ceiling."

"Not anymore, obviously."

She followed his gaze and laughed.

Of *course* Jas and Noelle were already putting on a show. Jas was sprawled out on the couch, one arm resting lazily along the back, the other tangled in Noelle's hair where she knelt between his legs. She kept her fingers twined at the small of her back, letting him guide her mouth up and down his cock in a slow, filthy blowjob that held Hawk riveted.

Judging by the affectionate look on Jeni's face, the only reason she wasn't emulating Noelle yet was because she was having way too much fun watching Hawk.

"This is pretty tame, you know," she murmured to Ryder. "You should be here some night when Lex and Jas go to town on her. The only thing more impressive than how crazy they make her is how smug Dallas gets about it. He likes being the king of debauchery."

"Of course he does. He built an entire empire around it."

He'd built an empire around liquor, and always claimed the debauchery as a selfish indulgence or, in his more cynical moments, political strategy. But contrasting Hawk's previous discomfort with his easy, confident demeanor now, it was hard not to see something else.

This wasn't just debauchery. It was freedom.

Noah and Emma might end up fucking in the corner, oblivious to watching eyes. Bren and Six would enjoy the view until they decided to take the party home behind closed doors. Zan and Tatiana would dance and cuddle and trade long, lazy kisses, but they wouldn't end up naked the way Finn and Trix would. And they sure as hell wouldn't end up in a tangle of limbs, the way Rachel, Cruz, and Ace might with Jared and Lili.

Whatever you needed, you could have. But you didn't have to take everything on offer, either. That was the magic of the world Dallas had created for them—a place where you belonged even if you didn't fit in, because the only qualifications for belonging were showing up, having each other's backs, and caring.

And being loyal to your king and queen.

"Come on," she said, spinning out of the circle of Ryder's arm. She grabbed his hand and tugged him across the dance floor. "We should pay our respects."

Lex looked up at their approach, then leaned over to whisper in Dallas's ear.

Dallas eyed Ryder and huffed as Nessa hopped up on the stage. "Lex says I can't give your boyfriend a hard time until I'm up to punching him in a cage."

Lex smiled. "Sorry, Declan. That's how you handle bona fide war heroes."

"Damn right it is." And because Dallas had been looking *so grumpy* about being coddled, Nessa did the opposite. She prodded Ryder to sit in the chair next to their couch and then dropped into his lap.

Dallas glowered at her. "You know, you used to respect me and do what I said."

"Yeah, when was that? When I was seven?"

He snorted and relented. "Just about. Maybe I should be wishing Ryder luck instead of dragging him into the cage."

Nessa replied by giving him both middle fingers.

Ryder trailed his fingers down the center of her back. "I'm not worried."

The warmth tripping through her could have been from the soft touch or the casual arrogance in the words—Nessa was learning that there was one time when confidence was really fucking hot: when Ryder was being confident about *them*. "Me neither. So lay off, Dallas. Because if you don't, I'm gonna tell you any time we bang somewhere in the distillery, and you'll never be able to go in there again."

Dallas damn near choked on his mouthful of beer, and Nessa waited for the explosion. But his near-death experience must have mellowed him—or Lex had worked her magic—because he only burst out laughing. "Goddamn, Nessa. You grew up mean."

"No. I grew up O'Kane." She hooked her arm around Ryder's neck and smiled at him. "And we go after what we want."

"One dream at a time," he agreed with a grin.

Silently, Dallas held up his beer. Nessa leaned in to clink their bottles together and took a sip. The beer was crisp and clean, not nearly strong enough for the newly kindled warmth low in her gut. That was the high of crossing that final invisible line, the one Dallas had drawn in his head years ago when he'd fixed her in his mind as a kid who could never grow up.

She was so high, she told caution to go fuck itself and kissed Ryder.

The chair jolted, and Nessa looked up just in time to see Lex kick it again. "Go dance," she ordered.

Poor Dallas. He was trying so hard not to look disgruntled. Nessa rose and swooped down to kiss his cheek, then dropped a second kiss to Lex's. "Yes, ma'am."

As Nessa dragged Ryder off the platform, she heard Dallas muttering that at least one of them got some respect, and giddy joy bubbled up until she was laughing as she spun to face Ryder. "So do super spies know how to dance?"

"Nope." He took her hand and spun her again, and

this time she landed against his chest. "But we can make it look like we do."

"You make it feel pretty convincing, too." Or maybe that was just the sensation of being pressed up against all those muscles. She still planned to soften him around the edges with her first spy mission—Operation Extra Desserts and Lazy Weekends—but his sturdiness had nothing to do with his perfect physique. It was a strength that went deep, the knowledge that she could crash into him...and he'd catch her.

Of course, he was also really good at improvisation. The beat changed to something low and intense, and the hand at her back pulled her close as his thigh slid between her legs. Dancing turned into swaying, the rhythm the slowest and sweetest kind of foreplay—and someone called her name twice before the familiar voice registered.

"Nessa!"

"Mia?" As soon as Nessa turned, her friend swept her into a fierce hug. Mia was effortlessly graceful in a stunning white dress that set off her dark brown skin and the sparkly gold nail polish Nessa had made for her personally. And she was *glowing*. Having the opportunity to apply her skills toward running Sector Eight obviously agreed with her.

Or maybe it was Ford, who stood silently at her shoulder, looking as serious as always, but not nearly as surly as he'd been before Mia crashed into his life. Nessa grinned at him. "Ford. Good to see you."

"You, too." His expression became a little more guarded. "Ryder."

"Ford. How are things in Eight?"

"Good." It was Mia who answered, and she was adorable when she got excited. "The systems Jim had in place were streamlined, but fairly compartmentalized. I suppose he couldn't risk letting any one person see too much of what he was doing. But now that we don't have that problem, everything's easier."

Remembering Jim's murder book, Nessa had her doubts that anything Jim really cared about had been in files Mia could access. "That's good. And I'm glad you could get away for the party."

"We wouldn't have missed it." Ford lifted his arm, flashing his O'Kane ink from beneath his sleeve. "For life, right?"

"For life." Nessa held up her hand, and Ford stared at it for about two bars of the music before giving her the world's most awkward high-five. He looked even more disgruntled when she laughed, so she threw her arms around him in a delighted hug, then gave Mia a second one. "You better go say hi to Dallas and Lex before Ford gets too grumpy with me. We'll catch up soon."

When they were gone, she turned back to Ryder and twined her arms around his neck again. But the tiniest bit of doubt wormed its way into her thoughts as she stared up at him. "I know everyone's been asking you about Five, but did they ever ask you about Eight? If you wanted it, I mean? You're Jim's heir, you know."

Ryder made a choked noise that exploded into laughter. "No. Christ, no. The only thing that ever made Jim crankier than secretly plotting revolution for decades was running those fucking factories. Mia can have them."

"She'll do awesome things with them." Nessa pressed closer, falling back into the swaying rhythm of the music. "And that frees you up to do awesome things with me."

"Speaking of which—" He whipped her around before settling into the rhythm. "I found the camera you wanted. It wasn't easy—or cheap—but it's yours now." He paused. "Walt Misham waited until *after* we agreed on a price to inform me that he learned the art of negotiation from Lex, of all people."

"Oh God, you bartered with *Walt*?" Imagining the two of them bickering over prices was enough to make her laugh again. "Well, I guess you're not rich anymore."

"I still am, barely. But only because that ornery old man likes me."

"Of course he does." She went up on her toes, sliding her chest against his. "You're smart and tough and funny and smoking hot."

Amusement and appreciation curved his lips up at the corners. "Are you saying Old Man Misham wants to steal me away from you?"

"Maybe." It would take more self-control than Nessa had ever possessed not to kiss that smile. His lips were warm and familiar, his kiss still as exciting as the first one had been. It made her heart race and her skin flush, and oh, she loved those butterflies now. They swooped and danced in joyous promise, even after she pulled away.

This close, the noise of the crowd faded away with the music. "Tell me a dream," she whispered.

"You know that bag I dropped off at your office before the party? It was the last of my stuff from Five. I gave Hector my keys this afternoon. It's all his." He paused. "So I guess that means I need a permanent place to crash now."

The dream rushed toward her effortlessly, and this time she didn't try to put on the brakes. She didn't tell herself it was *too dangerous* or try to hold back a little to protect her heart. She just...dreamed.

Ryder, living with her. Waking up every morning in her pillow-covered bed. Filling some of the empty shelves in her room with the things *he* wanted to learn about or explore, now that his life didn't have to be all about war. Picking up lunch from the market and bringing it to her office. Coaxing her out of the warehouse to have actual adventures, where she could see the damn world.

Falling into bed with her every night, and all the sexy-hot fucking that made her come alive. Scratch that—the sexy-hot fucking could happen in her office, too. And in the aging room again. Anywhere. *Everywhere.*

But that was *her* dream.

He went on. "I talked to Dallas. He knows I'm not going to join up, I've had enough of that for a while. But I have money, and he has places to invest it. And your boy could always use someone else around, telling him like it is."

Nessa stared over his shoulder at Dallas, who was talking to Lex, Bren, and Six now. As lonely as her life had been at times, Dallas had had it worse. The O'Kanes were honest with him, but loyalty and trust could be their own burden. People who believed in you didn't always see your flaws—or your mistakes. Lex carried as much as she could, but the weight had been crushing them both during this war.

Dallas didn't need another follower. He needed a friend. "Good. You'll be good for him."

"I hope so."

She brushed her lips over his. "What else do you hope for?"

"You," he answered simply.

The butterflies exploded. Into love.

She tangled her arms around his neck and laughed when he spun her again. The room swooped past in a blur, the smiling faces of her O'Kane brothers and sisters. Even when she had to close her eyes against dizziness, they were there with her—an afterimage etched on the backs of her eyelids. Her family, joyous and celebrating.

The music pounded in time with the blood in her veins, and she wrapped her legs around Ryder's waist and gave in to it. Primal and carefree, sensual and powerful, electrically alive.

An O'Kane. For life.

declan

There were advantages, Dallas realized, to having unlimited access to the resources and tools of Sector Eight.

He'd always been vaguely curious about how such a small number of factories turned out so many different types of goods and supplies—but not curious enough to go digging. Now he knew the answer.

Ruthless fucking efficiency.

The people in Eight could recycle *anything*. Break it down into its fundamental parts and then use their fancy printing machines to turn it into something new. Words like *rubble* and *garbage* had a different meaning there—*resources.*

Ryder had pulled a few strings for them, as had Ford and Mia. Dallas's share of Peterson's hoarded resources had done the rest. The Broken Circle was rising from the ashes, bigger and badder and a hundred times more debauched.

It sprawled across the lots that had housed both the old bar and the fight night warehouse, and rose five stories straight up. The massive basement held the new-and-improved fight arena, all set up for nightly betting and weekly blowouts. The ground floor would have plenty of space for dedicated drinking, but there was room for a dance floor now, too. And the shows would go on—on the main stage for the dancing, and exclusive stages where people could pay extra for something a little more hardcore.

Jared and Lili would rule over the second floor. Elite access for people who wanted to gamble with high stakes and drink Nessa's finest. And a lounge for the VIPs, decked out in all the leather and chains a celebrated deviant could want. Gia had even teased him about bringing her girls and boys over once a week to entertain—for a price.

A real den of sin. And it was gonna be fucking beautiful.

"The foreman left you another exasperated note." Lex walked in, with what was presumably the offending note clutched in one hand. "Still trying to pin you down on wall finishings." She wrinkled her nose. "Bare brick and wood were always good enough for us before. Don't know why that should change."

Dallas glared at the note. "Probably because he can charge us more if he talks me into something fancy. I'll put on my scary face and make it clear."

"Tread carefully. If you run him off, who knows where we'll find another."

"We'd make it work." He plucked the letter from

her hand, tossed it on his desk, and hauled her down into his lap. "I got a different kind of exasperated note today. From Markovic."

"Really?" She frowned. "Not a problem, I hope."

"More like polite nagging." He rested his chin on her shoulder and inhaled. After coming back from the dead, he wasn't taking this miracle for granted—the scent of Lex, the feel of her body against his. The way she'd taste when he finally got his mouth on her skin. "He's still arguing for a central government. All of us sector leaders parking our asses in those fancy townhouses and ruling from on high alongside him."

She coughed to cover a choked noise that sounded like a laugh. "I see."

There'd been a time when Markovic's offer would have seemed like the next logical step to Dallas, when the influence the man was offering would have seduced him. But that dark, power-hungry little part of him had almost cost him Lex, and the war had given him a bellyful of deciding who lived and died.

"I'd do it if you wanted to," he whispered against her neck. "It's as true today as it was the day I first made the promise. Beggar or king, Lex. I'll be whatever you want me to be."

She stroked his cheek. "I've only ever wanted you to be one thing—mine."

He inched his fingers under her shirt and stroked her skin, where his name was inked low on her abdomen. "That's a given."

"I mean it." She turned her head to meet his eyes. "I wanted you when everything you owned fit into one shitty little safe in your bedroom."

"And I wanted you when I caught you trying to rob it." He grinned at her. "Thank fucking God you did."

"Mmm. So what are you really asking me? If I want to live in some fancy place in the city and have people to bathe and dress me? Or if it's okay for you to want that?"

Trust Lex to ask the question that cut right to the heart of his turmoil. "More like if it's okay *not* to want it. I mean, I'm all for keeping an eye on what Markovic builds to replace the shit we tore down…" But damn near dying had a way of clarifying things. And after years of scrabbling, he finally knew what he wanted.

She grinned and cupped his face. "It's okay to be Dallas O'Kane, barbarian bootlegger. It's better than okay. It's perfect."

Knowing that Lex would always prod him to be the best version of himself was a comfort. But knowing she didn't want him to be someone else, that she saw him clearly and loved him for it—

Well that transcended comfort. Fuck, it transcended words. Maybe someday someone would invent one that felt big enough.

Until then, he used the ones he had. "I love you, Alexa," he murmured against her lips. "So let's settle down and rule our den of sin."

"For life, Declan."

She'd said it before, a dozen times. But now they could see past the threat of Eden, decide who they wanted to be. For the first time, Declan O'Kane saw the hazy promise of a future he'd never imagined possible.

Love. Laughter. Family.

Peace.

"For life," he echoed, and sealed the promise with a kiss.

SIX MONTHS LATER

Birthing babies still took forever.

Nessa accepted a coffee from Ryder and snuggled against him when he sat on the couch next to her. "Someone needs to keep an eye on Ace," she murmured. "Everyone thinks Cruz is gonna be the one to crack, but Ace has been storing it up."

"He'll be *fine*. Have a little faith."

Easy for him to say. The O'Kanes still didn't have a lot of experience with babies, though the fact that Eden wasn't spiking the water with contraceptives anymore might change that. Nessa saw pregnant women all over the marketplace these days—like everyone who'd ever wanted a baby had leapt at the opportunity.

Or maybe it was just the natural result of that first month of victory celebrations. She was pretty sure that was what had gotten Jas and Noelle, anyway.

The door opened, stopping all conversation around the room, but Jyoti was the one who stepped through. "Everything's going fine," she assured everyone. "Lex, can you come deal with Ace before Kora and Dylan kick him out of the room?"

"I'm on it." She rose, then leaned over Dallas with a grin. After a moment, she straightened, the flask from his pocket in one hand. "This is Plan B."

He snorted. "Plan C can be Zan and Bren sitting on him, I guess."

"Nah," Zan retorted. "Save us for when Cruz freaks out."

Nessa rolled her eyes. "If someone needs to sit on Ace, Lex will sit on Ace. She's plans A-Z."

"If he gets too shaky, I'll distract him by having *him* comfort *me*. Working smarter, not harder, remember?"

Ryder chuckled. "That's a tactic worthy of an evil mastermind. I'm impressed."

Lex followed Jyoti out of the room, and Nessa sipped her coffee. "I should have made you bet me. I know Ace."

"I'm not a betting man, darling."

She would have called him a liar, but Hawk was approaching with a nervous look in his eyes that she recognized all too well. He dragged a chair from a nearby table and spun it around before straddling it. "Ryder. Do you have a few minutes?"

"I don't think any of us are going anywhere for a while. What's up?"

"I was wondering if you could take the time to meet with my sisters." Even after nearly a year with the O'Kanes, Hawk could be reserved almost to the point of shyness. But he looked determined now. "They want to expand their business now that trade's opened up in Eden. They've been spinning and dyeing yarn, selling it as fast as they can make it. They need better equipment—and it's more expensive than what I can pay for."

Ryder considered that, and Nessa could almost see the wheels turning in his head. "Do they have a supplier lined up?"

"They have a few leads. A couple on livestock, too. Since Markovic went after the illegal farms for using child labor, a lot of those bastards are looking to unload for quick cash." Hawk quirked his lips. "We just need to get to them before someone else does."

"Why not?" Ryder shrugged one shoulder. "I'll meet with them, see what they have planned, and we'll make it happen."

Hawk heaved a sigh of relief, and Nessa bit the inside of her lip to keep from laughing. Ryder's investments were serious business, not in the least because she knew the O'Kanes trusted his instincts. Ryder would talk to Hawk's sisters, make suggestions where he saw the possibility for improvement, and help them achieve their dream.

Making his money back wasn't a priority for Ryder, but some of his investments were already paying off. The store he'd helped Tatiana open up inside Eden was the biggest success, but Ace's art gallery had notoriety going for it—and crowds of people showing up on the off chance he'd make an appearance and they could say they'd seen the infamous Alexander Santana with their own eyes.

With Ryder's help, some of the O'Kanes were

stretching their wings a little. Dipping their toes into passions they'd never thought to explore. With Eden's markets open to them, Dallas could afford to hire workers to pick up the slack—and help with increased production.

And Nessa could take the occasional day off. For adventures.

Hawk spent a few more minutes trading ideas and setting up a time before shaking Ryder's hand to seal the deal. As soon as he was gone, Jyoti wandered over to discuss some obscure question of trade with Ryder, and Nessa let their words form a pleasant hum as she cuddled deeper into his side and sipped her coffee.

Everyone in the room was talking. Six and Bren were sitting with Dallas. Mad and Scarlet were sitting with Jared, and Lili joined them with a plate of cookies. Hawk was back over there with Zan and Finn, undoubtedly discussing cars. Voices rose and fell, the cheer behind them so determined she could have almost believed it.

People were happy. But they also were carefully not looking at the corner.

Nessa's gaze slid there in spite of herself, and it was like a cloud drifting in front of the sun. Amira seemed serene enough, sitting between Jas and Noelle. Hana had crawled out of her lap and was stringing the words she knew together with a healthy amount of baby gibberish to tell Noelle something of the utmost importance, judging by the expression on her tiny, perfect face.

The last time they'd all gathered like this, it had been for her. Nessa could close her eyes and remember everything, straight down to Six's amusement and Ace's adorable panic.

It still hurt. Six months wasn't enough to mourn Flash. Six *years* wouldn't be. There was a hole in their lives now that they'd always have to step around, memories that had become bittersweet at best.

But they were living. As long as they were living, there was hope.

As if to underscore that, a baby wailed in the hallway. Conversation cut off abruptly, and all eyes swung to the door.

Lex came in first, smiling widely. She held the door open for Cruz, who followed with a screaming bundle of baby. Ace was right behind him with a second bundle, and he grinned at the expectant room. "Isaac already has my temper, and Rosalía here is perfect, like her mama."

The tension burst into laughter, and the O'Kanes rushed toward them. Nessa groped for Ryder's hand and turned to look up at him. "Isaac," she said softly. "It's Flash's real name. No one ever used it, but…"

His answering smile was soft and somehow serious. "The best kind of tribute."

Something that would keep him with them, honored, forever. Nessa dashed the tears from her eyes and kissed Ryder once, hard. Then she jumped to her feet and joined the jostling crowd of O'Kanes trying to get their eyeballs and hands on the newest members of their family.

"Come on, Ace," Dallas called over the noise. "You know who gets to hold her first."

"Yeah," Nessa countered loudly. "The person who's gonna give you a bottle of black cherry bourbon."

Ace looked back and forth between the two of them, then deposited his daughter carefully in Nessa's arms. "Sorry, boss," he told Dallas. "Got a better offer."

"Asshole," Dallas murmured, but Nessa barely noticed.

Rosalía was tiny and perfect, gazing up at Nessa with sleepy bluish eyes. She had a fringe of dark black hair and ten perfect fingers clenched into adorable little fists.

Nessa didn't want to puke on Ace anymore.

"Hi, Rosalía," she whispered. "I'm your terrible Aunt Nessa. When you're older, I'm gonna help you get into *so much trouble*, because overprotective dads can bite me."

Ryder leaned over her shoulder, his hands on her arms, as if he was afraid an embrace might jostle the baby. "That's another one for the list."

She smiled as she mentally added it to her list of dreams. *Be a terrible influence on this baby.*

That one? She'd have no problem pulling off.

Across the room, Isaac finally stopped crying. Nessa looked up to see Amira cradling him in her arms, a gentle smile on her lips. Noelle held Hana on her lap, intercepting the girl's hands as she reached eagerly for the baby.

"He's gorgeous," Amira whispered. "I'm so happy for you."

Ace leaned down to kiss the top of her head, and Nessa swallowed around the lump in her throat and remembered a promise she'd made. The tribute to Flash that she still owed. She twisted her head to look back at Ryder. "I need a favor."

"Anything, Nessa."

He meant it. Which was why she loved him.

The road trip was glorious.

Nessa hadn't admitted it to anyone—even herself—but she'd been scared. The harrowing trip from Texas still featured in nightmares that grew over years until the idea of leaving her snug fortress at the heart of Sector Four was unthinkable.

Maybe the war had given her a different standard for measuring fear. Or maybe it was just the promise—for Flash, she'd face down any terror. But from the first moment she and Amira bundled Hana into the car with Ryder behind the wheel, it was perfect.

Ryder knew *everything*. All of that education Jim and his mother had crammed into his head came out in the oddest ways. He knew pre-Flare history and geography, and he knew how to make it come to life. He told them about Reno as they drove past empty, decaying structures, and about how the thriving city had died when Eden and the Base redirected the river supplying it to irrigate their communes and farms.

He told them about the Sierra Nevadas, giving the distant peaks Nessa had lived with for half her life a name. Nessa rolled the window down as they drove along roads that seemed carved between jagged mountains and leaned out in an attempt to take it all in.

She couldn't. It was so much, so *vast*. They parked by the side of the road at a particularly high spot, where a pair of stone picnic tables had survived the elements. While Hana chewed on a brownie Lili had sent with them, Ryder smoothed a map—an actual, honest-to-God, *printed on paper* map—out on the table and traced their path for her, all three hundred and fifty miles from Eden to the vast swath of blue dominating the left side of the paper.

The ocean. Just like she'd promised.

Nessa had seen it in movies before, but vids and her imagination didn't do it justice. They parked in an overgrown parking lot just before noon on the third day, and she was overwhelmed the second she pushed open the door.

The smell—salt and something else she couldn't put her finger on, almost like the one time her grandfather had gotten his hands on some crabs and boiled them. And the *sound*—the waves crashed and surged, and birds flew overhead, crying out to each other in alarm.

Amira stood next to her, fingers pressed to her trembling lips. "Pictures make it look so calm."

Nessa wrapped her arm around Amira's waist. "And small. I thought the reservoir was big."

"It goes on forever, doesn't it?"

Nessa's eyes prickled as Ryder brought Hana around the side of the car. "Not forever. There's islands all through it, and land on the other side. We just can't see it."

"But it's there." Amira smiled. "It's beautiful. Untamed. That seems better than calm, somehow."

"Because it's like us. Wild." She squeezed Amira tighter. "Let's go get our feet wet."

She didn't know how Ryder had found them a stretch of quiet, sandy beach, but it was perfect. They kicked off their boots and socks and went right down to the edge of the water. Hana squealed the first time a wave rolled in and splashed her little legs with cold water, and Amira swept her up with a laugh.

It was the most beautiful thing Nessa had ever heard.

Later, stretched out on a blanket they'd flung across the sand, Nessa watched Hana offer Amira a fistful of dried seaweed and smiled. "Thank you for making this happen."

Ryder made a soft noise and cracked open one eye. "You're welcome."

"I mean it." She picked up another brownie and broke it in half, offering him part. She couldn't say she'd softened him up *too* much in six months, but she had time. Hopefully years. Decades. "I made a promise. You helped me keep it."

"I know." He rolled to face her. "It turns out, I really like your dreams. Especially making them come true."

For the first time in months, nervousness fluttered in her belly. She laid her hand on his cheek and rubbed her thumb over his lower lip to soothe herself. "I have another dream, you know."

"Does it involve swimming? Because that water is *cold*."

"Fuck, no. I don't even know how to swim." She almost asked him how *he* knew, but she could guess the answer. No doubt Jim had tossed him in the river or a reservoir or any handy body of water and told him not to drown.

They were both products of the way they'd grown up—too fast, too rough. But her life had gotten complacent and easy, and his had stayed dangerous. He'd learned patience and caution, and she'd learned to close her eyes and jump.

So she did. "I'm dreaming of ink. My first real tattoo." She took his hand and brought his fingers to her throat. The ink around Amira's neck didn't scare her anymore. If something happened to Ryder, she'd *want* the tangible proof for everyone to see. How much he mattered. How much he'd changed her. "I've been waiting for something I'm sure about. And I found you."

His fingers tightened for half a heartbeat. "Are you? Really sure?"

"That I want you to mark me? Absofuckinglutely." She covered his hand with her own. "I'm yours, Ryder. All you have to do is claim me. I love you."

He rolled over her, pressing her down into the blanket and the warm sand beneath. "I don't think I caught that," he murmured. "You're gonna have to say it again."

"I love—"

"I love you, too." He kissed her, long and slow and so, so deep. He kissed her with focus, claiming her without saying another word. She could put herself in his hands without fear, because Ryder's control was the gentlest, sweetest kind. In exchange for her trust and love, all he wanted was to keep her safe and happy.

So she wrapped her arms around him and dreamed about happily ever after. For him. For her. For everyone.

Together, they'd make that dream come true.

for life

Kit Rocha is the pseudonym for co-writing team Donna Herren and Bree Bridges. After penning dozens of par-anormal novels, novellas and stories as Moira Rogers, they branched out into gritty, sexy dystopian romance.

The Beyond series has appeared on the New York Times and USA Today bestseller lists, and was honored with a 2013 RT Reviewer's Choice

ACKNOWLEDGMENTS & THANKS

How do you make a million-word series? One word at a time. In the middle of 2012, in a fit of frustration, we threw up our hands and said, “Screw this, we’re writing exactly what we want for a couple weeks.” It was raw. It was filthy. It was dark and hopeful and it was going to change our lives, even though we didn’t know it then.

Nine novels, three novellas, two short stories, an outtake and one giant spin-off later...here we are. Saying our thanks for the final time from the VIP Lounge in Sector Four. Thank you to the friends, family and raptors who were there for the whole wild journey. Special shout out to Alyssa Cole, who not only beta read this book but responds to panicked 5 AM texts with grace and humor. Thank you to Sasha Knight for her editorial badassery and general cheerleading. Thank you to Sharon Muha and Lillie Applegarth, who have frequently backflipped through tiny deadline hoops to help us get these books out on time, continuity-checked and proofread. Thank you to Angie Ramey, who claims she’s our assistant but really is the Office Manager who makes sure the job gets done. Thank you to Jay and Tracy, who moderate the Facebook version of the VIP Lounge and have built it into a welcoming home for women to find their online family.

Most especially, thank you to the readers. Those of you who discovered the O’Kanes, loved them, cried with them and cheered for them. They live bigger and brighter because you are here to love their stories. If we told you how much that means to us, Nessa would definitely threaten to puke all over us.

We may be moving on to Sector One, but I hope we’ll always find time to sneak back to Sector Four and let you check in with the O’Kanes. Because as the saying goes...

BEYOND NOVELS

Beyond Shame
Beyond Control
Beyond Pain
Beyond Jealousy
Beyond Addiction
Beyond Innocence
Beyond Ruin
Beyond Ecstasy
Beyond Surrender

BEYOND NOVELLAS

Beyond Temptation
(novella — first published in the MARKED anthology)
Beyond Solitude
(novella — first published in ALPHAS AFTER DARK)
Beyond Possession

www.kitrocha.com

Made in the USA
Middletown, DE
04 June 2017